4.

Deke slipped his arms around her waist from behind.

She flipped around to say something but before she could speak, his lips were on hers. As if they had a mind of their own, her hands found their way around his neck. The pure unadulterated heat from the kiss left her knees weak and her pulse racing. Business partners did not kiss each other. She should step back, but her feet were glued to the cold dirt floor.

"How's that for romantic?" His voice was even deeper than usual and his eyes all dreamy as they locked with hers.

Like a flash of lightning, Rascal raced between the two rows of stalls, pushed his way between them, and put his paws on Deke's chest.

Thank God for dogs, she thought as she took several steps back and caught her breath.

High Praise for Carolyn Brown

"Brown always gives the reader emotion, eternal love, and all the excitement you can handle."   —FreshFiction.com

MERRY COWBOY CHRISTMAS

"A captivating cast of characters fills the pages of this sweet and funny novel."   —*Publishers Weekly*

"Jud is one sexy cowboy who will have readers falling in love."   —*RT Book Reviews*

HOT COWBOY NIGHTS

"Toby and Lizzy had sparks and a chemistry so hot that it practically burned up the pages of this amazing story... Toby was everything that a HOT, SEXY cowboy should be...I highly recommend Carolyn Brown as a GO-TO author for all things SEXY COWBOY. 5 stars."
—Harlequin Junkie, Top Pick

"The Lucky Penny Ranch sure is fun to visit and the characters are quite entertaining...I can't wait to read the next one."
—NightOwlReviews.com, Top Pick

"A sassy, sensual contemporary romance that will steal your heart...A charming tale, packed with plenty of heat, heart and hilarity, *Hot Cowboy Nights* is a must read for fans of contemporary western romance."   —Romance Junkies

WILD COWBOY WAYS

"With an irresistibly charismatic cowboy at the center of this story, Brown's latest is a sexy, fun read...The genuine, electric chemistry between Allie and Blake jumps off the page."

—*RT Book Reviews*

"A breathtaking romance filled with soul-sizzling passion and a heart-stealing plot. A five-star hit!"

—Romancing-the-Book.com

"Heartwarming and funny... *Wild Cowboy Ways* will pull you in and won't let you go until the end. I loved this book and recommend it to everyone. 5 stars."

—BookJunkiez.com

"A perfect read to just curl up with. The book is light, sweet and just the right amount of humor and emotions to keep you reading along. Carolyn Brown will get you falling in love with the characters before you can blink...It made me feel like I was watching a classic Hallmark movie. *swoon*"

—OnceUponanAlpha.com

ALSO BY CAROLYN BROWN

The Lucky Penny Ranch series

Merry Cowboy Christmas
Wild Cowboy Ways
Hot Cowboy Nights

Wicked Cowboy Charm

Carolyn Brown

Lucky Penny Ranch, Book 4

FOREVER

NEW YORK   BOSTON

Copyright © 2017 by Carolyn Brown
Preview of *Toughest Cowboy in Texas* copyright © 2017 by Carolyn Brown

Cover design by Elizabeth Turner
Cover copyright © 2017 by Hachette Book Group, Inc.

Forever
Hachette Book Group
1290 Avenue of the Americas, New York, NY 10104
forever-romance.com
twitter.com/foreverromance

First edition: January 2017

Forever is an imprint of Grand Central Publishing. The Forever name and logo are trademarks of Hachette Book Group, Inc.

The publisher is not responsible for websites (or their content) that are not owned by the publisher.

The Hachette Speakers Bureau provides a wide range of authors for speaking events. To find out more, go to www.hachettespeakersbureau.com or call (866) 376-6591.

ISBNs: 978-1-4555-3496-8 (mass market), 978-1-4555-3498-2 (ebook)

Printed in the United States of America

OPM

10 9 8 7 6 5 4 3 2 1

When my son was a little boy
I used to tell him that his good looks
would take him far in life,
but charm would get him
anything he wanted.
With that in mind, and since he is
a very charming cowboy,
this book is dedicated to him.

To Charles Lemar Brown
With much love!

Dear Readers,

Many of you fell in love with Deke in *Wild Cowboy Ways* and asked when he would get his story told. Then in *Hot Cowboy Nights*, you asked again, and by *Merry Cowboy Christmas*, it looked like a family reunion in the backyard as y'all gathered up to tell me that you really needed to read Deke's story. I loved your enthusiasm, and Deke, bless his sexy little heart, had waited long enough.

And then Josie came to Dry Creek, and poor old Deke met his match. Josie and I hit it off right from the first when I found out that she liked red lollipops. Even though I didn't know her very well at that time, she and I became really good friends.

I have to admit I dragged my feet a little when it was time to end this book. Sometimes that happens when I've really gotten to know a family and helped them work their way through several HEAs. But then my fabulous editor said that she'd be interested in a spin-off series with more Dawsons, and it wasn't nearly as difficult to finish the book. So keep your boots on and get your cowboy hat ready, because a new trilogy, the Happy, Texas trilogy, is on the way.

As I've said many times, a book does not appear by magic out of the clouds. It takes a lot of hard work, and not only from my sitting in front of my computer for days. Going from the idea to the finished product in my wonderful readers' hands is a process. So thank you to everyone at Grand Central for all their support and continuing faith in my stories. To Leah Hultenschmidt: When I count my blessings, you are right up there at the top of the list! To the Forever team that does copyediting, marketing, sales, and promotion: Thank you for everything from the depths of my heart. To my agent, Erin Niumata and Folio Management: You are all special to me. To my husband, Mr. B: I'm a lucky woman to have you in my life. To all my readers: Bless you one and all for reading my books, writing reviews, and telling your friends about them.

As I finished this book, spring was just pushing the daffodils up through the ground in southern Oklahoma. Y'all will be reading it in the dead of winter, so make a cup of hot tea or hot chocolate, get your favorite fluffy throw and socks, and settle down in your favorite recliner. And enjoy the journey with Deke and Josie as they figure out what they want out of life.

Happy Reading!
Carolyn Brown

Chapter One

Josie Dawson loved the smell of feed stores and the taste of red lollipops. The two together brought back memories of when she was a little girl and her father took her with him to get supplies. There was always a jar of free lollipops on the counter, and even if she had to dig to the bottom of the big gallon jar, she'd pick out a red one.

When the cold north wind pushed her inside the Dry Creek Feed Store that morning, she inhaled deeply and smiled when she saw the jar of lollipops sitting on the counter.

"Hey, Josie, what brings you to town this Friday morning?" Lizzy, her new cousin-in-law, asked from behind the counter.

"The Lucky Penny needs about twenty bags of cattle feed. Jud said you'd know what kind he gets."

The red lollipop was right there on the top, begging her to twist the lid off the gallon jar and grab it.

"You came at a good time. Deke Sullivan's in the back

getting bags of goat feed, so he can help load it for us," Lizzy said. "Want a lollipop?"

"Aren't they for kids?"

"Some of us never grow up." Lizzy grinned. "I like the yellow ones. What color?"

"Red."

"I can't let you eat alone." Lizzy handed her a red one and dug down to the bottom for a yellow one.

Josie peeled off the paper and stuck the lollipop in her mouth. "Ahh, it transports me back to when I was a little girl."

Lizzy nodded in agreement.

"Hey, Lizzy, will you open the door for me?" Deke called out.

"Sure thing." She started for the front door.

Nothing that Josie had heard about Deke Sullivan prepared her for the sight of him with a forty-pound bag of feed hoisted over each shoulder. Someone might have mentioned that he was taller than her cousins and her brothers, but with that cowboy hat tilted back on his head with a few strands of light brown hair falling down on his forehead, he looked like a giant.

"Well, hello!" Deke stopped right in front of the counter.

"Hey," she said around the candy in her mouth. "I'm Josie."

"Jud's sister?"

She nodded.

"I'm Deke. Right pleased to meet you. I've heard a lot about you, but no one told me you got all the looks in the family."

"Deke, hurry up. The cold air is coming right in," Lizzy yelled from the front of the store. "Oh, and Josie's going to need you to load some feed for her, too, if you don't mind."

"No problem," Deke answered, then strode out the door with his bags.

Josie was right in the middle of trying not to notice what a fine ass he had when Lizzy piped in with, "So are you really leasing the old hotel on Main Street?"

Josie pushed a strand of blond hair away from her face. "Yup, I'll need someplace for my oil crew to live while they're here."

"Oil? Do you really think it's true what Jud says about the Lucky Penny then?"

"Well, we'll find out. But until this rotten paperwork gets done, I feel like I'm twiddling my thumbs."

"Well, I'm sure those Dawson boys will keep you from getting too bored." Lizzy laughed.

"Oh, they've put me right to work," Josie answered. *But maybe it's a Sullivan boy I'd rather get busy with.*

* * *

Deke rubbed his hands together to warm them up as he walked back into the store. He crossed the floor in a few long strides, removed his hat, and hiked a hip on the countertop.

Lizzy handed him an orange lollipop. "Thanks for doing that for us."

"Mmm, my favorite," he said and popped the sucker in his mouth. He could barely take his eyes off Josie's full, red-stained lips. Her blue eyes locked with his for a second before he blinked.

"You comin' to the house tomorrow night for the New Year's Eve supper?" Lizzy asked.

"Wouldn't miss it." He planted both feet on the floor and settled his hat back on his head. "You going to be there, Josie?"

"Since I'm living with Jud and Fiona for the moment, I suppose I will be. Anything special I need to know about?"

"Not a thing. It's just family."

The phone rang and Lizzy reached for it. "Feed Store."

She listened for thirty seconds and then hung up. "That was Jud. Your goats are in my front yard. Guess they decided to come back home."

Deke started for the front door. "Dammit! Crazy critters."

*   *   *

Josie drove past the LUCKY PENNY RANCH sign and turned right into the next lane. Her cousins Blake and Toby and her brother, Jud, had bought the property last year and were determined to make it succeed despite its bad reputation. After all, if anyone knew about bad reputations, it was those three boys. And yet even they had turned around their wild ways and settled down—with the three Logan sisters, no less.

When she got to the barn to unload Toby's feed, she couldn't believe the sight before her eyes. Goats everywhere. Romping around the floor. Climbing bales of hay like they thought they were mountain goats. And her brother in the middle of the ruckus, cursing up a blue streak.

"This looks like it's more fun than herdin' cats." She laughed. "We could practice our ropin' skills."

"Laugh all you want. When Deke gets back, you're going to help us gather them up one at a time and get them in his trailer," Jud said.

"Where are Toby and Blake?" Josie asked.

"One of them is fixing the fence on our ranch. The other one is over there taking care of Deke's fence and shoring up the goat pen so this don't happen again," Jud answered.

It didn't take a genetics professor to see that Josie and Jud were sister and brother. They both had blond hair and blue eyes, but where his face was chiseled, hers was softer and her lips fuller. He was over six feet tall and she was just under that height. They had double degrees in geology and agriculture, and they competed to see who had the best nose for finding oil. Josie usually let Jud win when it came to ranching, but not by much.

The barn doors squeaked, and she looked over her shoulder to see Deke sliding his big frame through just enough space to let him into the barn. Fine-looking cowboy in those tight jeans and denim jacket over a plaid shirt with the tail hanging below it.

"Never pictured you for a goat farmer," Josie teased.

Deke glowered. "Hell, no! I am a cattle rancher. But to get Truman O'Dell's cattle when he gave up the ranchin' business I had to take this miserable herd of goats with them. I may barbecue every one of them."

"Aw, I think they're cute. Look at those two young ones up there butting heads and playing king of the mountain," Josie said.

"You want them? Today I'll sell them to you real cheap." Deke grabbed one by the legs and headed out to the trailer with it.

"No, she does not want them," Jud answered as he wrapped one up in his arms.

"I would if I already had a ranch," Josie said. "I love baby goats. When I get my own place, I'm going to have everything from chickens to cows."

She was busy sweet-talking one of the young ones when Deke and Jud returned. They quickly cornered the old ram, but he got away from them and butted Jud in the rear end, pushing him forward into Deke and sending them both falling face forward into the hay. Josie was laughing so hard that she could hardly breathe when the ram circled back around and head butted her forward. Deke had barely gotten back on his feet when Josie came barreling at him, sending both of them into a spiral roll that took hay bales with them.

"That was a wild ride." Deke flashed a brilliant smile at Josie.

"Did I stay on for eight seconds?" she asked.

"Didn't have the clock going, but it felt like it."

Josie sat up and spit hay out of her mouth, wiped the dust from her eyes, and shot a dirty look at the ram. "You sorry devil. You will pay for that."

Chapter Two

"Please pass the fried chicken. I see a thigh with my name on it," Deke said at the supper table on New Year's Eve.

"Overeating is a sin." Allie poked his shoulder.

"But it's not as bad as the sinnin' I usually do on New Year's Eve, now is it?" He waggled his dark eyebrows.

"Poor baby!" Allie teased. "So will you be going out dancing next weekend?"

Deke shook his head. "Remember that bull I was tellin' you about up in Montana? I'm going up there to look at him and if I like him as well as I think I will, I'm bringing him home."

"Is that your way of asking us to take care of your animals and old Rascal while you are gone?" Blake asked from the far end of the table.

"It is." Deke grinned. "But I'm taking Rascal with me this time, so you don't have to take care of my dog. After that debacle yesterday afternoon, Jud has proven that he's a goat whisperer and Josie is real good at catchin'

them, so if they get out again, just call on them to help
you."

"Of course, we will. You've taken care of stuff for us
so it's time for payback." Allie patted him with one hand
and reached over to rewind her daughter, Audrey's, baby
swing with the other. "Looks like she's going to sleep right
through New Year's Eve."

"They say that whoever you are with on New Year's
Eve, you'll be with all year long," Josie said.

Jud leaned over and kissed Fiona, his wife of only a
week, on the cheek. "Well, I sure like that idea."

Deke was right at home in the old house where his three
best friends, Allie, Lizzy, and Fiona, had grown up. It had
started out as a small hotel back in the days when the whole
area was an Indian reservation. In those days, the soldiers
at the fort needed a place for their families to stay when
they came to visit. And then times got tough and Miz Audrey, the proprietor of the hotel, hired six girls, trained
them well, and turned the hotel into a brothel. Generations
later, it became a home to the Logan family.

As of a week ago, it had lost its name—Audrey's
Place—and the property incorporated into Lucky Penny
Ranch when Katy Logan deeded it over to Jud and her
youngest daughter, Fiona. It might take a long time for
folks to stop calling it Audrey's, but in time the only Audrey anyone would remember was that sweet little red-
haired baby who had big old Deke Sullivan wrapped
around her little finger.

He stared his fill of the little girl and wished that he had
one just like her, only maybe with blond hair and big blue
eyes like her mama.

*Whoa, hoss! You're getting the cart way before the
horse.*

"Josie is interested in rodeo stock, too," Fiona said.

Deke glanced at Josie. "You plannin' to keep a bull in the backyard of the hotel?"

"Jud said I could keep whatever stock I want here on the Lucky Penny until I scrape up enough money to buy my own ranch. I've got enough put aside to buy a few good head of rodeo stock if I find something I like," Josie answered.

"Breedin' or takin' them to the rodeo rounds?" Deke asked.

"Breedin'. You?"

"Maybe both. I haven't decided yet."

"You a bull rider?" she asked. A vision of him on the back of a wild bucking bull jacked the room temperature up at least ten degrees.

"Dabbled in it. Riding was a hell of an adrenaline rush, but biting the dirt more times than I want to remember made me realize I wasn't ever going to win a big buckle at the Pro Bull Riding event. So now it's basically an armchair sport. How about you? Did you ever ride?"

"Few times, but it didn't take long for me to figure out that I wasn't coordinated enough to stay on the beast for eight seconds."

"Yeah." He grinned, and her heart kicked in an extra beat. "They say it's eight seconds, but when you're on the back of a bull, it's more like eight seconds past eternity."

"You got that right." She smiled. "I'm flying out of Dallas to go look at several really good animals—also in Montana. Where are you going?" She grabbed another chicken leg as the platter went around the table.

"North of Butte. How about you?"

"Going south so. Guess we won't be outbiddin' each other for the same animals."

*   *   *

Josie's phone rang and she glanced at the picture that came up on the screen. "I need to take this. Won't be but a minute. Excuse me."

"Kasey?" Jud asked.

Josie nodded and stepped away from the table.

Deke frowned. Did Josie have a boyfriend named Kasey?

Blake nudged him. "Kasey's our cousin. She was recently widowed and now she's on her own with three kids. She and Josie have always been thick as thieves."

"She and her brother are arguing and she wanted my input," Josie explained as she returned to the table.

"I'm sorry about her husband," Deke said. "How old are her kids? That must be really tough on them. I lost my parents when I was young and my grandparents raised me."

"Rustin is five. He'll be in kindergarten this fall," Josie said. "Emma is three and Silas is six months. And I'm real sorry to hear that about your folks, too, Deke."

"Six months!" Deke gasped.

"She was three months pregnant when her husband was killed overseas," Jud said.

Deke frowned. "That's terrible. She's lucky to have a big family to help her out."

"She's a great girl," Jud said. "She and Josie have been more like sisters than cousins."

"Y'all see each other very often?" Deke asked.

"Used to more than we will be now. I was working not far from Amarillo, so I could drive down to see her fairly often," Josie said.

"Well, I'm glad that you started off the New Year here

because that means you'll still be here next year when Fiona has her first baby," Deke said.

"What?" Josie whipped around to stare at her brother. "You are going to be a father and you didn't tell me?"

All the color left Jud's face as he whipped around to look at Fiona, who was just as shocked. Finally, Deke threw back his head and guffawed.

"It was a joke. We needed to lighten the mood." He swiped the sleeve of his shirt across his eyes and hiccupped. "That was amazing."

"And paybacks are hell," Josie said.

Fiona pinched him on the forearm. "Yes, they are!"

"Ouch!" Deke yelled. "You've always been the mean one and I was just getting you back for the last joke you played on me."

Josie had missed her brother when his contract was up with the job and now here she was in the middle of a big family on New Year's Eve. Maybe by this time next year Fiona and Jud really would be expecting their first child and Josie would have her new house built. And she'd be the favorite aunt.

She glanced across the table to find Deke staring right at her and be damned if he didn't wink. She wasn't naive. She'd been in love—twice, actually. She'd even considering moving in with her boyfriend the last time. But she wanted wild fizz and all those things that romance writers talked about in their books. She'd wanted that glow after sex and surges of desire when her man walked in the room. And until she got that, she'd focus on her work.

Her phone rang and she fished it out of her hip pocket. "Excuse me, again."

Deke pushed back his chair.

"You don't have to stand up. We're family." She smiled.

"Not me and you, darlin'. I'm barely considered shirttail kin," Deke said. "But I'm not being a gentleman. I'm going for the chocolate cake. You'd better not talk too long or there won't even be icing stuck around the edges of the pan. I don't waste anything when it comes to a sheet cake."

Josie walked up the stairs to her bedroom as she answered the phone. "That was fast. Did Brody come to his senses?"

"No, I haven't talked to him. I forgot to ask if you'd met Deke yet? Jud's talked so much about him that I wanted to hear your thoughts on him and on your new sister-in-law?"

"Jud is so in love with Fiona that if I found a fault in her, I'd never say a word about it or he'd shoot me on the spot. Deke is...well, think Blake, Toby, and Jud all rolled into one when it comes to flirting," Josie said.

"Holy smoke! I can't wait to meet him." Kasey sighed. "And now Rustin and Emma are fighting over the remote. Got to run. Talk to you tomorrow."

She hit the END button and went back to the dining room, leaving her phone behind. She really wanted that last chicken leg and then a piece of cake and she didn't want to talk on the phone anymore that evening. The rest of the family was all having dessert when she returned and settled back into her chair.

"Anything drastic?" Jud asked.

"Rustin and Emma were fighting over the remote, so if there was anything, we didn't discuss it," Josie answered.

They pushed back their chairs and talked about everything from food to goats for the next hour as they had after-supper coffee. When Josie was ready for dessert, Deke cut off another slab and poured a second cup of coffee.

"I'm not sure if a person can go to heaven if they let anyone eat alone. It's got to be a sin," he said.

"Deke has a sweet tooth that a truckload of chocolate couldn't satisfy." Jud chuckled.

"I wouldn't mind trying to see if that was the truth." Deke's one eyelid slid slyly shut when he glanced over at Josie. "My granny was a great one to keep baked goods ready and I learned to love all things that are sweet. When she passed on I was already hanging out over here a lot of the time, and Miz Irene made sure my sweet tooth didn't get to hurtin' too bad."

"You'll get to meet her and Katy tomorrow. They'll be here for Sunday dinner, and if Granny is up to it, they'll spend the night," Fiona said. "While Deke finishes up, you guys can take Audrey to the living room and we'll get the dishwasher loaded."

"All done." Deke pushed back his plate. "And I get to hold the baby first."

"I'll get the music ready," Blake said. "Got any requests?"

"Whatever you pick out will be fine, darlin'," Allie said as she picked Audrey up from the swing and handed her to Deke.

Shania Twain was singing "From This Moment On" when the four women finished in the kitchen and made it to the living room. Josie let the three sisters go on ahead and stood in the doorway, watching as they claimed their husbands and started dancing to the music.

Deke was sitting in a rocking chair and held Audrey in his arms. Looking at him with a baby in his arms, it was hard to believe all the stories she'd heard about him. The expression on his face as he looked at the little girl was a mixture of love, joy, and pure yearning to hold her forever. It was evident that Deke had been born to be a father, so why in the hell hadn't he settled down and started a family?

He looked up and she quickly looked across the room at Jud and Fiona, gracefully moving around the room in a country waltz. Blake held Allie so close that air couldn't find a way between them. Toby's eyes never left Lizzy's face as he whispered things that made her blush.

She wove her way through the couples and sat down on the end of the sofa next to where Deke was rocking the baby. "They look good together."

"We always dance on New Year's Eve. It's part of the tradition around here."

"Give me that baby girl." Blake took Audrey from Deke. "And go dance one with my wife. She don't wear out as fast as I do."

"I'll put her in the swing. You dance with your wife." Deke situated Audrey in the swing and crossed the room as the next song on the CD started. Chris Stapleton's "Tennessee Whiskey" was a slow, two-stepping song. He held out his hand toward Josie. "May I have this dance, ma'am?"

She put her hand in his and he pulled her up and then wrapped his arms around her waist, bringing her close to his body as they moved slowly around the room.

"Are you as sweet as Tennessee whiskey like the song says?" he whispered.

Lord, have mercy! His warm breath on her neck and the lyrics of the song in her head, plus his body pressed against hers sent sparks all over the room.

"Honey, I'm not a bit sweet, and you'll find that out pretty quick if you come around here very often," she answered.

When the song ended, a faster tune by Hunter Hayes titled "Everybody's Got Somebody But Me" started.

"You have to dance this one with me because it's the

story of my life today," Deke said as he swung her out to the upbeat music and sang along with the lyrics that said the whole place looked like a casting call for Romeo and Juliet.

"They are all so much in love that it would make even your sweet tooth ache," Josie said and laughed when he brought her back to his chest. "Poor old Deke. Do you want somebody to settle down with?"

"Are you proposing?"

"Not me. I don't have time for romance," she said.

"The New Year's Eve party starts on television in five minutes," Toby broke in before Deke could comment. "This is the last dance."

"Oooh, I like this song," Deke said as the music came on. "I can't believe that Jud said you were clumsy. Dancing with you is awesome."

"Blake Shelton. 'Sangria' is one of my favorites by him."

"You like sangria?" Deke asked as they moved around the floor.

"Sometimes. And sometimes I like that whiskey we heard about and sometimes I like beer," she said.

When the song ended, Deke bowed low and kissed her fingertips. "Thank you for the dance, sugar."

"Sugar? Ha!" Jud broke in. "She might know how to dance and come off as sweet, but don't let her fool you, Deke. That one can be mean as hell if she doesn't get her way, and she cusses like a sailor."

"Hey, now!" Josie protested. "And what're you tellin' Deke about me being clumsy?"

Jud held up his palms defensively. "Hey, when you were a kid you were all legs and arms and you were clumsy."

"And now?" Josie asked.

"Okay, okay, so you outgrew part of it. But you are still

mean. I'm tellin' you, Deke, she'll go to war with a Texas wildfire with nothing but a cup of water in her hand," Jud finished as he turned on the TV.

"I wouldn't want to be in New York City right now for anything," Lizzy said as she saw the throngs of people crowding Times Square. "There's more people per square block than what lives in Dry Creek," she said.

Josie was having so much fun that she didn't realize the countdown was going on until her brother and cousins paired off with their new wives.

"Ten, nine, eight," the announcer on the television said.

Lizzy slipped her arms around Toby's neck.

"Seven, six."

Allie rolled up on her toes and Blake drew her close to his chest.

"Five, four, three."

Jud held both of Fiona's hands and looked deeply into her eyes.

"Two, one!"

Josie was not going to miss a New Year's Eve kiss when there was a perfectly good cowboy right in front of her. She moistened her lips and got ready for a quick peck, but Deke wrapped her up in his arms so tightly that she could feel his heart thumping against her breast. He tipped up her chin with his fist and flat-out laid a kiss on her that left her breathless.

"Happy New Year!" everyone yelled as the old clock above the mantel chimed twelve times.

Chapter Three

Y'all ladies stayin' for the football game?" Deke looked across the room at Allie after Sunday dinner on New Year's Day.

"We'll be in and out to see how it's going. We're having a beer in the kitchen while we take care of the after-dinner cleanup," Allie answered. "Which way you goin', Josie? You want to watch the game or gossip with us?"

Josie picked up two beers and led the way to the kitchen. "Oh, honey, I never, ever turn down gossip."

Josie had heard all about Irene, grandmother of the former Logan ladies. But all the wild stories she'd heard did not prepare her for Irene Miller.

Irene pulled up a rocking chair beside the window. Evidently she had applied her own makeup that morning because she wore bright red lipstick that had crept into the wrinkles around her mouth. Her eye shadow looked like it had been applied with a putty knife, but her eyes were bright with happiness. Her gray hair sported a big red sequined bow on a matching headband, and her hot pink sweat suit had a beach scene on the front all done up in bling. She'd gone to church in that getup that morning and there was not one single raised eyebrow in the whole place.

"This is a wonderful day," Irene said. "I've lived to see one more year pass. Give me that baby and tell me I look beautiful. I dressed up special because I knew I'd get to go to church with y'all and have dinner here." Irene held out her arms.

Katy, the Logan sisters' mother, knelt beside her chair. "Mama, you are always beautiful but you look really good today. Hot pink is your color."

"Go in my room, look in my closet, and bring out the Jack? We should toast today," Irene whispered.

"You can't drink and hold the baby. What if you got woozy and dropped her?" Katy said.

"Shit, girl! I can hold my liquor better than that but I wouldn't want to breathe them fumes on her so we'll wait until later to toast the new year."

Allie put Audrey in Irene's arms.

Audrey cooed and grinned at Irene as she rocked the baby in the overstuffed rocking chair. "Look, Fiona? This baby has your red hair. She's going to grow up to be a fire-cracker just like you. Are you just here for the holidays or did you come home to stay? I've got this forgettin' disease and it plays hell with my brain."

"I'm home to stay. I married Jud last week, remember. And Mama gave us her house and the store. We live here now and remember, she bought a condo here in Wichita Falls so she can be close to you," Fiona said.

"*Condo*? Whoever thought up that word should be shot. It sounds like *condom*." Irene giggled.

"Granny!" Allie gasped.

"Well, it does and I'm old so I can say whatever I damn well please," Irene said. "Y'all sit down and visit with me." Irene motioned toward the chairs around the table. "I'm glad you aren't leaving again, Fiona. Tell me again about this tall one. I never knew Deke to bring a woman home. Is this serious?"

"Oh, no," Josie answered quickly. "I'm Jud's sister, Josie."

"Is Deke sick?"

"Why would you ask that?" Katy stood up. "I'm going upstairs and pack a couple of boxes to take with me tomorrow."

"Well." Irene rolled her eyes. "This girl right here is just his type. Tall, blond, and blue eyes and he's in there watchin' a football game instead of flirtin' with her. He must be sick."

"Maybe he's not my type," Josie teased.

"I like a woman with some sass." Irene giggled.

"Deke's kind of like a brother to all us girls so that makes her…" Lizzy stammered when Deke walked into the room.

Irene held up a palm. "Y'all are mighty quick to answer for poor old Deke today."

"Actin' just like older sisters, aren't they, Granny?" Deke chuckled. "Are you going to watch the ball game this afternoon?"

"When all that pregame shit is done, I'll come to the living room and take your money. I've got five bucks on the Cowboys," she said.

"Take my money!" Deke faked a gasp. "I'm going to take yours."

"If you do it'll be the first time." She grinned. "Got to do my good luck ritual." She broke out into the first lines of "I'll Fly Away." Deke joined in first and the rest of them followed his lead. Irene finished on a high note and then started an old Etta James tune, "At Last."

Everyone managed to keep up on the first and second songs, but Allie and Blake were the only ones who could sing all the words of the last song. When it ended, Irene frowned at Deke until he started the applause.

"Thank you." Irene nodded and smiled. "I went to Frankie's one time and I love Etta James. I bet you girls didn't know that, did you?"

Who was Frankie and what did Etta James have to do with him? Josie glanced around the room to see three slack-jawed women staring at their grandmother as if she had sprouted another eye right in the middle of her wrinkled forehead.

"Granny, you didn't!" Fiona gasped.

Irene shrugged. "I did and Dora June and Lucy went with me."

"We won't tell, Granny," Deke whispered. "You want me to tell Frankie hello for you next time I'm over that way?"

Irene cocked her head to one side. "Hell, no! I don't want you to go there no more, Deke. You ain't never goin' to find a wife in a place like that." She kissed Audrey on the cheek and handed her over to Allie. "Deke, you go protect my money and don't you lie to me when the game is over. I'm going to take a nap instead of watching the game. Where's Katy? I'm not sure which way to go."

"Right here, Mama," Katy said. "I could use a little nap myself. Let's go find a bed."

Irene's eyebrows knit into a solid line, as if she was trying hard to remember something. "Okay but if you snore, I'll kick your sorry ass out on the floor."

Katy looped her arm in her mother's and led her out into the foyer.

"What just happened?" Josie whispered.

It wasn't hard to picture Katy as the girls' mother. They were all built about the same and had the same shape face and bright smiles, but Irene was a different matter. That tiny little woman didn't look like she could have ever birthed a child.

"We were lucky today. Here lately, when she realizes that she's losing it, she just goes to sleep. But today, she was lucid for a long time," Deke said.

"That was so sad, but I bet she was a pistol before she got dementia," Josie said.

Deke filled a glass with ice and sweet tea. "I can sure tell you that she was as full of spit and vinegar as Fiona is."

"Oh, come on now," Fiona said. "She could outdo me any day of the week. I've never been to Frankie's."

"What's so bad about this Frankie place?" Josie asked.

"Did you have a bar in your part of the state where your mama would still take a switch to you if she found out you'd gone there?" Fiona asked.

"Sugar Shack," Jud said as he and Blake entered the kitchen.

"That's Frankie's in our part of the world," Deke said.

"So you are a regular there?" Josie asked.

Deke nodded. "I am. Y'all might as well come on in the living room and watch the ball game with us?"

"Maybe later," Allie said.

"When you do, you might bring in some snacks," Deke said.

"Aha, there is an underlying motive here," Josie said.

"I get mean when I get to craving something sweet, darlin'," he drawled.

"You've got two legs and two hands. You can come get it yourself," she told him.

"Whew!" Deke mopped a hand across his forehead in a fake gesture. "I bet she's got a broom parked by the back door."

"A brand-new 2017 model," Josie shot right back.

"You've met your match." Allie grabbed his arms and turned him around. "Go watch your football game and let us gossip."

Chapter Four

The cold winter wind continued to whistle through the dormant limbs of the few mesquite trees when Josie got out of her truck the next morning. The O'Dells' old house, nothing now but a blackened place on the ground, had sat in the middle of a yard surrounded by a white picket fence. A tiny splash of purple in the corner said that there had been a flower bed there at one time, and a volunteer pansy had popped up to tell the world that there was hope.

Josie bent for a better look and almost picked it, but then decided to leave the little flower right where it grew. She buttoned up her old stained work coat and jerked her stocking hat down over her ears. A braid on either side of her head shot out from the hat and floated on her shoulders. When she pulled a pair of leather gloves from her pocket a notepad fell out and landed right beside the pansy.

"Sorry about that, old girl." Josie picked up the pad, shoved it back into her pocket with the pen, and then put on her gloves. "Someday when I own this place I will plant more flowers, I promise."

It wasn't the first time that she'd gone to the old O'Dell ranch to look at the property, hoping that if the oil business worked out, she'd be able to buy it. She'd love to live so close to her family at the Lucky Penny, and she was already starting to see that Dry Creek would be an easy place to call home.

Speaking of the Lucky Penny, Josie figured she'd better get on with her chores. She'd told Toby that she would check the fence lines on his and Lizzy's part of the ranch, so she drove across the road, parked to the right of the cattle guard below the sign, and shut off the engine.

If something wasn't bull tight, she'd make a note of the location and take care of repairs when she returned from her trip. She started walking south, keeping the bitter north wind to her back. She made note of two rotted posts along the way. As she turned the corner and walked on, she found barbed wire was sagging in three places. Nothing drastic, but she'd alert Toby to replace it. The wind had not died down a bit when she started north, and it had started to mist. Not nearly a drizzle yet but the tiny cold droplets stung her face, so she pulled off the hat and flipped it out to make a face mask and put it back on, tucking her braids up under the edges.

Josie was no stranger to the weather and although she liked the spring and fall best, work had to be done in the heat of summer and the winter chill, also. Trudging on as the mist turned into a drizzle, she thought about the bull and the two broncs she wanted to buy. When the oil wells came in she'd buy a ranch. If not the O'Dell place then another one and the first thing she would build would be a state-of-the-art barn to keep her animals in. She could live in the old travel trailer that Toby had used until she could build a house. If she could talk the seller down a little, she might add another bull to the sale. From the pictures he'd sent via the Internet, the young bull had a lot of fight in him, which could be a great rodeo asset.

That picture of Deke's long legs slung across the back of a bull flashed through her mind again. Deke's muscles bunched as he wrapped the rope around his gloved hand and got ready to signal the crew to open the gate.

She shook the vision from her head and looked up at the skies, but there wasn't even a little ray of sunshine up there anywhere. Solid gray and a slow rain, which was good for the ground but not for the body. She'd started up the last leg of the journey and was about halfway up she noticed a movement out of her peripheral vision.

"Well, good morning. What in the world are you doing out in this weather?" Deke called out from across the dirt road.

She jerked her head up, gazed into his eyes and then down at his mouth, the only two things showing, since he wore scuffed work boots and a ski mask, just like she did, and camouflage-patterned coveralls. She liked the image of him on the bull much better.

"Walkin' the fence line. Crazy, isn't it, in this weather?" she asked.

"Maybe, but I get a lot of thinkin' done when I check the fences, and next summer, we will be begging for some of this rain. Too bad we can't harness it and make it fall when we need it most, ain't it?" Deke said. "I just finished up my morning chores and I'm headin' inside for a cup of hot chocolate and a morning snack. Want to join me?"

"I'd love something warm." She looked across the road.

"Just hop that fence and cross the road. I'll drive down to the end of the lane and take us to the house and then take you back to your truck when we are done."

She put one hand on the fence post and in a flash she was on the other side. "I'm hoping this doesn't turn to ice. I'd hate to miss my flight on Friday."

He pointed to his truck not fifty yards away. "What part of the state are you planning to go to again?"

"Just south of Butte, Montana, a little ways. Big place is selling off a couple of broncs and a few bulls. I've got one picked out that I really want. He's young and full of spit and vinegar. And I've been checking to see which cows might be best for breeding him with as I inspected the fences today. I've got my eye on a second bull, but I'll have to see how it plays out."

He kept a steady pace beside her. "How are you getting them home?"

"The seller has agreed to haul them anywhere in the United States. Not for free, of course, but I'll pay the price to get them down here in good health."

He opened the truck door for her and she crawled inside, glad to be out of the rain. He jogged around the front end and hurriedly slid into the driver's seat, slamming the door as fast as he could. "This is my ranch truck. Never leaves the ranch and it's a real workhorse. However, there's no heater or air conditioner anymore. So keep your gloves on until we get to the house."

"Not a problem. I grew up on a ranch, Deke. I know about work trucks."

"And oil? Think there might be some on my property, too?" he asked.

She cut her eyes around at him without moving her head. "Is that why you were flirting yesterday? You want to butter me up with sweet talk so I'll check your land for drilling sites?"

"Maybe." He grinned. "Or maybe you're just downright beautiful, Josie, and not to flirt would just plumb be wrong."

*   *   *

Josie peeled off her face mask and static electricity created a halo of blond hair out around her face. Even with no makeup and those two blond braids, she took Deke's breath away.

He was so busy looking at her that he veered off to the right and had to do some fancy adjusting to keep from hitting a fence post. "Trying to avoid a pothole," he murmured as he braked, put the truck in park, and hopped out to close a gate behind him.

When he got back behind the wheel, he paid more attention to his driving the rest of the way to the house. The rain had gotten serious by the time he parked, so he reached behind the seat and brought out a dark blue umbrella with the Dallas Cowboys logo emblazoned on it and hurried around to her side of the truck.

He popped it open and held it over her head, not making any attempt to keep the rain off him. When they reached the porch, he shook the droplets from his hair and hit the right little button to fold the umbrella.

"Welcome to my house." He threw open the door and let her go in first. "That would be Rascal over there by the fire. His arthritis is acting up in this cold weather, so I gave him the day off to rest while I did the chores."

The blue heeler thumped his tail on the floor a few times but didn't leave his warm rug by the open fire. Josie peeled off her gloves, shoved them into her pockets, and then Deke helped her remove her coat. He was so busy gazing at her hair and the curve of her neck that he almost dropped her coat and had to scramble to keep it from hitting the floor. When he turned around, she was kneeling beside Rascal and petting him. His old tail was doing double time and every time she said something else sweet to him, it went even faster.

"I'll make us some hot chocolate unless you'd rather have something else," Deke said hoarsely.

"That sounds great, thanks. How old is he?" Josie asked.

"Fifteen. He says it's time for me to get another cow dog, but I haven't found one as smart as he is. Truth is, I'm afraid if I bring a pup in here, he'll give up and die," Deke said sadly. "I've got some of Lizzy's Christmas cookies left. Want some with your chocolate? Being out in the cold uses up a breakfast pretty fast."

"Sure," she said but her eyes never left the dog.

He made the chocolate from his granny's recipe and poured it into two cups. With the plate of cookies on the top of one of the cups, he carefully made his way from kitchen to living room, purposely watching each step so he didn't spill anything. Something about her presence had him as clumsy as a fourteen-year-old on his first date.

"I want a dog. If you find a litter with pups as smart as Rascal, let me know and I might buy one," she said. "I can keep it at Jud's place until I get settled into the hotel."

"Won't never be a dog that smart." He set the cookies and hot chocolate on the coffee table and joined her on the floor in front of the blaze in the fireplace. "I use wood when I can. It keeps the fuel bills down in the wintertime. I just wish there was a way to use it to make the house cool in the hot summertime."

She picked up the cup nearest to her and took a sip. "This is really good. What do you do different?"

"It's an old family secret." He grinned. "If I told you how to make it, you might not come back another day for more."

"Oh, really?" She raised an eyebrow.

"That's right. I got you women folks figured out." He smiled.

"So you know women?" She reached for a cookie at the same time he did.

There was that jolt of electricity again when their hands touched. "Yes, ma'am, I do."

"Well then, smarty-pants, what have you figured out about me in the short time you've known me?" she asked.

"You dance like an angel. You love kids and dogs and you like hot chocolate and cookies. And you aren't afraid of hard work or getting cold if you need to walk a fence line to make it bull tight," he said. "And you've been in a relationship but you didn't commit because it didn't feel right."

She frowned. "Jud told you that last part, didn't he?"

"He didn't have to. You're too pretty not to have had a couple of serious boyfriends, but you are also smart enough to realize when something isn't the real deal," he said.

Josie's cheeks flushed an adorable pink as she searched for words. "What's the name of this ranch anyway? You don't have a sign up out there over the cattle crossing like most ranches do?"

"A tornado swept through here a few months ago. I'm sure that Toby told you about it. He and Lizzy got stuck in the cellar behind her store."

Josie nodded. "I did hear about that."

"Well, it took my sign with it when it left. It wasn't my

ranch then but my cousin's. He wanted to leave Dry Creek, so I sold my place to Lizzy and bought this one. I wasn't sure I wanted to keep the old name or register a new one. No one called it by anything but the Sullivan place, but still when my grandparents bought the place they decided to name it the Double Heart Ranch because they said it would take both of them putting their hearts and souls into it if they intended to make it work."

"I love that name and the story," Josie said.

"Thank you, ma'am. Now let's talk rodeo stock. I'm going up to Montana too, but I'm leaving Thursday morning."

"Driving?" she asked.

"Yes, and taking my stock trailer with me in case I get to buy the bull I want."

She took another sip of the chocolate and her expression said she really did like his recipe. "Where are you going?"

"Some little bitty place called Drummond on up north from Butte."

"Well, good luck. I'm flying. I don't have the time to drive and I don't want to ride that far anyway."

Deke had been about to ask her if she wanted to ride along with him, but evidently fate had just told him it wasn't a good idea. A little shot of disappointment hit him, but it was what it was, and it most likely was not a good idea for him to spend that much time with her in the cab of a truck. He'd almost wrecked the old work truck that morning just going from the pasture to the house.

"We might need to tighten up all our fences if we bring home a couple of wild bulls that will only be separated by a few strands of barbed wire and a dirt road," he said.

"Good fences make good neighbors," she quoted.

But they sure don't make for good relationships, he thought.

Chapter Five

On Thursday morning, Rascal followed Deke from the living room to the bedroom and sat on the rug beside his bed while Deke threw a few things in a duffel bag. Then he went back to the living room with him and watched as Deke made sure the fire was out and there were no embers left in the fireplace.

"You really do want to go this time, don't you?" Deke patted his head. "It'll be cold and we'll be runnin' long hours. It won't be like going to the rodeos in the travel trailer. You'll only get to stretch your bones when we get gas. You'd be much warmer right here in the house, and Blake will come by twice a day to let you outside."

Rascal's answer was to lie down on his favorite rug and put his paw over his nose in a pout.

"Okay, but remember, if you get cold or whine, you asked for a long turn-around trip and you'll have to use the leash."

Rascal's head popped up and his tail thumped against the floor.

"I guess that's settled then. I'll be glad for the company. Looks like everything is taken care of, so you go on and wait for me by the truck." Deke opened the door and the old dog shot out of it like a puppy. He crossed the porch in record time and sat down, straight and tall by the truck's passenger door.

One more glance at the fire to be sure it was completely cold. Adjust the thermostat so the central heat would kick on when it got cold. Pick up his duffel bag and that new fluffy red blanket he'd given Rascal on Christmas morning. Checkbook and ranch credit card in the side pocket of the duffel.

He locked the door and hurried across the yard. Rascal jumped into his place in the passenger's seat as soon as Deke tossed his blanket inside.

"Don't be askin' me how far it is or if we are there yet." Deke chuckled.

Rascal yipped and pointed his gray nose straight ahead.

"I might need your advice on this bull I'm lookin' at, so keep your wits sharp."

Rascal watched the road for two hours and then he curled up on his blanket and shut his eyes. Every so often his tail would twitch and his old legs would quiver, but he didn't wake up. Used to be when the country music on the radio stopped for the news, his eyes would pop open and he'd growl.

"I guess you're chasing rabbits in your dreams. I won't wake you, but we just crossed over into Oklahoma," Deke said.

The next song on the radio reminded him of Josie. There had been talk that they might all get together a couple of evenings that week and do some painting at the hotel, but the plans had fallen through and he hadn't seen her since he'd taken her home on Monday.

He kept time to the music with his thumbs on the steering wheel, singing along when he knew the lyrics. When he got back home late Saturday or sometime in the early hours of Sunday morning, he figured that his infatuation with Josie would be all done.

"And next weekend I'll be ready for a trip to Frankie's for sure. I bet the ladies miss me." Deke smiled at the long, straight highway ahead of him.

"Then again, I'd give it all up if I could have what Fiona and Jud have. Or Allie and Blake or Toby and Lizzy. All of them make my heart hurt to have someone to go home at night to like they do," he said. "I should have listened to Granny Irene when she kept telling me that I couldn't find a woman to settle down with in the bars."

*　　*　　*

Cheyenne, Wyoming, was bitter cold that night when he stopped at a small motel with a neon sign that said truckers were welcome. That usually meant they wouldn't fuss about a dog, and besides it was past nine o'clock. The manager was most likely eager to rent out whatever rooms he could at that point.

"Help you, sir?" An older lady looked up from the check-in desk.

"Just need a room. Be out early in the morning, but I do have a dog. He's housebroken and old, so he won't cause any damage."

"Ten-dollar fee for any animals. It's not one of those yippy little dogs, is it? I only got one room left and it's right next door to an elderly couple. Wouldn't want them calling me because your dog barked all night."

"No, ma'am. He's a blue heeler and he'll be glad to curl

up and sleep all night." Deke filled out the paper she passed across the desk to him and handed her his credit card along with a ten-dollar bill. "I don't reckon I'd feel right about charging Rascal's fee to my business card."

"You are an honest man. Ain't many of them left in the world." She handed him a key card. "Room one oh one, right at the end. You can park your truck and trailer out in the back lot. There's a place for your dog to take his nightly walk behind your unit."

"Thank you." Deke smiled. "Breakfast?"

"There's a truck stop that serves a good plate of food for a decent price up the road about a mile. There's a coffeepot in your room so you can get your eyes open with a couple of cups before you leave. Put your key on the top of the television and have a safe trip."

"Thank you, ma'am." Deke pulled his cowboy hat down tighter on his head when he opened the door.

Ten minutes later, he and Rascal were in the room. He quickly unfastened the dog's leash from his collar, and the old boy sniffed out every corner, made sure there were no varmints hiding in the bathroom, and then hopped up on the end of the king-size bed.

"Wait right here and I'll get the goody bag out of the truck." Deke turned up the thermostat on the wall heater. "No barking. We've got old folks for neighbors."

Rascal flopped down and put his paw over his nose.

"Back in less than five." Deke eased out the door.

When he returned the room was already beginning to warm up. "Bologna sandwiches for me, and I've got your favorite dog food right here plus since you were such a good traveling companion today, you get a piece of bologna for dessert. But only if you eat all your food first."

He'd gotten off the fast-moving interstate somewhere in Colorado, found a nice-size grocery store, and bought supplies to last the whole trip. Bread, lunch meat, cheese, dog food, chips, and one of those cheap coolers so that his perishables wouldn't ruin. It wasn't his first cross-country trip, and although he didn't mind café food, he hated to leave Rascal in the truck by himself. They had stopped for hamburgers at a McDonald's in the middle of the afternoon. Deke had two bacon cheeseburgers with everything on them. Rascal had two with meat and cheese only. They'd shared a big order of fries, but Rascal didn't want any of Deke's strawberry shake. He did however have about half a cup of coffee, lapped right out of Deke's cup when it had gotten cold.

*   *   *

On Friday morning, Josie packed a carry-on bag for the airplane with a couple of extra shirts, one pair of jeans, pajama bottoms and a tank top for sleeping, and a couple of pairs of underpants along with toiletries for an overnight trip to Montana. Her flight took her from Dallas to Cheyenne and from there to Butte, where she had reserved a rental car and a night in a nearby hotel. On Saturday morning, she'd drive south to Silver Star to look at the rodeo stock. She had a red-eye flight booked so she'd be home in the early hours of Sunday morning.

She remembered to pick up her heaviest coat on the way out of the house that morning. Jud was out helping Blake take care of Deke's cows as well as those belonging to the Lucky Penny. Fiona had left for work at the convenience store right after breakfast, so there was no one to wave good-bye to as she drove away.

Josie had visited the hotel several times over the past few days and was very pleased with the way the fresh new paint had spruced up the downstairs. With Fiona's help, they'd chosen a nice neutral carpet that would be arriving in a couple of weeks.

She was glad to be leaving Dry Creek for a few days. Jud and Fiona needed some time together—alone. They'd only been married for three days before Josie had arrived to stay in the house with them. She was sure they were more than eager for the clean-up to be finished on the old hotel—not that they weren't sweet as pie and perfectly hospitable. But yes, sir! A couple of days alone would be great for them.

She sighed wistfully at the thought of being a newly-wed...someday.

"But"—she inhaled deeply and let it out slowly—"not right now."

She drove straight to the airport, parked in a long-term lot, and was sitting in the gate area twenty minutes early. At five minutes until boarding time she counted the people in the airport—thirty total. No kids and two cowboys, neither of which was nearly as sexy as Deke. Her thoughts shifted over to that New Year's Eve kiss and a hot little shiver inched its way up her backbone.

She wondered if he'd made it to his destination and pulled out her phone to check a map from Dry Creek to Drummond, Montana. Fourteen hundred miles. If he traveled halfway he'd have stayed in Cheyenne, Wyoming, last night. Then this morning he would have gotten up early and headed out again. Was he planning to stay in a motel tonight and go on to the ranch to check on his bull tomorrow morning?

"But I'm going to have the better bull when we get home." She grinned.

My bull's better than your bull, the voice in her head singsonged.

She giggled, not even caring if several people stared at her.

"Group one, now boarding," the lady behind the counter said.

The two cowboys followed her down the long corridor to the entrance of the plane, where a smiling flight attendant welcomed her aboard. She found her seat, stowed her small suitcase in the overhead compartment, and sent up a little thank-you to the universe for giving her one of those exit seats with lots of legroom.

"Mornin', ma'am." One of the cowboys settled in beside her. "You sure you want to be sittin' here? You got to be strong enough to help people if we go down."

"I'm sure," she said.

"Well, I guess it is a small group of passengers and I could take care of them by myself if I had to."

"I'm able to hold up my end if we start to crash," she said.

"If you say so." He grinned.

After takeoff the cowboy tucked his chin to his chest and went right to sleep. When they landed in Denver, he awoke with a start, was gentlemanly enough to get her small case down for her and let her get off the plane before he did. She had exactly thirty minutes to catch the next flight. Thank goodness the gate was only a short distance from where she'd disembarked.

The flight from Denver to Butte was full without a single empty seat. Outside forces made for a turbulent ride, and her legs ached by the time they landed. She went straight to the car rental, picked up a Chevrolet Cruze, and checked her phone for directions to the hotel where she had a reservation.

The skies were totally gray when she went from car to hotel lobby and the air felt cold and damp even though the clouds weren't spitting out a bit of moisture. It was the prelude to the storm that was approaching for sure and she hoped the flight home on Sunday evening wouldn't be delayed.

She dropped the clothing she was wearing on the chair in the hotel room and padded naked and barefoot to the bathroom, where she took a long, hot shower. After drying off, she pulled on a pair of bikini underpants and a nightshirt that reached to her knees and pulled her phone from the hip pocket of her jeans before hanging them in the closet.

Jud had called while she was in the shower and there was another missed call, but she didn't recognize the number. She called Jud first and he told her that the storm was coming in faster than expected. It wouldn't be there until Sunday morning, so she shouldn't have to change her plans.

Then she called the second number.

"Dayton Ranch," a female voice answered.

"This is Josie Dawson returning a call that I missed."

"Oh, I'm so glad you called back. You are the last one on my list. We've called off our cattle sale scheduled for tomorrow. The storm that's coming this way has spooked our buyers and there simply was not enough to have a sale. I'm sorry if it has inconvenienced you."

Josie wanted to kick something but she sweetly said, "No problem, ma'am. Would you know of any other sales within a hundred miles that are still on schedule?"

"There is one up around Drummond. I can give you the number. It's scheduled for noon tomorrow. He's only got some rodeo bulls and a couple of broncs left, but he hasn't canceled yet."

"Thank you, I'll take that number," Josie said.

She wrote it down and wondered if she'd see Deke at the sale. Now wouldn't it be a hoot if they had a bidding war for the same bull?

Chapter Six

She checked the distance on her phone from Butte to Drummond. It wasn't much farther than what she'd planned to drive south, so she called the number and sure enough the man said the sale was still on. The next morning a few snowflakes were drifting from the sky when she crawled into her little red rental car. It was so pretty along the side of the road that she stopped long enough to take a picture of a bright red cardinal sitting in the white, undisturbed snow.

Twenty miles on up the road it had gotten serious and the roads were getting slippery, but she checked her GPS and it was closer to go on to the Drummond place than to go back to Butte. When she reached Drummond, she stopped at a service station and called the number for exact directions.

"Everett speaking," a rough old voice answered.

"I called last night about your rodeo stock. I'm in Drummond. Is the sale still going to happen?"

"No, it's canceled. This damn storm has hit a day earlier than they said it would."

"Could I come out and at least look at the stock?"

"You can but you are probably askin' for trouble," he said.

"Just give me the directions," she told him.

"Turn south on Highway One. I'm about two miles down the road on the right. You'll see the ranch sign if the snow ain't gotten ten feet tall in the next ten minutes. Miller Ranch. Turn in there, and the cabin is a quarter mile back down the lane. Drive easy now."

The phone screen said that Everett had hit the END button. Using her phone for a GPS she drove about half a mile in blinding snow up to an intersection and slid around the corner on a slick road. Two miles wasn't that far, she kept telling herself. She'd check the stock he had for sale and then be out of there in no time. It might take her all afternoon to drive seventy-five miles back to Butte but she'd driven in snow and ice before.

Fifteen minutes later, she finally reached the sign, with icicles hanging from it. She made a turn and the lane led her up to a small cabin set in the middle of a pine grove. Smoke spiraled up from the chimney and lights flowing from the windows threw off a yellow cast on the six inches of snow already on the ground.

Leaving her bag in the car, she turned off the engine, wiggled into her coat, and then opened the car door to the coldest, wettest snow she'd ever had hit her smack in the face. It didn't take long for her to jog from car to front porch and rap on the door.

The man who swung it open and motioned her inside didn't even come up to her shoulder. A thin rim of gray hair circled from one ear around to the other, leaving the top of his head bald. Freckles started there, and Josie couldn't have put a pin down without touching at least half a dozen that inched their way all down his face. His jeans hung on his small frame like a tow sack on a broom handle and the sleeves of his red plaid flannel shirt were rolled up to the elbows, revealing a thermal shirt beneath it.

"I'm Everett, and you must be Josie. Have a seat over there at the table and I'll pour you a cup of hot coffee. You can hang your coat on that extra nail by the door."

"I'd really like to see your stock and then get back on the road before this gets worse," she said and then noticed the dog lying in front of the fireplace.

"Rascal?" Surely she was seeing things. This could not be the same place that Deke had been headed—or could it?

"That's what I hear his name is." Everett chuckled.

"Josie!" Deke came through the back door with a load of firewood in his arms. "What are you doing here?"

"Same thing you are, I expect," she said. "My sale was called off and so I drove up here. Have you seen the bulls?"

Deke shook his head.

"I guess y'all know each other?" Everett asked.

"Oh, yes. His ranch is right across the road from my brother and cousins' place," Josie answered.

"Well, that damn sure proves that it's a small world." Everett laughed. "There'll be time to see them bulls later on this evening," Everett said. "Lots of time, matter of fact. This storm is going to be the mother of all past blizzards. Y'all ain't goin' anywhere for a week or maybe longer. We'll all just hunker down and wait it out."

"But if we left right now?" Josie said.

"Can't. Radio is saying roads are closed, and that the flights in and out of Butte and as far as Denver have been cancelled," Everett told them.

"What are we going to do?" Josie asked.

"Like I said, we'll all hunker down and live through it. I've got supplies and I'll be mighty glad for the company. It gets lonely up here in the wintertime," Everett said.

Josie looked around the cabin, her eyes coming to rest on the single bed shoved up against the wall.

Everett chuckled again. "I've got a little bunkhouse about twenty feet from my back door. You kids can stay in it."

Josie swallowed hard.

"Bunkhouse ain't as big as my cabin, but it's got a set of bunk beds and a bathroom and a real good fireplace with a full wood box right beside it and lots more stacked up by the door. Deke can start a fire and it'll be warm in just a little bit. And there's a table and two chairs and I keep a deck of cards and a bunch of books out there. Summertimes, I hire a couple of boys to help me out and they get their room and board with their salary," he explained. "And old Rascal over there, why he can either sleep in here with me or he can go with y'all. My last old dog died a few weeks back and I wouldn't mind if he chose to keep me company."

"You don't even know us," Deke said.

"I'm pretty damn good at readin' people. Y'all ain't the kind to hurt an old man. We'll have a good time. We'll go out in the mornin' and evenin' to do the barn chores and get to know each other through the day. Got to warn you though of two things. Blizzard like this is going to knock out the power by mornin' so we'll only have daylight and lamplight. The hot water tank out in the bunkhouse is small, but it is propane powered. Still you'll need to take real quick showers."

Josie locked eyes with Deke, not knowing what to do or say. There didn't seem to be a way out of the situation, and yet, sharing a room with him for days on end? Lord, did she have that much strength?

"Thank you for your hospitality, but we'll be glad to pay you for room and board," Deke said.

"Bullshit! You'll help me with chores and keep me company. That's enough payment," Everett said. "I made up a big pot of stew this morning and a loaf of home-made bread. I guess Mama Fate was tellin' me to get ready for company."

Josie's chest tightened when she thought about spending a whole week with Deke in a bunkhouse that was even smaller than the little cabin.

Chapter Seven

Deke polished off two bowls of soup and several thick slices of bread before he finally pushed his chair back. Mama Fate, as Everett said earlier, had sure enough dealt him a loaded hand and he wasn't sure how it would play out.

He'd thought he was over the attraction to Josie, but the way his old heart reacted when he walked out of that bathroom and saw Josie—well, it reminded him of the lyrics of that new country music song that said, "I looked up and an angel stood across a crowded room." The room was not crowded by any means with only Everett and Rascal there with Josie but she still looked like an angel with that blond hair and those big blue eyes.

"Poor old Rascal," Everett said. "Look at his face. He thinks he's not getting any food. Does he like dry dog food or human foot better?"

"Oh, no! I've only got a small bag of dry food and two cans." Deke slapped his forehead. "I thought I'd buy more on the way home if we ran out."

"Don't worry. Folks that live up here keep a good supply laid by, enough to last a whole winter if we need it. My old dog left behind two fifty-pound bags of dry food and two cases of canned stuff. But I bet old Rascal here would like a bowl of stew. He can have the dog food tomorrow night or when he don't like what we've got cooked." Everett went to the small stove and brought back a bowl that he'd dipped up earlier. "I reckon it's cool enough that it won't burn his mouth."

"You're spoiling him." Deke grinned.

"I miss my old dog. Having Rascal here going to help me as much as you kids keepin' me company the next few days," Everett said.

"How long do you reckon this will last?" Deke asked.

"Well, last time roads weren't cleared off for three weeks and then only the big roads. Highway One didn't see a snowplow for a month, but this one ain't nearly that big and we did get some warnin'. Thought it would be a day later getting here, but the weathermen ain't always spot on when it comes to that stuff. I bet this little old duster just keeps us snowbound a few days or a week at the most."

"Oh, no!" Josie said loudly.

Deke laid a hand on her shoulder. "It's okay. Maybe it won't be as bad as they think. Have you called Jud to tell him? I managed to get a call out to Blake, but it was real scratchy."

Josie grabbed her phone from her hip pocket and called the car rental place first to tell them that she was stranded and wouldn't have the car back until the roads were clear. Then she hit the icon to call Jud. Fiona answered on the first ring. "Blake just called and told us that Deke got stuck in that big storm blowing through the north. Are you at the airport?"

"No, I'm right here with Deke and it looks like we'll be staying with Mr. Everett Miller until the roads are clear."

Everett waved a hand to get her attention. "Might as well tell her that cell phones ain't worth jack shit up here in a blizzard. Might be good for another hour or so but listen to that wind. My house phone will be deader'n a roadkill possum before the night sets in too. This much wet snow will put the phone lines and the power lines on the ground for sure."

"I heard all that and, Josie, I'm real glad Deke is with you," Fiona said. "I'd trust him with my life. But how in the world did this happen?"

Josie got one word out before the phone went black and a NO SERVICE message popped up. Then the electricity went out and the little cabin was as dark as night even though it was only a little after one in the afternoon.

Everett grabbed a box of matches from above the stove and set about lighting oil lamps—one in the middle of the table and one at the end of a table between a recliner and a sofa.

"Time to hunker down. At least your folks know you are all right."

"How far is it out to the barn where you keep the cattle?" Deke asked.

"Not too far, but goin' out there now in this blinding blizzard ain't about to make a bit of sense. We have to go about five to take care of the stock so we'll wait until then to go. We'll have to break the ice in their water and give them some feed and milk the cow. And in the mornin' we'll do it all over again, but from what the weatherman said on my squawk box up there"—he pointed to the radio on the mantel—"this will settle down right over us for three days before it moves on off to the east. There'll be three feet of it before it stops and we'll have some shovelin' to do."

"How do you get from here to the barn in all that?" Josie asked.

"With snowshoes and right easy." Everett smiled. "Both of y'all look tired. If you want, you can go on out to the bunkhouse and have a little nap this afternoon. I most usually take one from about two until three. Be nice if old Rascal stayed in here with me. His old bones don't need to be travelin' back and forth any more than mine does. You'll find everything you need to start up a fire, and there's lots of good quilts on the bunk beds to keep you warm."

Josie headed for the nail where her coat was hung and Deke had to rush to get there before she did. He pulled the heavy work coat from the nail and held it for her to slip her arms into. His fingertips brushed her bare neck when he pulled it up and the chemistry he'd felt when she plowed right into him and knocked them both to the floor was still alive and strong.

"Did you bring your ski mask?" he asked.

She shook her head. "But my coat has a hood and I can draw it down tight. I'll be fine in that short distance."

"So does mine and I brought a mask. You can use mine." He pulled it from his pocket and shoved it down over her head.

"I got extras," Everett said. "Like I said, up here we stay prepared." He went to a chest of drawers at the foot of his bed and brought out a bright red one. "I always buy bright colors in case I fall into a drift. If someone was to come to check on me, it'd make it easy to find my frozen body."

He tossed it across the room toward Deke, who caught it midair and pulled it down over his head. "I should go out and bring in my things. It'll take a couple of trips to get it all. If you'll wait right here, I'll get your stuff with my last load."

"It's only one suitcase and my laptop and thanks, Deke," she said.

"No problem," he said.

"Quickest way is to bring it right back through here," Everett said.

Deke nodded and pushed his way out the door. When he cleared the porch, he started to mutter. "Hellfire and damnation! How am I supposed to survive days on end with Josie in a bunkhouse smaller than that cabin?"

He pulled his suitcase and a bag of leftover food from the truck and carried it all up to the porch, muttering the whole way. Barely opening the door enough to shove them inside, he almost slammed it on his hand when he shut it. His truck already had a snow cap on the top that was three inches deep. That trip took the rest of his stuff plus Josie's into the house.

Everett went over to the back door but he didn't open it. "You stay between the cedar trees. The path will take you right up to the bunkhouse porch. Matches are on the mantel in a tin box. I expect between the two of you, you'll make it out there with one load. Me and old Rascal here, we'll take us a nap and then start up supper so it'll be ready when we get done with the chores. And don't forget to turn on the two-way radio when you get out there so I can holler at you when the food is ready."

Both Deke and Josie stepped out into snow up to the tops of their boots in a fierce blizzard that obliterated everything from their sight. The cedar trees were at least ten feet apart and Deke was afraid if Josie fell he'd never find her.

"Stay close!" he shouted above the violent wind. "If either of us fall we're in trouble."

*   *   *

It seemed like they were moving in slow motion, but finally the porch came into view. With her long legs, Josie took the four steps up onto the porch in two long strides, threw open the door, and then quickly closed it the second that Deke was inside.

"Sweet Jesus!" she said as she undid her hood and ripped off the ski mask. "This is only half as big as his cabin. We won't be able to cuss a cat in here without getting a hair in our mouth."

"I haven't heard that saying in years. This isn't as big because it doesn't have a kitchen. His hired help eats with him in the big house," Deke said.

" 'Big house,' my butt." She went straight to the mantel and lit the oil lamp setting beside the tin box with matches inside. "That is barely a cabin. It doesn't qualify as a house. You reckon he's going to kill us or throw us out in the snow to freeze to death?"

"Nope." Deke reached inside the wood box, brought out several heavy logs, placed them in the fireplace, and added kindling.

Josie could hardly take her eyes off his strong arms as he carried the wood the short distance from the box to the fireplace. To have those arms around her, to cuddle up next to him on one of those bunk beds—she shook her head to get the picture out of it and reached for the tin box of matches on the mantel.

"How many do you need?" she asked.

"Just one," he answered.

"Confident, aren't you?"

"Not confidence, just practice, ma'am." He got the fire going with the first one.

"Impressive," she said.

"This tiny little place will be warm enough we can take off our coats before long."

She sat down on the sofa facing the fireplace and took stock of the whole place. A set of bunk beds covered the wall to her right. A doorway into a bathroom was to her left along with crudely made bookshelves with about a hundred well-worn paperbacks. A deck of cards was in the middle of a card table with a couple of folding metal chairs on either side. A second table was fitted into the small corner from the end of the bunk beds to the wall and another oil lamp had been placed in the middle of it.

"We'll survive," Deke said.

"Who are you trying to convince? Me or you?" Josie asked.

"Both of us. It's better than freezing to death in our vehicles. Lord, I wish I would have turned around and gone right back home when the first snowflake hit my truck window," he answered.

"Me too, but I just knew I'd have time to drive seventy-five miles and get back long before my flight." She threw one arm over her head and groaned.

"Top or bottom?" Deke asked.

"Well, now that depends on lots of things," she said before she thought.

Deke whipped around, his eyes as big as silver dollars. "What did you say?"

She blushed and quickly covered her blooper. "I don't care. I could sleep right here, especially if it was only for a nap. Maybe I'll go to sleep and wake up to find this is all a dream and the sun will be shining."

"Okay then, I'll take the bottom bunk. Rascal gets restless if he's not sleeping right beside the bed on his blanket or else on the foot of it. And, darlin', if you wake up for a nap and find this is a dream, please don't leave me behind."

"You think that old codger is going to let Rascal come out here with us?" Josie asked.

"He'll be sorry if he doesn't. Rascal has to go out at least once in the night and he don't care if he's making yellow snow or killing grass. He might not make it six inches off the porch but he will go out." Deke sat down on the sofa beside her. "It's starting to warm up real good. I reckon we could take our coats off."

She reached over and touched his cheek. "I'll give it five more minutes. You still feel like ice."

"Your hands are either warm or else they just feel that way because your touch just made my whole face tingle," Deke said.

"Forget those pickup lines, cowboy. You are stuck with me for the duration of this damned storm."

"And you, darlin', are stuck with me."

"You're right." She yawned.

Deke removed his coat and boots and pulled back the quilts on the bottom bunk. He slipped in between the flannel sheets, laid his head on the pillow, and shut his eyes. "It's right cozy in here. Things will look better when you wake up."

"Promise?" she asked.

"Cross my heart." A smile tickled the corners of his mouth.

She quickly removed her coat, hung it on one of the two nails beside the door, and then set her boots beside the fireplace. The end of the bunk bed was slatted to create a ladder and the wood wasn't as cold as she figured it might be. She quickly scrambled up, pulled back the covers, and got comfortable in between the sheets.

"Feels like Everett sprung for good memory foam mattresses, doesn't it?" Deke whispered.

"It's pretty comfortable, whatever it is," she said. "And just for the record, I'm glad you are here, Deke. I'm not afraid of Everett but..." She paused.

He snored, and she shifted her position to look over the edge of the bed. Heavy lashes rested on his high cheekbones. His chiseled face was softer when he slept, but his lips seemed even more kissable. What would it be like to feel those lips on hers?

She eyed the books across the room and silenced a groan. Every one of them was most likely westerns or murder mysteries, and she liked neither one. However, after a couple of days of blizzard and a week of cabin fever she might be willing to read the Bible backward to relieve the boredom.

Shutting her eyes did not mean that she would sleep, but she tried anyway and was amazed when the snoring below her stopped, bringing her to a sitting position. "Jud, is it already morning?"

"I'm not Jud and it's afternoon, not morning, darlin'. What world did you wake up in?"

She fell back on her pillow. "Jud snores. When it stops it means it's time to get up and get busy with the morning. You snore and you stopped. I thought I was back in the trailer that we shared out in the panhandle."

He swung his legs over the side of the bed, and, careful not to bump his head, he eased out of the bottom bunk. "So y'all stayed in a little travel trailer some of the time?"

"We shared a pretty nice two-bedroom trailer. It was a lot bigger than this place." She watched him put two more logs on the fire and run his fingers through his hair. "So what are you thinking about? That this would be a good honeymoon cabin with the right woman and a big old king-size bed rather than these things?"

"You read my mind, only I think a honeymoon would be better with a bunk bed, darlin'." He grinned.

She managed to spread the bedcovers back as she got out of the bed. "You are a rascal, Deke Sullivan." She made her way down the ladder and sat down beside him on the sofa.

"I've been called worse by women who weren't nearly as pretty as you. It looks like we will have no technology for a few days and we will have to listen to Everett or read all those books over there." He nodded in that direction. "You want first pick or can I have it?"

"Go on. I don't expect there's a thing over there that I'll like anyway."

He stood and crossed the small room in two long strides. "You read anything by Jill Shalvis? I've got two here, and there's a Meredith Wild that looks like it might be a romance type of book."

"I'll take both of them." She was almost giddy with relief.

He handed her the two books, and she opened up the one by Meredith Wild. Sweet Lord, it was good, but it was too easy to see herself as the character named Erica and Deke as Erica's lover. When she found herself almost panting, she looked across the sofa to see Deke reading a different book by the same author. He probably thought *Hardwired* was going to be some technology book.

A deep crimson blush crept from Josie's neck to her

face. She laid her book aside and went to the bookcase, found a Nicholas Sparks book, and took it back to the sofa.

"Man, I didn't know romance was this good," Deke said. "But I'll have to read it in short doses. Those scenes where they're having..." He hesitated.

"The sex scenes?" she asked.

His Adam's apple bobbed a couple of times when he swallowed hard.

"Was there something there you didn't know how to do?" she teased.

"Oh, honey." He grinned. "I could teach that Blake fellow a thing or two."

"Bullshit," Josie said, but then wondered what it would be like to have Deke pull her body so close to his that she could feel the hardness behind his zipper.

"I think maybe I'll tackle a James Patterson. I like a good mystery." He went back to the case and returned with a thick book that looked like it had been read a hundred times. "I can't imagine high school boys reading that romance stuff."

"Maybe they should," Josie said. "It might make them less clumsy."

"What would you know about that?" He turned, and their gazes locked midway between them.

"Oh, honey, I was clearly the author's model for the heroine," she said.

"Well, then if we ever got together, we should set the whole world on fire."

The radio squawked behind them. "Breaker, breaker, bunkhouse folks. I'm makin' supper so if you guys are hungry, you might want to bundle up and come this way."

Deke pushed a button and said, "Be right there."

"Good deal."

"Can he hear us?" Josie asked.

"Only if we push the button. Didn't you ever have walkie-talkies as a kid?"

"Not me. I always wanted a new chemistry set for my birthday and Christmas."

Josie wondered what kind of chemistry they might create in the cozy little cabin. She only hoped things wouldn't blow up in her face.

Chapter Eight

Josie didn't argue when Deke drew her close to his side on the walk from the bunkhouse to the cabin. With visibility at about two feet at the most, she rationalized that it was for safety. But she really did like the way that big strong arm felt around her waist, giving her support and at the same time creating all kinds of crazy vibes. It had been a very long time since anyone had made her feel special or since someone had flirted so blatantly, and both felt pretty damn good.

Rascal met them at the door with a welcome dance. Tail wagging so fast it was a blur and a few twists and turns to show that he was right glad Deke hadn't given him to Everett. Deke dropped down on his knees, removed his snow-covered gloves, and rubbed Rascal's ears. "Has Everett taken you outside? Do you want to make a trip before I take off my coat?"

"You're dripping water all over," Josie said as she hung her coat on a nail. The snow that had stuck to it quickly melted in the warmth of the cabin and dripped onto a frayed towel that Everett had spread out to keep puddles off the floor.

"Rascal and me took a little walk when we woke up from our nap. We only got about a foot off the porch and it didn't take him long, but we've been outside," Everett said, answering Deke's question. "Josie, you know anything about cookin'?"

"Little bit," she said.

"Can you make good biscuits?"

"Yes, sir."

Everett motioned for her to join him in the kitchen area. "Good, because no matter what I do my biscuits turn out like hardtack. I do like a good biscuit or homemade yeast bread, but I ain't got a hand for either one. So you can make us up some biscuits for supper to go with these chicken fried steaks and mashed potatoes. I got a jar of wild plum jam up there in the cabinet that Martha brought me last spring."

"Who's Martha?" Josie asked.

"That would be my lady friend." Everett grinned.

Josie smothered a laugh at the thought and crossed the room to the small kitchen area. It was nothing more than a stove on one end of a line of cabinets with no doors. Dishes and food alike were organized so well that she felt like she was picking items from the grocery store shelves as she lined up what she needed for biscuits.

"Milk?" she asked.

"Refrigerator." Everett pointed toward a narrow door at the far end of the area. "Got smart after the first year I was up here and fixed a little room to hold it and my freezer."

The small room held a chest-type freezer and an upright on one end and a refrigerator on the other. Two rows of pots and pans, big bowls, and all kinds of extra dishes lined two rows of shelves surrounding the whole room. She shivered as she chose a big metal bowl and then opened the refrigerator to find several gallons of milk. She set one inside the bowl and hurried back to the warmth of the cabin, carefully closing the door to the little room behind her.

"Why did you put the refrigerator out there?"

"No electricity," he answered. "Came close to losin' a whole beef and two hogs that first winter, so come spring, I built me a refrigerator room."

"Did you raise a family up here?" she asked.

Rascal went back to his blanket, which was now on the foot of Everett's bed, and curled up, but his tail kept wagging. Deke quickly hung up his coat, rolled up the sleeves of his plaid shirt, and washed his hands.

"What can I do?" he asked.

"Open that jar of green beans and dump them in that pan on the back of the stove. Turn the fire on under them and add some butter. It's on the table already and let them boil hard for fifteen minutes," Everett said.

"Back to your question, Josie." Everett finished beating on three round steaks with a cast-iron tenderizer. "I almost had a family. That was the plan forty years ago when I bought this place and built this cabin on it. I married the sweetest girl in Montana that summer. Her name was Lorraine and I loved her with everything in me, my heart, my mind, my body, and my soul." Evidently the old guy didn't get many visitors in the wintertime because he sure liked to talk. "I was plannin' to add a real bedroom to the place because we were going to have our first child that next summer. I had visions of a sprawlin' cabin with two wings and an addition on out toward the bunkhouse."

He poured milk into a bowl, cracked two eggs in it, and

added salt and pepper. Dipping out a cup of flour into a second bowl, he went on with his story. "We got a late freeze that year and we had a new calf out in the barn. Lorraine was on her way out there to see him when she slipped and fell. One minute she was alive and the next she was gone from me. The doctor said that she didn't suffer. The preacher said that she and our baby went to heaven immediately."

"I'm so sorry," Deke and Josie said in unison.

"Me too," Everett said. "She's buried at the cemetery in Hall and I just couldn't leave her. Not until this past year when she come to me in a dream and told me that my bones were too old to be enduring Montana winters. She said that her spirit would go with me wherever I went, so that settled it. I'm selling off my rodeo stock. I want to wait until summer to leave, though." He put two large spoons of shortening into a cast-iron skillet and turned on the burner under it. "You about ready to put them biscuits in the oven? That way all this will be done about the same time."

Josie pinched off the last of the dough between her thumb and forefinger and plopped it down in the pan he'd already prepared. He opened the oven door and she shoved them inside.

Josie looked up from the sink full of warm water where she was busy washing up her biscuit bowl to see Deke wipe his eyes. She wondered if it was the steam from the boiling potatoes and beans or if it was Everett's story that was getting to him. It sure enough had not been the biscuit dough that put the lump in her throat. Poor old Everett; he must have felt like Lorraine took his heart with her.

That's what Josie wanted. A love so strong that death couldn't break its bonds.

"And"—Everett swallowed hard—"this might seem

crazy to you kids, but it's in the summertime that Lorraine's spirit comes back the strongest. I swear I can feel her sittin' beside me on the porch step and I imagine that we're talkin' about things. It brings me comfort, but she's said that unless I leave before another winter that she won't never come back to me again."

Josie patted Everett on the shoulder. "Then you are doing the right thing. Did you know Lorraine your whole life?"

"Lord, no." Everett shook his head. "I was thirty years old and quite the rounder in those days. I was livin' in bunkhouses, working on ranches, mainly breakin' horses and doin' odd jobs, ridin' a few bulls at the rodeos and savin' up to buy my own place. Then a buddy of mine found Jesus."

The first steak he put in the hot grease filled the whole skillet. He glanced at a clock on the wall above the mantel. "Thank goodness they make a battery-powered clock for times like these. Three minutes on each side. That gives the beans time to boil, and Deke time to drain and mash those potatoes and your biscuits time to cook."

"What did your buddy finding Jesus have to do with Lorraine?" Deke asked.

Josie had been about to ask the same question and waited for Everett to go on.

"He was as big a rascal as I was, but he got to goin' to church and fell in love with the preacher's daughter. And he pestered the hell out of me to go to a church social to look at good girls. That's what he called them, and I told him I wasn't interested in no good girls. I liked my one-nighters just fine and dandy."

He flipped the steak over to brown on the other side. "You go on and set up the table for us, Josie."

She took three plates from the bottom shelf and gathered up enough mismatched cutlery to set the table for three.

"But you went?" Deke drained the potatoes and added butter and salt and pepper.

Everett handed him an old-time potato masher and Deke went to work with it.

"Had to. I owed him a debt, which we ain't goin' to talk about tonight. So I went with him yankin' and pullin' on me the whole way, and Lorraine was there. She was the new schoolteacher down at the Hall school and it was love at first sight. I looked at her and she looked at me and the whole world disappeared. We was married six weeks later right there in that church," Everett answered. "Now let's talk about you two? When did you meet each other?"

"Josie just moved to Dry Creek," Deke answered. "But I've lived there my whole life. My dad was a long-distance truck driver and my mama was a nurse. Daddy died in a car wreck on icy roads when I was seven, and then Mama had an aneurysm when I was eight. Granny and Grandpa raised me up on the ranch from then on. Then when they passed on they gave me my folks' place and my cousin got their ranch. His wife wasn't much for country life, so last year I sold my ranch and bought the old home place."

A lump was suddenly in Josie's throat that wouldn't disappear no matter how many times she swallowed. She couldn't begin to imagine life without her parents. Tears dammed up behind her lashes, but only one escaped, and she quickly wiped it away with the back of her hand.

"Why'd you move from one ranch to the other?" Everett asked.

"Grandpa was my guardian, and when I got old enough he turned my folks' ranch over to me. But I always dreamed of owning the ranch where I was raised. Luckily, things worked out because one of my best friends bought my parents' place and I had the money to buy my grandparents'."

"And you, Josie?" Everett turned to her.

"Lived out in Hereford, Texas, but there are Dawsons all in that area, with most of them being near a tiny little town called Happy," she said, amazed that she could speak at all. "I went away to college, then came back out as far west of Amarillo as you can get without being in New Mexico to work for an oil company. Finished up my contract with them and came to Dry Creek to be near my brother and to drill for oil," she said.

"Think there might be oil there?" Everett asked.

"Every test we've run has come back positive. We've got the paperwork filed, but it takes time before we can actually start the drilling," Josie answered.

"Well, I reckon there ain't no better way to get acquainted than being snowed in for a week." He chuckled. "You want to do some bull talking now?"

Josie nodded. "Yes, sir!"

"They're mean and tough and cowboys love it when they find out they'll be ridin' one of my bulls. The bulls have a real good reputation, so if y'all buy one or all four of them, then you'll be gettin' some good stock."

"What about your broncs?" Josie asked.

"One of my friends called just before y'all got here and said he wanted to buy them, so they're off the table. A word of advice to you kids. If you're going to have bulls, then have good bulls and don't go into the market for broncs. Specializin' is the name of the game these days. Bulls do better than broncs when it comes to what you'll make on them, and they're sturdier. They are good breeders and they will make you some money if you want to start making the rounds with them." Everett laid the first steak on a paper towel-covered platter and glanced at the clock when he put in the next one.

*　　*　　*

Deke wanted all four bulls the minute he laid eyes on them. They'd give his ranch a fantastic start, and their names were already known among the whole crowd of rodeo people, both promoters and riders. The Resistol Rodeo wasn't too far from Dry Creek and he had connections with the rodeo crowd from his riding days, so leasing his bulls for a weekend at a time to stud wouldn't be difficult.

"Meet Barbed Wire," Everett said, introducing the first big solid black bull. "You might as well try to ride a bale of barbed wire as this boy. Only had six riders so far that stayed on him the full eight seconds and he comes out of the chute with both hind feet in the air every single time. Got an average buck-off time of just under four seconds."

He moved to the second huge stall. "And this is Critter. He's Barbed Wire's son and the youngest bull of the four. He meaner than the devil and his average buck-off time is four point one seconds. He's still workin' on matchin' his daddy for tough, but he'll get there."

Deke heard Josie gasp when they reached the third pen. He couldn't fault her for that. Right in front of them was old Lucifer himself in all his brown-and-white-spotted glory. Everett didn't need to tell them his stats. They were known everywhere—but who would have guessed they'd find him in northern Montana.

"Guess y'all done know about Lucifer. I bought him three years ago and he's been a moneymaker. He'll make a cowboy upward toward ninety points with all his twists and turns. Y'all live right close together, right?" Everett pulled his stocking hat up over one ear. "The wind whistlin' makes it hard for me to hear."

Josie raised her voice. "Deke's ranch is across the road from my brother's place, which is where I'll keep my stock until I get a place of my own."

"Go into business together. Make it the JD Bull Business or some such thing and you can share the profits at the end of the year." Everett jerked the hat back down over his ears and went to the last stall. "And this is my pride and joy. He's Lucifer's offspring and he's only been in two rodeos, but he's done me proud. This here is Winchester. Give him another year and he'll be a force to reckon with."

Deke could tell by the wary look in Winchester's eye that he'd give a rider a lot of bang for his buck. Buying all of them, especially with Lucifer in the lot, he could start making the statewide rounds with them in the spring. Maybe Everett had a good idea about him and Josie going into business together. But he had a feeling that she would never go for that. He only hoped that when the dust—or, rather, this rotten damned blizzard—settled, she wouldn't make an offer to buy the whole lot and leave him driving home with nothing but an empty trailer.

"Where is Dry Creek?" Everett asked. "I been thinkin' about moving to Texas when my place sells. I'd still have seasons, but the winters wouldn't be this fierce." Everett hung the galvanized milk bucket on a post and opened a gate. "I'm going to take Lucifer out of the stall and y'all can clean it out, put down some fresh straw, and throw a little bale of hay in his trough."

"Will the others trust us to lead them out?" Deke asked.

"You'd better get your bluff in on 'em if you're plannin'

to buy them," Everett said. "If you get done with Lucifer's
pen before I finish milkin', you can start by putting him
back in the stall. Don't be pettin' his back, though. First
sign of pressure and he thinks it's time to buck. Last kid
who tried to help me almost got himself stomped."

Deke picked up a wide shovel and went to work on the
wet, messy straw, digging every bit of it away from the
cold dirt underneath and piling it into a weathered old red
wheelbarrow.

He caught a glimpse of Josie's well-rounded butt when
she turned away from him and his chest tightened. He
leaned on the shovel handle for a moment and then inhaled
deeply and went back to work. Who would ever believe
that mucking out a stall could get him so turned on?

*   *   *

Josie headed to the center of the barn, stopping long
enough to look at the two broncs and wishing that they
were still up for sale. They were fine-looking horses with
good lines and lots of fight in their eyes.

She picked up a pair of wire snips from a worktable in
front of the hay bales, stuck them in her hip pocket, and
then slipped her gloved hands under the wire on a bale
of hay. Everett had stacked the bales that were lighter in
weight and color on one side of the big barn and the heavier, darker bales on the other side. Light for bedding; dark
for feeding.

Carrying the light bale back to Lucifer's stall, she
passed Deke pushing the wheelbarrow toward the back of
the barn. She stopped long enough to watch him muscle the
door open against the wind and snow and manhandle the
load out into the corral. He treated that heavy weight as if

it were no more than a stack of feather pillows. His arms didn't even strain the seams of his coat. And he whistled the whole time he worked, making it clear that the work wasn't drudgery but something that he enjoyed. Another side of Deke that most women would never see.

Suddenly it was too warm in the barn. She unbuttoned her coat and wiped her brow with the back of her gloved hand. Maybe they should set Deke outside naked and let her look at him for a couple of hours. The heat from her body would melt every bit of the snow on Miller Ranch. She stopped fanning her face with her hand when he pushed the wheelbarrow up to the next stall.

"You look like the Abominable Snowman," she said. "Or maybe Shrek."

"Oh come on, now, I'm not that ugly." He rolled back his mask, leaving it stuck on his head like a stocking hat.

"But you are that big." She started past him to go for the heavier bale of feed hay.

"So does that make you Fiona?" he asked.

"No, Fiona is married to my brother." She giggled.

He tilted his head to one side. "And it's also Shrek's lady friend."

"You've watched the movie?"

Deke nodded, his eyes on her lips. Suddenly, her mouth felt warm, slightly bee-stung and moist.

She took a step forward, like a moth inching its way toward a flame.

Lucifer's loud bellow startled her and she whipped around too fast to check on him. Her hip hit the blade of the shovel sticking out of the wheelbarrow. She could feel herself falling and grabbed for the stall. Her heart raced with panic and then strong arms circled her and before she could blink she was plastered against Deke's broad, hard chest.

She pushed back with intentions of thanking him but his eyes were on her lips again and it was as if time reversed and they were right back in the moment again. Then his gloved hand tipped her chin up and his eyes fluttered shut.

She wrapped her arms around his neck and rolled up slightly on her toes until her nose was only a couple of inches from his. He tilted his face to the left and she went to the right and their lips met in the middle in a kiss that made a sizzling sound like steak hitting a hot grill. The last time her pulse had raced so hard was when she was on the back of a horse riding hell-bent for leather across the open plains out near Amarillo, Texas.

When the kiss ended Deke ran the edge of his hand down her cheek and hugged her before he dropped his hands to his side. She took a step back and leaned against a stall fence and filled her lungs with air that smelled like used bedding.

"That good, huh?" he asked.

"Wouldn't know. I haven't kissed a man in a year, so I don't remember what it's supposed to feel like." Her voice sounded strange, as if she'd been running.

He took a step forward and kissed her again. Her arms went around his neck. His dropped to the small of her back, penning her against the stall. The energy surrounding them swept Josie away from all common sense and she would have been making out with him the rest of the day if he hadn't finally taken a couple of steps back.

"Now you have something to compare it to. How was that?" he asked with a wicked grin on his face.

"Not bad." She shrugged nonchalantly, her fingers crossed behind her back like a little child who'd told a lie.

"We'll have to practice." Deke grinned.

"No, Deke."

"Is it because of my reputation or your fear?" he asked.

"Maybe both. Do either of us have time for this? And even if we did, I'm just not sure it's a good idea."

"Change is possible and fears can be overcome," he said.

She pushed away from the stall. "A philosopher as well as a cowboy."

Deke opened Barbed Wire's gate and led him to the center of the barn. "I'm just full of surprises," he threw over his shoulder.

She jerked off a glove and touched her still-warm lips. So this was why they called it chemistry between two people. Put two people together. Add a few soft brushes of skin and then two kisses. Boom!

Chapter Nine

Josie wasn't sure a person could go to heaven if they went to bed at eight thirty in the evening. It seemed like it ought to be a sin for sure and she didn't expect to fall asleep for at least two hours when she put on her pajama bottoms and a tank top that evening. Deke blew out the lamps, putting the room in semidarkness.

She flipped from one side to the other a couple of times, trying to get comfortable and convince herself that it was close to eleven o'clock, which was her normal bedtime. The wind still whistled like a freight train outside the bunkhouse and it looked as if the blizzard might hang around until the heat of summer arrived.

"Hey, wiggly britches up there. Are you thinking about those kisses?" Deke asked.

"I am not," she answered.

"Well, I am. They were pretty fine in my book," Deke said.

She scooted to the edge of the bed and peeked down at

him. Half his face was in dark shadow, but the flickering fire gave a little definition to the other side. He looked up at her and gave her one of those sly, sexy winks.

"Like what you see?" he asked.

"Of course, but I'd be dead or blind not to," she answered honestly.

"And that means?"

"Deke, you could charm the panties off a woman and I believe you probably know that," she answered.

"If they wear panties." He grinned.

She flipped back on her bunk, head on pillow, eyes straight ahead and face burning. She'd walked right into that one, so she couldn't blame anyone but herself.

"How about you, Josie? Could I charm your cute little bikini under britches off you?" he asked.

She glanced at the clothing hanging on a makeshift line Deke had stretched across the room. There was her underwear, along with the rest of the day's laundry, silhouetted against the embers of the fire.

"Good night, Deke," she said.

"'Nite, Josie. And those were some damn fine biscuits you made for supper. I hope Everett sweet-talks you into making them every morning for breakfast while we are here," he said.

"Thank you. The end," she said.

"And that means what?"

"It's what Mama always told me and Jud when we'd keep talking after she tucked us into bed," she told him.

"I ain't been tucked in so I reckon I can talk some more."

"The end," she said.

His chuckle let her know that he thought he'd gotten the last word even if it wasn't a real one. She shut her eyes and this time went right to sleep. She awoke the next morning to the smell of coffee close enough that she could feel the steam from it on her face.

"Wake up, beautiful," Deke whispered.

"What time is it?" She sat up and rubbed her eyes.

"Four thirty. I found an old blue granite pot and a pound of coffee on the bottom shelf of the bookcase. Guaranteed to wake you right up."

She sat up and wrapped her hands around the mug. "And it's warm. How did we miss seeing it last night?"

"Have no idea. I imagine that Everett is already up, since we all went to bed so early. Ready for bacon and eggs?" He smiled.

No, but she was ready for another kiss or two after those scorching hot dreams she'd had about him through the night. Really, now! This whole scenario was because they were stuck in a storm. If she'd been one of dozens of women in a country bar, he probably wouldn't give her a second glance.

He was already dressed in wrinkled jeans that had come off the clothesline and a clean shirt. He picked up the walkie-talkie and said, "Breaker, breaker. Is Rascal up and ready to get the day started over there?"

Everett came right back with, "We're both up and had our coffee. Rascal likes his in a bowl with a little cream in it. Y'all come right on over when you are ready and we'll get some breakfast started. We got to have sustenance if we're going to go back to the barn this morning."

"Be there in fifteen minutes," Deke said.

"You've got to be kidding me." Josie sighed. "I haven't had my morning shower and my hair dryer doesn't work with no electricity."

"You take a shower, get dressed, and bring me the hairbrush. You can sit close to the fire and I'll brush it out for you. The heat will dry your silky hair in minutes," he said. "I already had mine this morning, but there's been time for the water to reheat."

She must've been sleeping pretty hard not to have heard Deke up and around, taking a shower, putting away his clothing off the line, making coffee. A picture of him doing that wearing nothing but a towel around his hips flashed through her mind. Good Lord! She had to get ahold of herself.

She crawled down the ladder at the end of her bunk and padded to the bathroom. Then she remembered that she should take her clothing with her, so she went back to the clothesline and picked off jeans, shirt, and underpants. She went back to the bathroom and didn't have her toiletry kit, so she had to go back to her suitcase a second time.

Deke had picked up his book and was reading by the light of an oil lamp. His long legs were stretched out toward the blazing fireplace, warming his bare feet. Bare was the word that kicked off the picture of him in the towel again and no amount of blinking or shaking her head would dislodge it.

"If you can't lick 'em, join 'em," she murmured. Everett was right about the hot water. She had to rinse the last of the shampoo from her hair in downright icy water.

"I miss electricity but not as much as hot water," she whispered as she wiped the steam from the mirror above the sink. With only the oil lamp that Deke had left burning on the back of the toilet, the reflection staring back at her was nothing but a dark shadow with very little definition.

After quickly drying off, she jerked on jeans so stiff that she had to work her legs down into the legs and a knit shirt that was anything but soft. She added a clothes dryer to the list of things that she really missed. She gathered up her toiletry bag and carried it back to the suitcase, keeping out the hairbrush. Sitting down with her back to the fire, she started to brush out her long blond hair. But she'd given her hair only a couple of strokes when Deke laid aside his book, sat down behind her, and took the brush from her hand. He ran it through her wet hair—slowly, pulling it upward so that the heat from the fireplace could dry the individual hairs.

How could something as common as brushing hair be so sensual, expose every raw desire in her body, and make every nerve tingle? Warmth spread from her scalp in waves all the way to her toes and it had absolutely nothing to do with that crackling fire behind her.

"Twenty minutes and it's all done. We'll be only five minutes late." He reached over her shoulder, handed her the brush, and kissed her on the cheek. "You sure are a pretty thing sitting there in front of the fire in the light of the oil lamp."

"Well, thank you, Mr. Sullivan." She bounced up on her feet. "If you are buttering me up for breakfast biscuits, you are doing a fine job of it. Let's get our boots and coats on and brave the storm. You think it will quit today?"

"Not according to what Everett heard last night. The weatherman says maybe by Tuesday it will move on out of the area."

Josie slipped her arms into her coat, put on her gloves, and stretched the ski mask over her face. "Would you buy this ranch?"

"Hell, no!" Deke said quickly. "Summers might be pretty, but I'll put up with the sweltering Texas heat before I'd move to a place that has winters like this. Keeping rodeo stock in the barn is not my idea of a good thing. They need to be out in a pasture or maybe in a corral. Would you buy it?"

"Double hell, no!" she said. "A pretty summer isn't worth this crap. You ready for me to open the door?"

"Might as well be."

She swung it to the inside and groaned. It had served as a backstop for at least two feet of snow. Her boots came up to midcalf but there was no way she'd make it to the cabin without getting her jeans wet. And then there was the job of going to the barn for chores. What she'd give for a pair weatherproof coveralls right then couldn't be measured in dollars.

One minute she was standing there, dreading raising her foot for the first step, and the next Deke had scooped her up in his arms like a new bride.

"Not a bit of sense in both of us getting wet. Besides, I can move faster with you in my arms rather than holding on to your arm," he said.

He stepped out, shut the door behind him, and trudged through snow up to his knees. Josie wrapped her arms around his neck and listened to the steady beat of his heart.

Deke loved babies, had a soft spot for the elderly, and carried a woman through the snow. It wouldn't take much to fall hard for a man like that. She was a bit disappointed when he tapped the cabin door with the toe of his boot and Everett opened it. He gently set her on the floor but stomped his boots on the braided rug inside the door, shaking off as much snow as he could.

"Now that was right neighborly of you." Everett smiled.

"I wanted a pan of her biscuits, and I'm hungry. If she was wet from the knees down she'd want to get dried and warm before she'd make them," Deke told him.

"Well, then I am grateful to you because me and Rascal have been thinking about them biscuits ever since we got up this mornin'," Everett said.

Deke crossed the floor and hugged the dog. "Rascal, you old traitor. You didn't even come give me a welcome."

The dog's tail thumped on the sofa where he rested on his red blanket, but he didn't move.

"He says that he welcomed you yesterday and today it's your turn to go sit on the sofa and talk to him," Everett said. "That way you can get them britches legs dried off in front of the fire while me and Josie make some breakfast. I reckon we'd best fire up the tractor to get out to the barn this morning."

"Where is it?" Deke asked.

"Parked right up next to the side of the house. I've got good heavy coveralls, so I'll get it ready and y'all can get in with me right off the porch but Josie will have to ride in your lap because it ain't got but two seats.

"I'll fry the ham steaks if you'll make a pan of biscuits. Maybe some hash browns and scrambled eggs would be good with it. I hope the hens ain't goin' on strike in this storm. We're down to about three dozen out there in the fridge. And tomorrow I reckon we'd best skim the cream off that milk out there and freeze it to make butter out of later on."

"Today is Sunday, right?" Deke asked.

Everett checked the calendar on the wall with a big *X* through each day. "Time is crazy in a storm like this but yes, sir, today is Sunday."

Rascal moved over close enough that Deke could rub his ears. "Seems like we've been here a month."

"Happens that way when the sun don't come out and

you live in a routine rut. That's the reason I mark off each day just before I go to bed every night," Everett said. "When we can get out more it'll straighten itself out a little. When it stops blusterin' around, we'll put the plow on the tractor and make us a path to the barn. We'll have to use a couple of shovels for the path between the bunkhouse and cabin, though. Tractor can't get between them cedar trees I planted for a wind break."

"Rascal, do you and Josie want to make a snowman with me?" Deke asked.

"Hell, no!" Josie said loudly.

"Sassy, ain't she? Reminds me of my Lorraine. She didn't swear very often, but when she did I knew it was time for me to go to the barn and let her cool off." Everett grinned so big that it erased several wrinkles from his hollowed cheeks. "Just for the record, I wouldn't build no snowman, neither."

Josie stirred up the biscuit dough and tuned out Everett's chatter. Not having a phone or her laptop made her absolutely antsy. What was going on with the preparations for the oil well? Had they heard back from the environmental folks yet? Had the carpet been installed at the hotel yet? And how was Kasey doing?

"Josie!" Everett said loudly. "Are you with us or has your brain plumb frozen?"

"I'm sorry. What did you say?"

"I asked you which one of them bulls you got an interest in," Everett said.

"All of them," she said.

"You kids talked about whether you might go into business together? I wouldn't feel right sellin' all of them to you when Deke got here first."

"We haven't but we will. If you'll open the oven door

for me, we'll get these to cookin'. Don't know about y'all but I'm starvin',*" she said.

"I like a woman with an appetite." Everett hurried to do her bidding. "Don't you, Deke?"

"Oh, yes I do, and one that can make a mean pan of biscuits is just that much better." He grinned.

"And who knows her way around a barn." Everett nodded.

"Flattery won't get you anywhere," Josie told them. "What have you heard this morning about the weather? I looked out the window when I was hanging up my coat and my rental car is almost covered up."

"More of the same," Everett said. "It's your turn to love old Rascal now. I'll take care of the rest of the breakfast."

By the time they finished eating, Deke's jeans were almost dry. While Josie washed up the dishes Everett zipped himself into coveralls, pulled on hip-wading boots that she'd only ever seen fly fishermen wear, gloves, and a face mask, then brought out a pair of snowshoes from under the bed.

"Sorry, kids, but I ain't got but one pair. If I'm still here another winter, I'll buy a couple more sets just in case something like this happens again."

Josie reached for the cell phone that was always in her hip pocket to take a quick picture of him and then remembered she'd left it in the bunkhouse. Not that it would do her a bit of good anyway, since it needed charging and the electricity was still out.

No electricity and no television, either?

She scanned the room and located a television hanging on the wall at the end of his bed. In the semidarkness and set back in a corner it was almost invisible.

Everett chuckled. "I don't have cable, but I watch a lot

of movies and TV series on DVD. I got every one of *Justified* and a bunch of other ones like *CSI* and got all of those *NCIS* ones. The Gibbs one is still my favorite, but I'm likin' that one down there in New Orleans pretty good too. When the power is on, the sound of their voices helps me make it through the loneliness."

"Hey, those are some of my favorite shows, too," Deke said.

They both looked at Josie. "Okay, I watch them, too, but I also like *Castle*."

"Got that one too. Martha bought all the seasons of it for my Christmas. Ain't even had time to start watching it. Too bad the electricity is out. We could watch the episodes together." Everett headed for the door.

"I feel like I'm living in the Old West days," Josie said.

"You are, but the thing about this is that it'll be over and we can jump forward to the present. Them folks just had to keep enduring it. I think old Rascal could use an outing this mornin'. Deke, you carry him to the tractor and he can ride between us. He won't mind bein' crowded and he'll love bein' able to prowl around in the barn."

In a few minutes the sound of a tractor engine cut through the noise of the wind. Josie began to worry about Everett when the engine didn't start getting louder like it should when moving toward the front of the house. Idling meant Everett was inside the cab, but after it warmed up, the sound should change.

Rascal hopped off the sofa and sat by the front door, eyes straight ahead.

Deke stomped his feet down into his cowboy boots. "I'm going out to help him."

Josie reached for her coat. "I'll go with you. If he's fallen or hurt, it'll take both of us to get him back in the house."

The tractor engine went from a gurgle to a growl and Josie giggled, not from happiness but from relief. "Thank you, Jesus." She rolled her eyes toward the ceiling. "And I mean that quite literally."

"And I'll add the amen." Deke picked up Rascal.

She was totally surprised when she opened the door and found only a few inches of snow on the porch. "He's been sweeping it regularly."

"Probably for Rascal."

"I'm ashamed of myself for ever thinking he was..." She hesitated.

"Me too," Deke said.

"He's just a lonely old guy without any family."

"By the time this all blows over, he may be giving thanks for that," Deke said.

"Somehow, I doubt it."

The blade of the tractor was on the ground, making a pathway, when it came to a stop in front of the house. Josie waved and stood back while Deke waded through a couple of feet of snow and put Rascal in the cab. She started to take a step but Deke yelled at her to wait a minute. He whipped around and came back in the same footsteps, threw her over his shoulder like a bag of chicken feed, and carried her to the tractor. When he got inside and sat down she fell into his lap perfectly.

"Well, that was romantic," she said breathlessly.

"So you are thinking romance?" Everett chuckled.

"No, sir, I am not." Josie peeled off her mask. Lord almighty, it was hot in the tractor cab. Rascal was shoved up against her left side. Deke's breath was even hotter than usual when he exhaled against her cool cheeks. And Everett had the heater going full blast.

Blade still down, he turned the tractor around, leaving a

pile of snow right in the middle of the yard. "There's a pile of snow for your snowman, kids. You just have to bring something out to shape him up when this quits."

"Romance?" Deke whispered softly in her ear.

"Partnership?" she said.

"Did I hear partnership?" Everett asked. "It would be a good thing, I'm tellin' you. I wished a lot of times that I'd had a partner to help me with that end of my business."

"We're talking about it," Deke answered.

Everett plowed right up to the doors and turned off the engine. "I'll hold on to old Rascal while y'all go get the barn doors opened up."

Josie quickly slid out with Rascal right behind her. So much for Everett keeping the dog in the cab. Everett slipped in behind him, and Deke shut the door. Twisting and turning like a puppy, Rascal jumped on hay bales, chased out a rat, ran back down the aisle where the bulls were and sniffed the stalls, and then came tearing back to Deke.

Everett unzipped his coveralls, removed them, and hung them on a nail inside the barn door. He took down an old coat hanging beside them and took time to button it up all the way to his neck. "I'm going to check on the hens before I milk."

"They are in the barn?" Deke asked.

"No, they got their own yard, but it's attached to the end of the place. Y'all come on with me and I'll show you how we take care of things up in the cold part of the world."

Everett led them to the tack room at the end of the barn. He picked up a bucket with hay in the bottom and pointed toward a dozen hinged flaps located on the far side of the room. He unfastened a latch at the side of the first flap and smiled. "Guess they ain't got nothing to do when it gets like this but sit on their nests and gossip like old hens do." He brought out an egg from behind each flap. "We'll have plenty to do some bakin' this afternoon if you've got a mind to help me, Josie?"

"Be glad to help. I love to bake," she said. "We could even make some extra things to put in the freezer for later, but I have to warn you about Deke's sweet tooth. There might not be any extra with him in the cabin for a few days."

Deke nodded emphatically. "I'm not good in the kitchen but I'll sure help with cleanup if you'll make cookies or cakes or pies or brownies. And Josie is right, I do love good desserts."

"Then it's a plan. Y'all go on and feed the bulls and broncs. I only clean out the stalls at night, so you'll be done by the time I get through milkin' the cow," Everett said.

Josie stopped at Lucifer's stall and stared at the magnificent beast. She wanted all the animals, and forming a partnership might be the right thing to do. Those bulls in Butte couldn't be a bit better than Lucifer or the other ones, either. Every one of Everett's bulls had good lines, a fantastic reputation, and she could probably make a fortune using them for breeding stock for her own herd plus charging other rodeo folks to use them. Then if she wanted to make a rodeo with them a couple or three times a year, that would be even more money.

Deke slipped his arms around her waist from behind. She flipped around to say something but before she could speak, his lips were on hers. As if they had a mind of their own, her hands found their way around his neck. The pure unadulterated heat from the kiss left her knees weak and her pulse racing. Business partners did not kiss each other.

She should step back, but her feet were glued to the cold dirt floor.

"How's that for romantic?" His voice was even deeper than usual and his eyes all dreamy as they locked with hers.

Like a flash of lightning, Rascal raced between the two rows of stalls, pushed his way between them, and put his paws on Deke's chest.

Thank God for dogs, she thought as she took several steps back and caught her breath.

"Well?" Deke asked as he rubbed Rascal's ears.

"It's better than being slung over your shoulder like a bag of cattle feed," she called to him as she headed toward the feed bin to fill a bucket for Lucifer. It wasn't a lie, but she wasn't about to tell him just how much his touch or his kisses affected her. Her knees felt like they had no bones in them, her heart was pounding, and her palms were sweaty, so she'd say his kisses caused an emotional upheaval in her body.

If that meant romantic, then hell, yes!

Chapter Ten

As Deke figured it, a low bid on the four bulls would be about seventy-five thousand and the high somewhere up around a hundred. At seventy-five thousand, he could go half on the partnership deal if he tightened his belt and didn't buy that tractor he'd had his eye on for the past year.

He checked the wood box of the bunkhouse, found it nearly empty, and geared up in his coat, hat, and gloves to go out and bring in a few armloads. Last Sunday evening he was in Texas, where it was cold but the ground was clear. With the blizzard raging, it was hard to imagine there was another world outside of Everett's small cabin and the bunkhouse, or that he'd only been there a couple of days. It seemed like forever.

"Need some help?" Josie asked from the corner of the sofa where she was propped up with a romance book with a picture of a cowboy on the front.

He shook his head and asked, "Who are you reading?"

Josie held up the book. "Laura Drake. She writes amazing westerns."

A picture of a cowboy and a cowgirl, both wearing black hats and just about to kiss, was on the cover. Except for the red hair, the girl could have been Josie.

"Got time to lay it aside to open the door for me when I kick it with the toe of my boot?" he asked.

She nodded but didn't look up. "Sure thing."

He loaded up a stack of wood on a flat board, picked it up, and headed for the door. It opened the second he was close enough to walk right in with the wood. She held the lid of the wood box up while he carefully shifted the armload inside.

"Half full," she said.

"One more armload, but good news. The blizzard is letting up. I can actually see Everett's cabin."

"How much snow did you have to shovel off the top of the wood pile?" she asked.

"It was up to the eaves. But this time will be easier. See you in a few minutes." He pulled the face mask down and squared his shoulders. Not once in all his life had he been in weather like this but the physical storm was nothing compared to the one going on inside his heart and mind. One was freezing cold; the other was hotter than the barbed wire fence on hell's back forty. And there didn't seem to be a happy medium with either one.

The second load filled the box so well that the lid wouldn't close all the way. He hung his coat back on the nail and laid the ski mask and gloves on the stones in front of the fireplace.

"So what do you think..." Warming his hands by the fire, he started to ask about the partnership, but a knock on the door stopped him.

Josie hopped up and covered the distance to the door in three long strides, flung it open, and Rascal bounded across the room, hopped up on the sofa, and actually looked like he grinned at Deke.

Everett followed him inside. "Rascal was restless. The storm is letting up and he's worried that you'll go off and leave him here. Not that I'd mind one bit. Me and him would get along just fine, and I miss having a partner around here." Everett brought Rascal's red throw out from under his arm and spread it out on the sofa.

Rascal curled up on it with Deke beside him, rubbing his ears. "So you finally missed me, did you?"

"Come in and have a seat. We can put on another pot of coffee," Josie said.

"No, sweetheart. I don't drink coffee this late and it takes too much energy to take off these coveralls and put them back on in half an hour. Besides, I'm at a real good spot in my book. I see you got a Laura Drake over there. She's a right fine author. I like her because she writes about rodeos."

"You read romance?" Josie gasped.

"I read good books. If there's a love story I always pretend that it's me and Lorraine in another place and time." He grinned. "Y'all have a good night. I expect by morning it'll all be over but the cleanup business."

"Good night," Josie said. "See you at breakfast."

"Good night, and if Rascal decides to stay when y'all go in a few days, he'd be right welcome."

"Not a chance," Deke said, "but I don't have a doubt that you'd spoil him rotten."

Everett pulled up the collar of his coveralls and eased out the door with a wave over his shoulder.

"It is slowing down." Josie's tone was full of excitement.

"Do you think we can start back home by the end of the week?"

"Maybe," Deke said. "It'll depend on how fast the folks can get the roads cleared for traffic. They'll take care of the interstate highways first and then the smaller roads. If the weather stays below freezing, it'll be a long time before this melts."

"Spring, probably." She groaned. "Please tell me we won't be here until summer."

"We won't even be here until spring. I can't promise Valentine's Day, though, and I might not be able to get to the flower shop or the store to buy candy for you so what else can I do to make the day special?" he teased.

She rolled her eyes and fell back on the sofa beside Rascal. "Don't even think like that. I'm so far behind on work already that I can't even think about Valentine's Day, but that's a whole month away. My eyes are tired. Talk to me. Tell me why you want those bulls out there in the barn."

He grabbed the dog by the ears and kissed him on the top of his head. "I'm glad you came home to me, old boy. I was getting worried. Now to your question, Josie. I rode bulls right out of high school. By damn, I was going to be the best of the best, win the buckle and the money at the big rodeo in Las Vegas and maybe even buy the Lucky Penny, since it butted up to the ranch I owned." He paused to scratch Rascal's ears.

"Did you get bucked off and lose your dream?" she asked.

"Got bucked off lots of times and have a broken wrist and ankle to prove it. Damned things still pain me when it's cold like it is here. Took a lot of pain to convince me that I was not nearly good enough to ever make it to Vegas."

"So you gave up? That surprises me," she said.

"I didn't give up. I faced reality. I still like to break a bronc or ride a bull in the pasture sometimes, but it's not for anything other than the fun," he answered. "Now, tell me why in the hell an oil woman like you would want those bulls?"

"I've been going to rodeos since I was a baby. The trip to Vegas for the National Finals was our family vacation most winters. I fell in love with the bulls, but I also loved the broncs. It's all I can do to sit a horse without falling off, so there never was a time I wanted to be out there on the broncs or the bulls, but I loved watching the events."

"Owning a bull and watching them kick and buck are two different things," he said.

"I see it as an investment. Take them to the rodeo and lease them a couple of times a year to make them happy. Then use them for breeders. Do you know how much a stock owner would pay to breed a cow to Lucifer? With his reputation he would earn out whatever we pay for him in a couple of years at the most."

"Your parents ever have rodeo stock?"

"No, but Kasey's did for a while. Then her grandpa died and her granny Hope Dawson had to cut back on things. Running the ranch was enough for her. She still went to the rodeos but she sold off their stock."

"Your parents still living?"

"Oh, yeah! Alive and ranchin' out near Hereford, Texas. They've got a couple of thousand acres that grows off Angus cows and pumps a little oil for them," she answered. "James and Amelia Dawson, and the ranch is the Flat Rock Ranch."

"Never heard of that one. Got brothers other than Jud?"

She shook her head. "Just the two of us. Daddy would have liked more kids, but it didn't happen. He can't wait for grandbabies so I hope Fiona and Jud have a yard full someday." Josie inhaled deeply and let it out slowly. "Now, let's talk about this partnership idea."

"I'm ready when you are. How much do you think he'll ask for all four?"

"Seventy-five and up," she answered. "But it's not the money. It's the partnering up that worries me."

"I'm an honest person, and I don't owe a penny on any of my land or cattle. I never run in the red, and I don't believe in borrowing money. If I don't have the cash to buy it, then I figure I don't need it," he said. "Looking at those bulls, though, and seeing the potential to make money with them, well, I got to admit, a bank loan to buy them don't seem to be so bad."

"So do you have the half to go into a partnership?" she asked.

"It would deplete my working cash down pretty slim, but I can do it," he answered honestly. "How about you? You and Jud have probably put a lot of money into this oil venture. And you've leased the hotel. That means some pretty high utility bills plus upkeep on that old building. Are you going to have to go to the bank if we buy all four of them?"

"I have enough left to go halves on all four bulls, but it would come close to draining my savings account. If the oil well comes in like I think it will, I'll replace that and add lots more to it in a few weeks. But I try not to bank on tomorrow's egg crop."

"So do we shut our eyes, hold hands, and take the plunge?" Deke asked.

"Let's talk to him tomorrow morning and see what his asking price is and then we'll discuss it again. I don't mind having a partner, especially if you agree to keep them at your place. But you do know that once we go into business together, there can't be any kind of romantic things going on. If that went south, it'd get messy."

"I guess we'll worry about that bridge when we get to it. Right now we just need to know what Everett is asking and whether we can even afford to buy any of the stock," Deke said.

"One step at a time?" she asked.

"That's all we can do. Worrying about it or fretting about how much money we need to come up with, it's all in vain," he said.

"Ahhh, the sexy cowboy is showing off his philosophical side again." She grinned.

"So I'm sexy?"

"Deke Sullivan, wipe that innocent grin off your face. You can't pull that naive stunt with me."

He tucked his head shyly and looked up at her from under heavy brows. "Well, shucks, ma'am. It means more to me to hear you say I'm sexy than all the other women who've said the same thing."

Josie shook her finger at him. "That innocent attitude won't wash with me."

The smile tickling the corners of her full lips said otherwise. Impulsively, Deke leaned over Rascal and kissed her on the cheek.

"You just kissed the dog with those lips." She wiped at her face.

"That makes you privileged."

"Well, thank you so much."

"That can be my good-night kiss. I'm going to bed now," he said.

*   *   *

She cut her eyes around to watch him go from the sofa to the bunk bed. Even in baggy pajama pants and a thermal shirt he made her mind go to places that set her heart to thumping.

"I've got a friend at the Resistol Rodeo over around Waco who would give us some business through the summer. The guy who's been supplying the rodeo with bulls is going into straight broncs, so I bet we could get a toe in the door real easy," Deke said.

"And I've got some contacts out in west Texas around the panhandle area." Riding bulls wasn't on her mind as much as riding a cowboy.

Holy shit! the voice in her head shouted loudly.

Okay, okay, I hear you, but dammit it would be fun.

"We would have to buy another trailer or a bigger one that would haul all four of the bulls and there would be travel expenses and gas money," he said.

"And our vet bills and feed and keeping them healthy," she added.

"I'll tell them bedtime stories every other night." He grinned.

She laughed. "I'll take them midnight snacks. I thought we said good night."

"Looks like we'll make a good set of partners," he said. "I can't shut my mind off and besides, it's not really night until you get into your bunk."

Rascal hopped off the bed and went to the door, where he sat down and whined.

Deke threw back the covers and crawled out of the bunk. "That's my cue to take him out for one more trip, which means putting on my jeans again." He dropped a kiss on her head as he passed by the sofa on the way to the bathroom to change.

"What's that for?" she asked.

"One more good-night kiss." He put on his coat while Rascal acted like a puppy, turning circles and yipping. However, when Deke opened the door and the poor old feller saw all that white stuff—again—he lowered his head and Josie could have sworn she heard him sigh.

She padded across the wood floor in her socks and crawled up into her bunk. Even more than her cell phone, she missed her queen-size bed so that she could spread out. And she missed Kasey and Jud. There was so much she needed to tell Kasey, to get her opinions about and hash out with her.

How would her brother feel about her going into business with Deke? He and both of her cousins, Blake and Toby, were best friends with Deke and thought that he was a real stand-up cowboy. She heard the squeak of the hinges and glanced that way. Rascal beat Deke into the house and shook from his nose to his tail twice before he meandered over to the fireplace and stretched out in front of it. Deke carefully removed his coat, hung it up again, and placed his boots, gloves, and hat back on the stones to dry in front of the fire.

"I would rather sweat in the summer as have to get bundled up every time I walk outside in the winter. You could not *give* me a ranch in this country." He disappeared into the bathroom again.

Shutting her eyes, she imagined his muscular body as he changed from jeans and shirt into nightclothes. Tingles tiptoed up her spine and her breath came in short bursts. Her eyes popped open and she stared at the fire, at Rascal, even at the snow-covered window over to the left of the fireplace. She made herself think about making biscuits and about walking in snow up to her butt, or even buying all those bulls.

It did not work.

Thinking of the fire put a picture of his bulging biceps as he carried in an armload of wood. The idea of snow put a visual of the way he filled out the butt of those tight-fitting jeans when she was thrown over his shoulder like she didn't weigh more than a feather pillow.

Rascal made his way from fireplace to the lower bunk and hopped up on the foot of it, turned around a couple of times, and curled up for the night. Deke would be sleeping in that bed in a few minutes. Was there room for her and Rascal if she decided to forget the partnership and sample the forbidden fruit?

Sharing rights to Lucifer—well, that made her think of the kisses they'd shared in the barn that were hotter than hell. Fitting enough, since Lucifer himself lived in the barn.

Deke came out of the bathroom and put his folded clothing on the end of the sofa. "I'll do wash tomorrow evening. You've been a great sport about having to do laundry by hand every single evening, Josie. Most women would be whining about that even more than the cell phone."

"If we don't get out of here by Saturday, you're going to hear lots of whining," she said. "I can hold up for a week, but past that my nerves are going to be frayed."

"We'll be out by Saturday if we have to ride Lucifer all the way to Texas," he promised.

The visual of her sitting on that bull with Deke's whole body pressed up against her back as he held her with one hand and the reins with another jacked up the temperature in the room at least twenty degrees.

"You better live up to your word if you don't want to hear the whining begin. Good night, Deke." She blinked, but the feeling of his body against hers did not disappear.

"Good night, Josie. And Rascal just wagged his tail, so that means he says good night too. Got to admit, I'm real glad to have him back at the foot of my bed."

I'd rather have you in my bed, she thought as she got comfortable. *Maybe that's what I need. One good romp in the sheets with you and then I could get you out of my system.*

Chapter Eleven

Everett picked up the plate with a dozen biscuits stacked on it, took two off the top, and passed it to Deke. "I'm going to miss these every morning, but I'm going to miss you guys and old Rascal even more. I was tellin' Lorraine last night that we've become real good friends in the past four days. It's like I've known you all of your lives. Don't look at me like that." He split one biscuit and laid it on his plate, covered it with sausage gravy, and then passed the bowl to Deke. "Me and Lorraine talk every night before I go to sleep. Truth is I have not been— what's that word? Celebration? No, *celibate*. That's it. And some things me and Lorraine don't just exactly talk about."

"I thought you told her everything," Deke said.

"I do, and what I don't, well, she knows anyway and there ain't no need to discuss that part. I figured when she thought it was time for me to move on, she'd let me know, and she did. Last night she said that I'd spent far too much time alone," Everett said seriously.

"Does that mean she's not going to talk to you anymore?" Josie asked. If she and Deke got married and she died, she would never, ever give him permission to sleep with another woman. Heaven did not look good in that shade of green.

"I'm not sure. It'd be kind of awkward for her to visit with me if Martha was in my bed. I told you about her, didn't I? I'm just hoping that Lorraine still talks to me when I'm out in the barn or when I'm by myself," Everett answered.

"I bet Lorraine still talks to you," Deke said.

"I hope so." Everett's head bobbed up and down a few times. "Now let's visit about your partnership business."

Deke buttered a biscuit to eat with his scrambled eggs and bacon. "We've talked about it and we like the idea, but we should hear your price first."

"Well, I been thinkin' on that a lot since you kids showed up here, and that's what I was talking to Lorraine about last night. I was asking more for the whole lot of them, but I'd be willing to take less if you go along with my plan."

Josie's heart threw in an extra beat. "And that would be?"

"I won't have trouble selling this place come summer because several folks have asked about it before now. The neighbor over to the north would like to expand his spread, and he'd give me a fair price. And there's a couple of young folks at the church who are fixin' to get married, and I might make them a real good deal on it just to see them stay in the state." Everett rubbed his chin, as if trying to decide just who he would entrust his property to when summer came around.

Lord have mercy! Josie thought. *Just spit it out and stop beating around every snow-covered bush between here and Texas.*

"I'll take fifty thousand for all of them. Half down and half when I deliver them, soon as I get things squared away here. Might be late May or early June when we could get there with them, but you could go on and get a schedule for them to be in the summer rodeos in your area. I've got a real nice trailer that they all four fit in real good and a big old pickup truck to pull it with."

Josie could hardly believe her ears. "Are you sure about this, Everett? Lucifer alone is worth almost that much."

Everett drew his mouth together and said tersely, "Don't try to talk me out of this. Lorraine has spoken, and she gets a little touchy when I argue with her. So hear me out."

"Go on. I'm listening," Deke said seriously.

"I like you kids and I like them bulls. So here's the deal that goes with them. I'll bring them to Texas to you. Give me a room in your hotel, Josie, so I'll have a place to hang my hat while I look around for some property around Dry Creek."

"Everett; you've only known us a few days. We'd be taking advantage of you," Josie said.

"You willin' to give me a place to live?" he asked.

"You can stay in my hotel for free anytime you want for as long as you want, but that's not the issue here," Josie said.

"Okay. Deke, you willing to help me find a little spread? Nothing too big. Maybe fifty acres so I can just play around with it without having to work too hard," Everett asked.

"I'd gladly do that for you," Deke said.

"And as partners are you both willing to let me come over to the pasture or the barn and visit with the bulls anytime I want?"

Josie nodded. "Of course."

"Then I don't see no advantage being took with any of

us. You can each write me a check for twelve thousand five hundred dollars. I will hold them until I get to Dry Creek and set up a banking account there. And I'll bring the bulls and my trailer, which you kids can keep on your ranch for me until I get my own. But you are welcome to borrow it until you can buy one or roust up enough cash to buy that one from me."

"I feel like I fell into a fresh cow pile and came out smelling like a rose," Josie said.

"Me too." Deke grinned.

Everett stuck his hand over the table. "With what all y'all are going to help me with, I feel the same. We'll shake on it. I can hear Lorraine humming in the background."

Deke pumped Everett's hand up and down several times. "We'll be glad to have you in Dry Creek."

When Deke let go, Everett extended his hand to Josie. "Handshake is good as money in my books."

She grabbed it and pulled Everett toward her for a sideways hug. "In mine, too, but a hug is even more."

As if on cue, the electricity came back on. The news station anchor on the television started talking in the middle of a sentence about the storm that had passed through the northern part of the state and was headed east. And the motors from the refrigerator and freezers started to whine.

"See there. We've got a good plan. I expect that Lorraine talked to the right people up there in heaven. If she didn't like it, we wouldn't have power until spring." Everett chuckled. "I'm right glad it's back on. I need to do some laundry. You are welcome to use my washer and dryer so you don't have to hand wash your things any longer."

"Thank you and I will definitely take you up on that offer." Josie looked around the one-room cabin.

"It's behind the door over there." Everett pointed to what she'd figured was a closet for his clothing. "One of them stack-up kind, but it's big enough for my stuff."

Deke straightened up in his chair and his eyes went to the wall phone hung by the kitchen sink. "Does that mean the phones are working?"

"Naw," Everett said slowly. "We won't be able to get phone service for a while longer, which means my computer won't work. But we can get the news or watch a movie. I got lots of them."

"You have a computer?" Deke asked.

"Of course. I ain't too savvy with it but I can get around enough to send messages to Martha and such," Everett said. "And I got me a cell phone too."

Josie's burst of adrenaline over having a phone quickly drained.

This, too, shall pass, she thought, which was her favorite quote. *Complete power will be restored. I will get out of this place. Someday it will be just a funny story that I tell my grandchildren.*

"Time to dig out?" Deke asked.

"Yes, it is. You want to take the first run at plowing us a fresh path to the barn? Me and Josie, here, will do up the breakfast dishes while you do that and then we'll all go do chores. I'm going to miss you kids being here to share in that with me," Everett said.

"I'd rather plow as wash dishes any day of the week," Deke said.

"When you get to the barn you might take a turn around the cabin and the bunkhouse so old Rascal will have a place to snoop around. Hell, make a maze if you have a mind to. He's getting cabin fever and needs to get outside for a little while a couple or three times a day."

Deke pushed back the chair and carried his breakfast dishes to the sink. "I can't remember when I've done so little for so long. The days are run together when all we see is snow and more snow. Rascal isn't the only one getting cabin fever, are you, old boy?"

Rascal left his warm place on the sofa and trotted over to the door.

"You wait until I get a good path up and I'll come and get you." Deke pulled his coat on and reached into his pockets for his gloves, stopped long enough to pat Rascal on the head, and went outside. Rascal hung his head and went back to the sofa.

"See there. I told you Rascal was getting cabin fever. He's sick and tired of being cooped up and he wants to go chase rabbits, whether they are real or not," Everett said.

Josie placed two plates in the drainer and Everett dried them with a white dish towel. "We're all pretty much tired of being inside. It's hard to believe that we only met a few days ago, isn't it?"

Everett nodded. "We ain't known each other but a short time, but the way I figure it is that we've been together up near a hundred hours. That means if we'd been seein' each other at church on Sunday mornings that would amount to about two years' worth of knowing each other."

"Hadn't thought of it like that." Josie sighed as she wrung all the water from a dishrag and ran it over the floral oilcloth covering the kitchen table.

Everett dried a coffee cup and set it up in the cabinets. "I reckon we know each other well enough that I can ask you a question. What's bothering you this morning?"

"What makes you think something is on my mind? The sun is peeking through the clouds. The electricity is back on. I don't have to do laundry by hand the rest of the time we are here. I've had good food, a warm place to sleep, and good company." She smiled.

"You need to talk or you are going to explode," Everett said. "I ain't wantin' to clean up blood and guts and besides, it would upset Rascal. Who better to tell your troubles to than an old man you won't see for weeks and who'll probably forget that you ever talked to him? I got to admit every so often anymore I have to rely on Lorraine to tell me things. I go to the refrigerator and can't remember what I was going to get, so I just say, 'Okay, darlin', help me out' and be damned if I don't see just what I needed. Are you worried about me to moving to Dry Creek?"

"Oh, no!" Josie said without hesitation. "I can't wait to introduce you to Herman and Lucy Hudson. He's about your age and still as much of a go-getter as you are."

"Then what is going on with you and Deke?"

"I've only known him ten days. What makes you think anything is going on?"

"I'm old, not blind or deaf," Everett answered. "Deke is a good man and he's struggling with something too. And I bet it has to do with this attraction you have for each other."

"What makes you think that there's an attraction?" Josie asked.

"That's plain as the nose on a pig's snout so tell me what's wrong and let me help fix it. I can't stand to see you sad."

Josie sighed again. "I don't know how to even begin."

"Well, I knew Lorraine was the one for me the minute I laid eyes on her, but she was a fine, churchgoing woman and she wasn't too sure about someone like me who didn't have a nail to hang his hat on. She finally came to trust that I was ready to settle down and told me that it was the future that mattered," Everett said.

"Okay, I'm attracted to Deke, but maybe it's just because we've been thrown together all these days. What if all that changes when we get home and back into our own settings?"

He chuckled. "Time, sweetheart, is the thing you need. Don't rush into anything, but don't slam the door to opportunity. It's damn hard to catch when it's already gone down the road a mile, so invite it in and feed it chocolate cake. You can always kick it outside if it misbehaves."

Josie wasn't sure if Everett had advised her to give in to her attraction, feed Deke chocolate cake, or kick him out in the yard, but she appreciated him for caring enough to notice that she was having a problem that morning.

"Bottom line is to always listen to your heart, sweetheart," he said seriously. "It ain't got no ears or eyes. It don't see the past or the future. I ain't never known it to steer a body wrong."

Rascal's ears stood straight up when the noise of the tractor engine made its way right up to the porch. He hopped off the sofa and waited at the door. When Everett cracked the door a few inches Rascal wiggled through the opening and hopped up into passenger's seat of the tractor.

"I'm off to take care of the distance from here to the barn. Y'all should be able to walk out there in about ten minutes," Deke yelled.

Everett slipped into his coveralls. "By the time we get bundled up, we can go. It won't take long for him to clean off the path to the barn."

Josie put on her coat, hat, and gloves and thought again about what Everett said about the heart. It would definitely take time to sort out everything that had happened in so short a time, and the way she'd always figured things out before was by hard, physical work.

What was it her granny Dawson used to say about planning?

Oh, yes.

Man plans; God laughs.

Chapter Twelve

Deke was once again behind the wheel of the tractor after they'd finished taking care of the livestock that Wednesday morning. His job was to clear the snow out of the corral so the bulls could be turned back outside. Once that was done then they could turn the bulls out and wouldn't have to shovel out the stalls every day. The bulls would be much happier outside than cooped up in stalls.

Everett was spending the morning in the tack room doing some cleaning and getting serious about moving. Josie had gone back to the house to start a pot of oven stew and make a pan of yeast rolls for the noon meal. Deke missed having her close enough to talk to, or even to catch a glimpse of as she worked in the barn with him.

Rascal had declined an offer to ride in the passenger's seat with Deke, opting instead to follow Josie back to the warm cabin. Deke couldn't blame him, not when the temperature was still in the single digits that morning. He turned on the radio, and the DJ's voice startled him. The station was coming in loud and clear so he didn't mess with trying to find another one. Especially after the DJ announced that it was a country music station.

He kept the beat of the fast music for several minutes and then a woman gave the local news, which said that the schools in Drummond and Hall would not resume classes until Monday, January sixteenth. The roads were still closed but the plows were out working, and most of the roads would be cleared by Friday.

Then the music started again with Thomas Rhett singing "Die a Happy Man." Deke lost himself in the song, pretending that he was singing it in Josie's ear as they danced in their bare feet on the soft green grass of spring.

The song ended and then Chase Bryant's "Little Bit of You" started playing. The song finished but Deke was still thinking about how the words to the song related to him and Josie and almost missed an advertisement from an animal shelter. The lyrics said that he was a little bit restless and couldn't get her off his mind.

When he started paying attention to the woman on the radio, he heard that the shelter had a black Chihuahua who needed to be placed with a new friend. He was only two years old and was housebroken. Deke wondered if maybe he and Josie should go adopt the dog for Everett so he wouldn't be lonely when they were gone. A little dog like that would keep him company.

Chihuahuas are yappy little beasts, his grandmother's voice in his head said. *So think about that in the hotel when Josie's oil crew is trying to sleep.*

"There's a little backyard and besides he won't be there long because I know a couple of small places for sale in

Dry Creek that he's going to love, then the dog can yap all he wants," Deke argued.

He made a mental note to talk to Josie about it that night. They could pick up the dog at the Drummond shelter and backtrack to Everett's place to deliver it before they pulled out for Texas.

The bulls' pen was cleared out by midmorning. He opened the big doors of the barn, drove the tractor inside, and parked it. Then he carefully opened the door to Lucifer's stall, threw a rope around his massive neck, and led him out the smaller door to the corral.

Lucifer was so happy to be outside that he acted like he'd just gotten turned loose from the chute and there was a cowboy on his back. He turned this way and that way, his back legs straight up in the air at one time.

Deke agreed with the old guy but if he really wanted some action, Deke could provide it. He pulled on the rope, leading Lucifer to the side of the corral. Then Deke climbed to the top of the railing and eased down on the bull's back. He barely had time to wrap the rope around his hand and get the other one in the air before Lucifer really did show off. He kicked. He twisted. Both hind legs went straight up in the air.

And five seconds into the ride, Deke went flying off his back, landed on the icy ground, and slid halfway across the corral. Lucifer continued with his antics until he realized all he was fighting was a rope before he settled down, threw back his head, and told the whole ranch how tough he was.

Deke was almost up on his feet when his slick-soled boots slipped and he had to grab the fence to keep from falling again. That's when the applause started from the barn door. He slapped his thigh with his hat and carefully took a bow.

"You done good," Everett yelled. "Five seconds is mighty fine to stay on Lucifer's back."

"He's a good one," Deke said.

"Are you all right?" Josie hollered.

"Sure I am. It was just like falling into a feather bed," Deke drawled.

"Looked more like a concrete driveway to me," she said.

"If you'll kiss it and make it all better, I'll get back on him," Deke teased.

"Sounds like a challenge to me." Everett laughed. "I'll leave you two to take care of that dare and I'll go get Barbed Wire."

Every muscle in his body was going to ache tomorrow but right then he was able to make it from the corral to the barn door. "So?"

"I don't want you to get back on that wild thing so I'm not kissing it and making it all better," she declared.

"How be if I get on Barbed Wire? I might stay with him eight seconds. Hell, for a kiss, I wouldn't care if he threw me off in two seconds."

"Did you tell all the girls that when you were in the bull ridin' business?"

"I only wish I'd have thought of it then." He grinned. "What brought you and Everett out here anyway? I wasn't expecting an audience."

"Everett said he figured Lucifer would show out some when he got outside and he wanted me to see it. He's one mean bull. I can see where the cowboys would love to draw his name for a ride. They could rack up some points with him," she said.

"We've bought us a keeper for sure."

Everett brought Barbed Wire out and turned him loose in the corral. He loped around the thing then threw back his head and bellowed. Lucifer did the same and then they both went to the hay trough and looked back at Deke.

"Guess that's your cue to feed them. I'm going back to the house to finish my job," Josie said.

"No kiss?"

"Not right now, cowboy." She smiled.

He finished his chores and headed for the house at noon. The path was clear, with dead grass crunching under his boots but on either side of him was a snowbank that still stood over four feet tall.

"I may never leave Texas again," he said.

Not even to get to spend a week with Josie? There was that pesky voice again.

"I'm not going there," he answered. "Hello! Rascal, where are you?" he yelled as he opened the front door to the cabin.

For the first time since he'd arrived on Saturday, the place felt strange. The blaze in the fireplace was still going strong. The aroma of yeast bread filled the cabin, and there was a pot of stew bubbling on the stove. Everything to testify that folks lived here, but it felt so empty without Everett, Josie, and Rascal.

He hurried to the back door and swung it open to see a path from the cabin to the bunkhouse cleared off so well that the dead grass was visible. Deke closed the door and rushed out across the path.

"Josie," he called out.

Rascal bounded from the sofa to the door to meet him and Josie glanced up from the sofa. "You're late to dinner. I spilled some water and then stepped in it so my socks were wet. I came out here for a dry pair."

"The cabin was empty. Where's Everett?" Deke asked.

"He said if you weren't here in five more minutes he

was going out to the barn to get you. Did you get a wild hair and ride another bull or what?"

"No, I was getting the stalls cleaned and ready in case Everett needs to put them back inside before winter ends. I'm starving."

Josie kept pace alongside of Deke, but he missed the times when he carried her back and forth. He'd liked the feel of her body next to his and the way their hearts beat in unison. When Everett slung open the front door to the cabin, Rascal didn't even slow down until he was on the sofa in front of the fire.

"Must've missed you somehow. Me and Rascal went out the back way to go check on you," Everett said.

Deke and Josie shucked out of coats before they sat down where Everett waited. He said a very short grace and then handed the soup ladle to Josie. "This looks so good. I like a good hearty stew." He raised his bowl for her to fill it. "How do you like that job Josie did out there shoveling a pathway between the cabin and the bunkhouse, Deke?"

Deke handed Josie his bowl. "If you would have waited I could have done it or at least helped you this afternoon."

"After that bull ride, I expect you'll be sore as the devil pretty soon."

"Might need to work some of the soreness out," he said with one of those grins that jacked up the temperature in the room.

She could think of all kinds of ways to work that soreness out and not a single one of them had a thing to do with a snow shovel.

"I've been blessed," Everett said, breaking the silence. "God sent me you kids and old Rascal to keep me from dying from cabin fever this week. And then He went and blessed me double by giving me a plan to move to Texas." He finished off his dinner and brought the cinnamon rolls to the table for dessert. "I'd been looking to go that way, but Texas is one big state and I didn't know anyone down there except some business acquaintances. Now I've got friends and a future."

Josie rolled the kinks out of her tight shoulders. "And we're just as glad as you are. You'll love Dry Creek. We have cold winters and hot summers but not this kind of thing."

"All that work is talking to you, isn't it?" Deke asked. "It's kind of like the first days of hay hauling in the early summer. That first week is torture on the upper arms and shoulders, but when the second week rolls around the muscles are usually accustomed to the hard work."

"Yes." She nodded. "But I'd be willing to bet dollars to cow patties that you are just as sore."

"I'm going to miss y'all when you leave in a couple of days," Everett said slowly. "They've started clearing the highway up from Butte and plan to get up to us pretty soon."

"How do you know?" Deke asked. "No phones and you can't tell me you've got walkie-talkie radios that reach that far."

"I got an old CB radio out in the tack room along with a little generator. I use it at times like this to talk to Martha and other folks. We check in on each other to be sure everyone is still kickin'. At our age, it's necessary, not luxury."

"Does that mean we can go home tomorrow?" Josie held her breath.

"No, not tomorrow but maybe on Friday." Everett sighed. "Martha's phone is working, but she lives on the other side of Hall, and the servicemen get to the town folks first."

"One more day and we can go home." Josie hugged herself in joy.

"I know y'all are eager to get back to your lives but it makes me sad." A smile stretched out some of the wrinkles in his weatherworn face. "Not that I care so much about losing you two but I'll sure miss old Rascal."

Deke chuckled down deep in his chest. Everett did the same and Josie giggled. Then they were all laughing so hard that they were wiping tears from their eyes with paper napkins.

"Well, I *will* miss him." Everett hiccupped. "And it's not a damn bit funny that you're taking him from me."

"I think you've been sipping on something you got hid out there in the tack room," Deke said.

"Or maybe you and Martha were sweet-talking on those CBs," Josie said between gasps.

"Cowboy like me don't kiss and tell." That set Everett off into another round of laughter. When he could catch his breath, he said, "Okay, now seriously, I'm going to miss y'all."

Josie came to the conclusion that she was worrying herself crazy over the little things and the old adage said not to sweat the small stuff. She should live every day without fretting and enjoy what that day brought into her world, not let what might be, or what would not be, ruin her joy. Partnerships. Relationships. New family members. It would all work itself out without her stressing over any of it.

"Laughter is good for the soul," Josie said.

"And stew is good for the body," Deke echoed.

"Then I'll just say that good yeast bread and cinnamon rolls is good for everything," Everett added.

"Need some butter?" Josie asked.

"Something this good don't even need butter," Everett said. "Some things are perfect just the way they are and don't need a bit of help. Take Lorraine, for instance. She didn't need all that makeup stuff or fancy dresses. She looked beautiful in a pair of blue jeans and a flannel shirt."

That is exactly what Josie wanted when she got ready to settle down permanently. A cowboy who thought she was beautiful in her jeans and flannel shirts. Whoever it was had some big shoes to fill if he was going to make her feel like Everett did Lorraine.

She glanced over at Deke, who was staring right at her. Their eyes locked for several seconds then he winked.

"I kinda like women in blue jeans and flannel shirts myself." Deke picked up a roll and bit into it. "My God, these are wonderful. Will you marry me, Josie?"

"There you have it. The man is proposing right here in my little cabin," Everett said.

"No, he is not. He's teasing," Josie said.

Everett's old eyes twinkled. "Well, if he is, then will you marry me? Anyone can make rolls like this and shovel snow both, why, I'd marry that woman in a split second. Hell, I'll even get on the CB and have a helicopter bring in a preacher man in the next hour if you'll say yes."

"Both of you finish your dessert and hush," she said.

The adventure would be over in two days. She'd go to the airport and see if she could get a flight out to Dallas. Hopefully, the airline would reimburse her for part of the ticket that she hadn't used and it wouldn't cost her an arm and a leg to get home. Deke and Rascal would haul an empty trailer back to Dry Creek and they'd go their separate ways, seeing each other only at family functions or in passing.

She shook her head in disagreement. She and Deke were friends.

Friends? The voice in her head sounded an awful lot like Kasey's.

Yes, friends, Josie argued. *So we kissed a few times. That doesn't mean we are anything more than friends.*

"Are you fussing with yourself or has the butter gone stale?" Everett asked.

"Fussing with myself," she answered honestly. "I can't decide which one of you I should marry, now that you've both proposed to me."

"Should we have a pistol duel out in the backyard?" Everett winked at Deke.

"I didn't bring my pistol. You got two? I reckon she's worth fightin' for," Deke answered.

Everett narrowed his eyes. "But is she worth dyin' for? I'm a right fine shot."

"I reckon she just might be," Deke answered.

"I'm sitting right here," Josie raised her voice.

"Darlin', neither one of us is blind." Everett chuckled. "We can see you right fine. I'm going to stand down, since I'm an old man and I done had my Lorraine. Deke, you do right by her, though, or I'll come gunnin' for you for sure."

Josie's forefinger shot up to point at Everett. "I'm still sittin' right here. Both of you have another cinnamon roll or I will refuse to make any more," she said.

Chapter Thirteen

Josie stopped in her tracks the next morning when she got to the cabin. The scenario in front of her looked like a photograph from an old tintype picture. Everett's grin covered his whole wrinkled face. But who in the hell was that woman smiling up at him like he hung the moon and the stars?

"Josie and Deke, I'd like you to meet Martha. She hitched a ride on the snowplow this morning and brought her overnight bag with her. Guess she missed me," he said.

"Right pleased to meet you kids but I didn't miss this old coot as much as he'd like to think. I came so I could get to know you two before you go back to Texas. Roads will be cleared tomorrow and you could leave, but I forbid it." She slid a pan of biscuits into the oven and poured two cups of coffee.

She motioned for Josie and Deke to take a chair. "I come from superstitious folks and I will not have you guys traveling on Friday the thirteenth. That's why I brought my bag to stay until Saturday. I don't go anywhere on Friday the thirteenth neither. And before you ask, I'll drive two miles out of the way when a black cat crosses in front of me."

"Bossy, ain't she?" Everett said with pride.

Martha washed her hands and dried them on her bibbed apron. "Better bossy than bad luck."

"I wish all next week was filled up with Friday the thirteenths," Everett said.

"So do I." Martha's bright blue eyes lit up.

"I figured you'd be ready to get rid of us," Deke said.

"I told you earlier, I'll miss Rascal."

At the sound of his name, the dog raised his head and yipped.

"See, he understands my language." Everett grinned again.

"Hey, Rascal, you ready to go home?" Deke asked.

The old boy got up and headed for the door.

"Traitor." Everett chuckled. "I thought me and you was buddies."

"You are." Josie nodded. "He's ready to go home where it might be wintertime but it's not over his head in snow. Besides, I told him that you would be joining us real soon, so he knows that it won't be long until he sees you again."

"That's right," Martha said. "There's a lot of work to be done by May or June, so you'll be busy."

Josie joined Martha at the stove. "So you caught a ride with the snowplow man?"

"I did. He's the grandson of my friend who leads the singing at the church on Sunday morning. On the way we had a nice visit about his new baby daughter. She was born on Thanksgiving Day and is growing like a wild weed in the springtime."

Josie caught a whiff of the same perfume that her grandma wore. They looked nothing alike. Josie's grandma was tall and thin. Martha was short and at one time would have been considered curvy. But the way she flitted about the kitchen with a kitchen towel over her shoulder made Josie think of her own grandmother.

"Don't tell Everett." Martha lowered her voice as she removed the biscuits and casserole from the oven and shoved in the pan of muffins. "But I'm going to Texas with him. I'll ease into it so that he thinks it's his idea."

Josie nodded slightly. "You think you'll like it there."

"I'll like anywhere that Everett is," Martha whispered. "Okay, fellers, we are bringing the food to the table."

She and Josie carried food to the table, where Martha laid a hand over Everett's and said, "I will say grace this morning." She bowed her head. "Thank you, God, for sending these kids to us so Everett wouldn't be lonely and for this food. Amen."

Josie had barely gotten her eyes closed when the prayer was over. She looked up from the corner of one eye to see Deke grinning.

"My kind of prayer," he said from the corner of his mouth.

"Oh, yeah." She nodded as she put two biscuits on her plate. "What is in this casserole? It looks and smells scrumptious."

"Sausage, eggs, cheese mainly. Sometimes I add a little hot sauce, but the sausage smelled like it had enough spice in it," Martha answered. "It's Everett's favorite."

"Can't beat it on a cold morning like this," Everett said.

Martha dipped heavily into the long casserole and dished out a healthy portion on each of their plates. "After breakfast, you boys can get on out of here and do the chores and whatever else you've got on your agenda this morning. Me and Josie are going to make cookies. I checked the bins and they're all empty."

"Man cannot live on bread alone. He must have cookies." Everett chuckled.

"Amen," Deke said reverently. "And I do mean that in the most serious way."

"You okay with that, Josie?" Everett asked.

"I'm fine with it. My sweet tooth might even be bigger than Deke's."

Deke laid a hand on her knee under the table. "Ain't possible, darlin'."

Sparks flitted around the table like fireflies on a spring night. Two more nights. Two more days. And then they would be back in Dry Creek and things would be normal again. No kisses. No sparks. Only seeing Deke at family functions and with the bulls, but that was business, not romance in any form.

Boring, the voice in her head said. *Admit it. This has been exhilarating!*

Okay, you win. It's been fun.

And you will miss the kisses and the sparks?

Yes, I will miss them but I'll get over it.

Bullshit!

Josie set her mouth firmly and refused to argue anymore, but Deke's touch on her knee had left a warm spot that might never cool down.

*   *   *

Deke found all the bulls eyeing him when he took the feed out that morning.

"I know I'm late but not a one of you have lost a pound

since yesterday so stop eyeballing me like you might have my arm for breakfast." Deke chuckled.

"Fussy this morning, ain't they? Those broncs are acting like it's the end of the world," Everett said right behind him. "Ain't much to do this morning after we get done, so I thought we'd fire up the heater in the tack room and have us a game of checkers. How's that sound?"

"We could play in the cabin by the fire," Deke answered.

"We need to leave them women alone this morning. Martha might burn a pan of them if we happened to be in the house and she was talking to me rather than watching the cookies. Or worse yet, she might add a teaspoon too much baking soda, and I hate it when that happens to a good cookie," Everett answered.

"We could stay in the bunkhouse," Deke argued.

Everett shook his head. "They got to believe that we are out here working real hard. If they caught us in the bunkhouse, they'd know that they are getting under our skin."

"And that means...?"

"Martha almost pushed me out the door. They need to talk about us," Everett answered. "By noon, they'll be sweet as honey."

Deke cocked his head to one side. "How'd you get to be so smart and how do you know that Josie is getting under my skin?"

Everett wrapped his hands around the handles of the wheelbarrow and started toward the two horse stalls. "I might be old, son, but I ain't dumb. Besides, a man your age would have to be blind or just downright stupid if he wasn't affected by Josie Dawson."

"Amen," Deke said.

Lucifer bawled and Deke nodded. "I understand, old

boy. I was hungry this morning, too, but I think your aggravation is from being cooped up. You are ready for a rodeo and the excitement of a noisy crowd."

And you? The voice inside Deke's head asked bluntly.

Yes, he was ready for a rodeo with Josie by his side.

Josie? Why didn't you feel like this with Fiona when she came home at Thanksgiving or even Lizzy after she and the preacher broke it off?

They were like sisters, he argued. *Josie is special.*

Everett tapped him on the shoulder. "Hey, you about done? I got a little bottle hid in with the saddle soap, so we can have a nip while we wait on the warmth to spread."

"Just have to put up the tools and shut the door," Deke answered. "Be there by the time you get the fire going."

The room was warm and the checker game was on the table when Deke arrived. He removed his black cowboy hat and raked his fingers through his hair. Out of habit, he ducked to clear the top of the door into the tack room.

"Never had to do that one time in my whole life, not even with a sod house, and their doors are really short," Everett said.

"I was over six feet tall before I ever got to high school. Sometimes it's a blessing. Sometimes it's a curse," Deke said.

"I could see how that would be the case. Sometimes being short is the same two things. I put a pot of coffee on top of the old woodstove. When it gets to boiling we can have a cup but until then." He dumped out screws and rusty nails from a couple of small jars, blew the dust out of them, and poured two fingers of amber-colored liquor into each. "It's Martha's best recipe. Got just a hint of apple and cinnamon and guaranteed to warm you up. Don't toss it back. Sip it and enjoy the heat."

"Martha brews moonshine?" Deke gasped.

Everett nodded seriously. "Didn't think your women from down in Texas had a franchise on making good moonshine, did you? She only makes what we can use in a year's time, so it's legal, or at least mostly so."

Deke was no stranger to apple pie 'shine. He'd had a few shots of it at Frankie's place many times. He turned it up and let a few drops rest on his tongue before swallowing. The fire was there, but it was every bit as smooth as what Frankie made.

"Fine stuff, huh?" Everett asked.

"Never had better," Deke answered.

"You might want to explain that." Everett set his jar to one side and set up a checker game on the workbench.

"There's this old beer joint in Texas named Frankie's and he has moonshine with an apple flavor, but it don't stand up to this," Deke said.

"You will have to take me there so I can taste it for myself."

"I can do that, but you have to promise you'll leave the hookers alone. I got a feelin' that Martha would shoot me if she found out," Deke said seriously.

"You got that right. Martha would kill me dead if I came dragging home smelling like booze and wild women." Everett laughed.

"This game looks like it's been played a lot."

"When Lorraine was upset, I used to come out here and play myself."

"I thought Lorraine was an angel who never got angry."

"She was a woman, for God's sake," Everett said. "All women get angry. I swear, they start a fight just so they can get us into the bedroom to make up. Ain't you never been in a serious relationship?"

Deke shook his head. "Not me. Serious relationships lead to the altar, and that place gives me the hives."

Everett frowned. "Then you'd better get them stars out of your eyes when you look at Josie. And don't lead her on. She deserves better than that. You can go first."

"I don't have stars in my eyes, Everett." Deke pulled up a sawhorse and used it for a bench. Everett dragged an old rusty metal chair across the floor and sat down in it. He pushed a red checker into place after Deke made his move and crossed his arms over his chest.

"Have you been leading Martha on all these years?" Deke asked.

"Hell, no! We had us a long talk in the beginning, set down the rules on both sides, and declared that if we had a change of heart that we'd voice it rather than letting it sit and simmer until it became a problem. Your turn."

Deke moved a black disk. "You never had a change of heart?"

"Not yet, but seeing her today, well, I got to admit that it kind of took the wind out of my sails and I'm not as gung ho about leaving her behind as I thought I was. I've got a few weeks to decide what I want to do about that, though. And if I get down there to Texas and don't like the heat and the cactus, I can always come back here and buy me a little place in town. A man can change his mind even if he is old," Everett said.

"You think a man can change more than his mind? You think he can change his whole outlook on life?" Deke asked.

"If he couldn't, there wouldn't be a married man in the world." Everett laughed.

*   *   *

Martha was clearly the lady in charge of the cabin that morning but Josie didn't mind. The little lady was full of energy and life that filtered all through the small cabin. And besides, it had been days since Josie had had a woman to talk to, even if it was about cookie recipes.

Martha handed her a white apron with ties around the neck and the waist. "Here, you'd best put this on or you'll have a messy shirt. And come on to the pantry with me to help carry the stuff. I'd rather work in my kitchen where there's lots of room, but the table will have to do for our workstation."

Josie picked up the bins full of flour and sugar, leaving the smaller things for Martha to tuck inside the tail of her apron. After they'd both carried their load to the table, Martha motioned for her to follow her to the pantry again.

"Get the molasses for the gingerbread and the powdered sugar and brown sugar and don't forget the chocolate chips," Martha said. "That should do it with what I've got here and if you'll bring that quart jar up there on the top shelf, I won't have to get out the step stool. Everett says that he puts it up high so that he'll have to work at getting to it."

"What is it?"

"Little something to sip on while we cook. Like that song says, it is five o'clock somewhere." Martha giggled.

"Whiskey?" Josie cocked her head to one side.

"Oh, no, honey, that is the best batch of apple pie moonshine that I ever made. I tried peach this year but I don't like it nearly as well as the apple pie." Martha headed off to the kitchen with spices, salt, and other cookie-making ingredients tucked into the basket she'd made from the tail of her apron.

"Sweet Lord," Josie murmured.

Martha had organized the ingredients on the chairs around the table and had two glasses waiting beside the sink when Josie brought out the moonshine and the rest of her list. She carefully set it all on the cabinet and handed the 'shine to Martha.

"How long have you been making this stuff?"

"My mama taught me to make it when I was a kid. Her mama taught her. My granny was downright religious, so she called it medicine and used it to cure sore throats, coughs, and whatever ailed a body. If she mixed it with honey or with cinnamon or heated it up with lemon, it saved a trip to the doctor. Money was mighty scarce in those days and this medicine wasn't hard to make," Martha answered as she poured three fingers of the amber-colored liquid into each glass and handed one to Josie. "Now sip it easy like or it'll go to your head real quick. Got to give a body, even a tall one like yours, time to absorb the heat."

After the first sip, Josie fully well understood what Martha said about the fire. It burned from her tongue to her stomach, and that was just the first sip, but the aftertaste was heavenly, just a touch of real apple pie covered with a layer of sugar and cinnamon. If Josie could learn how to make this stuff, she could forget about oil wells and rodeo stock and go into the business of making moonshine.

"How in the world did you get the taste of real pie in that bottle?" Josie asked.

"Now that's a family secret that I don't tell anyone."

"Not even your oldest daughter?"

"Never had kids. Lorraine and me, we planned on having four kids a piece. I was going to have all boys and she was going to have all girls. I'd have the first one and then she'd have a girl so that when they grew up my boys would marry her girls and we'd share our grandbabies. God had a different plan." Martha sniffled and then said, "But this ain't no time to be crying over spilt milk. If things work out in Texas maybe I'll adopt you and teach you to make decent 'shine."

"You only met me today," Josie said.

"When a person gets as old as I am then they see things a little different. Most of their lives are on the past side of living and there's not much in the future side, so we get clearer vision. Kids don't understand that so mostly we just let them go on and make their mistakes like we did ours. But know this." Martha looked up from sifting flour into a bowl. "I can see that you are in turmoil about this partnership with Deke. It will work out just fine. I feel it in my bones."

"And you got all that from just eating breakfast with us?"

Martha set the sifter down and added a teaspoon of baking soda to the flour. "Honey, I can get more than that out of one church service. Me and Everett make bets on who's liking who in our community and how soon they'll be holding hands or when the first kiss might be."

"Who wins most of the time?" Josie asked.

"Me"—Martha winked—"but sometimes I let Everett win so he'll keep playing. Now you tell me about this hotel you've bought in Dry Creek. I understand that Everett is going to stay there for a spell until he can find a ranch. Is that right?"

Josie opened a package of chocolate chips and handed them to Martha. "Dry Creek was the center of a fort years and years ago when Texas was being settled as a state. Downtown only has one block of stores and lots of them are empty. There's a feed store, a café, a convenience store/ gas station combination, beauty shop, and day care and that's it. I'm not planning on running the hotel like a real one but using it as a bed-and-breakfast for my oil crew. I've got it leased for a year and then will decide whether I want to buy it outright or not."

"Hotel in a little bitty town?" Martha asked.

"Actually, Dry Creek used to have two hotels. Audrey's Place was one during the days when Texas had a lot of forts in that area," Josie explained. "Then it was a brothel when times got tough. Then it was just a big old house where the Logan family lived. The hotel I'm talking about is on Main Street, in downtown Dry Creek. It's old and has been empty for years, but it's got rooms I can use for my oil crew," Josie explained.

"You taken Deke into one of those rooms yet?" Martha's eyes twinkled.

"Martha!"

"I'm old enough to have done it all and enjoyed most of it," Martha said. "But we'd better get on with making cookies or when those two fellows come back, they might think we've spent our morning talking about them. That wouldn't be a bit good for their egos."

Josie nodded. "You got that right. Hey, I've got an idea. Let's make a batch of sugar cookies and replace half the milk with this." She held up the apple pie moonshine. "I bet they'd taste wonderful."

"Now that sounds like a fine idea. We'll finish these chocolate chip cookies and then move on to the apple ones next. I never thought of trying that." Martha broke two eggs into the mixture. "I like trying new things in cooking as well as..." Another giggle.

"Did you love Everett before he married Lorraine?" Josie asked.

Martha dropped dough onto a cookie sheet. "Every

woman in the state of Montana loved Everett. He had this charm about him, and being kind of short for a man, he had this cocky attitude that drew women to him like flies to a honey jar. Of course, I loved him, but there was no way I could tame him. Only Lorraine had the ability to do that but then, well, let's just say when I got my chance I did not let it pass me by. Now don't get me wrong. I loved my husband with my whole heart, and me and him, well, we had as good a relationship as two married people ever had and I can't wait to see him in eternity, but I know him well enough to know that..." She paused and took a deep breath. "He wouldn't want me to be grieving my whole life away. He was too good a man and a husband to want that for me."

Josie took another swig of the 'shine. It slid down her throat as smooth as whipped cream and warmed every fiber of her body.

"I've got an idea," Martha said. "Let's add some walnuts to the recipe for our new apple cookies and maybe substitute brown sugar to give them an undertone of caramel, roll them into balls, and bake them long enough for them to crust over, then roll them in powdered sugar and more ground-up walnuts. They'll be like Everett."

"Why would you say that?"

Martha slid the first pan of cookies into the oven. "Hard and crispy on the outside. Soft on the inside. Sweet with just a hint of bite. Makes for an interesting man, don't it? Kind of like Deke."

"It sure does," Josie said honestly. "Now tell me what to start with and I'll make the dough for our brand-new recipe. I bet we could win a prize with this one."

"But we couldn't take it to the church bazaar, now could we?"

Josie's laughter filled the room. "Of course we could. According to the experts the liquor cooks out in the oven so no one would get plastered on the little bit of booze in the mix."

"There's one lady in our church who swears a drop of liquor has never touched her lips and never will. She says that she and St. Peter have an agreement about whether she gets into heaven or not. I figure that she's sown her wild oats in other ways, like in the hayloft with the hired hands when she was younger." Another sly wink. "So that's why she's making bargains with St. Peter in her old age."

"Martha!"

"Please, sir, do not kick me down to hell." Martha threw the back of her hand over her forehead in a dramatic gesture and kicked up her tone a notch until it was nasal and whiny. "I know that I screwed around like a horny little bunny when I was young, but I never drank liquor, so let me through the pearly gates on that ticket."

Josie's laughter echoed off the walls and became so contagious that soon Martha was wiping her face on the tail of her apron.

"You should be a comedian," Josie said when she could breathe again.

"That's what Everett tells me all the time, but I get stage fright when I step out in front of people. It don't matter if there's one person or five thousand out there in the audience. Now let's get these chocolate chip ones done so we can play around with our new recipe and then we'll make ginger snaps."

"What are we doing for dinner?" Josie wiped at her eyes with her apron like Martha had done. "Maybe fried chicken?"

"And you could make about half a dozen loaves of

your yeast bread today. What we don't eat, we can freeze. Everett has been raving about it," Martha said. "I can make biscuits that melt in your mouth but me and yeast hate each other. It don't rise for me no matter how hard I cuss at it."

"I'd be glad to do that," Josie said.

At straight up noon the kitchen door opened and Rascal rushed into the house, stuck his nose up in the air, and sniffed his way to the stove. Everett did the same, taking time to plant a kiss on Martha's forehead on the way.

"We've got fried chicken, Deke. Martha makes the best fried chicken in the whole state of Montana. Do I smell apple pie?"

"No but you do smell apple cookies." Josie winked.

"That smells like your moonshine, woman. Did you put it in the cookies?" Everett asked.

"It was Josie's idea," Martha said proudly. "And they turned out wonderful. Be right tasty with some hot coffee after we have dinner."

Josie was careful not to look at Deke even though she wanted to so badly. If Martha could really read people as well as she thought, then she'd see that Josie did like him—a lot—and that they'd already shared many hot and steamy kisses.

Chapter Fourteen

Those two old toots wore me plumb out today." Deke yawned and slumped down into the old worn sofa in the bunkhouse.

"I think that might have been the plan." Josie plopped down beside him and kicked off her boots. "Get the kids so tired that they'll go to bed and go to sleep so they wouldn't hear Everett's headboard bumping against the wall in the cabin."

Deke shuddered.

"Or maybe they wore us out so we wouldn't knock boots," she teased.

"I like that picture better." He grinned. "We've only got one more night in this bunkhouse after this one, Josie. I dread that trip back to Texas all by myself. Why don't you forget about flying and go with me?"

"I'm too tired to make that decision tonight. Can I think about it until morning?" She yawned.

"You can think about it until time to exit off the highway

toward the Butte airport. You'll have to drive your rental car back there but you could return it and then go with me. Rascal and I would love the company." He stretched and winced at the same time.

"Thanks for the offer. I will definitely give it some thought when my brain is not fried on too many of those moonshine cookies and heavy food."

"Don't forget the Scrabble games. Lord, who would have thought Everett would know so many crazy words?"

"Or Martha. I'll tell you a secret if you promise not to tell Everett."

Deke drew a cross over his heart with his forefinger and held two fingers up in the air. "Cross my heart and hope to die."

Her eyes glittered. "You don't have to go that far."

"What is it?"

"Martha says she's coming to Dry Creek with Everett. She talked about it a lot today. Said that a lot of her friends have died and she's not going to sit in her house in Hall, Montana, and dry up like a prune. She says that when it all comes about, that Everett will think it's his idea."

"I think it's an awesome idea. Maybe they'll even be willing to help out with the hotel, giving you more time to spend at the oil wells." Deke laced her fingers into his and squeezed gently. "Martha is a fantastic cook and Everett is damn fine at fixing things. It could work out to be a pretty sweet deal."

"I would have never thought of that, but it could work." She whipped around and planted a kiss on his cheek.

He quickly removed his hand from hers and cupped her cheeks in his, looked deeply into her eyes, and then lowered his mouth for a real kiss—one of those that set her nerve endings on fire. With his tongue doing a mating dance with hers, his hands left her face, and he shifted her body to his lap. Each kiss jacked the heat up in the little bunkhouse another ten degrees until finally, panting and gasping for breath worse than she had in the middle of a bout of hot sex, she felt Rascal cold nose her bare foot and she jumped up.

He groaned. "Well, I feel exactly like a high school sophomore."

"Only it was Rascal who caught us and not Everett and Martha." Her head was spinning and her pulse racing when she flopped back down on the other end of the sofa.

"I still got my pants on and your bra is intact." His smile got bigger, but when he reached out to pet the dog, he grimaced again.

"In another ten minutes, Rascal would be blushing. That's twice now that you've winced. Did you really hurt something when Lucifer bucked you off?"

"Rascal, quit blushing..." Deke ignored the question.

"When did Rascal stop blushing?" Josie asked.

"A long time ago," Deke said honestly but he kept his eyes on the blaze. "Listen, Josie, we both know I'm a sinner, not a saint."

"And?"

"And I don't know what the future holds. Do you?"

Her head moved slowly from side to side. "But I know when you are hurting. So 'fess up."

"It's my shoulders. Guess I landed on them," he said.

She scanned the room. The sofa was too short. The beds wouldn't work. Finally, her eyes came to rest on the floor. She stood up and picked up a spare quilt from his bed.

"What are you doing?" he asked.

She spread it out on the floor in front of the fireplace. "Lie down on your stomach."

"Why?" he asked.

"I'm going to work on those sore muscles."

He quickly shucked his shirt and stretched out on the quilt. "Well, darlin', I never refuse a massage."

She straddled his hips and dug her fingers into his shoulders, working out the knots in his muscles and working up a heat inside her body at the same time. The air in the cabin got thinner and the blaze, only a few feet from them, got hotter. She took several deep breaths and let them out slowly as she kept telling herself that this was nothing more than a massage and there was not a damned thing sexual about it.

"Have you been in a serious relationship?" He groaned.

"A couple. Am I hurting you?"

"Hell, no! It feels great. What ended them? Fear of commitment?"

"I don't think so. I honestly think that deep in my heart I knew it wasn't right. Mama has taught me that any man is not always better than no man and to be careful when it comes to picking out the right one," she said honestly. "How many relationships have you been in?"

"None, but it's not fear of commitment. It's fear of making a mistake and being with the wrong woman for the rest of my life. I can't imagine waking up one day and figuring out that I was with someone and wanted someone else," he said.

"Kind of like that old Conway Twitty song?"

"Exactly. It wouldn't be fair to the woman I was with or the one I wanted to be with, so I never let myself go past a weekend stand."

His shoulders began to relax as the knots disappeared.

"So you are like a weekend drunk, only instead of booze it's women?"

"Oh, you can throw the booze in there with the women." He chuckled. "And Josie, I've never told anyone that before in my life. I only realized it myself since we've been here and I've listened to Everett talk about Lorraine."

"And if you found your Lorraine?"

"I imagine I'd throw my weekends out the window, drop down on my knees, and ask her to marry me. If I ever have a serious relationship, that's what it'll have to be. I'll go all in or I won't go at all," he said.

"I'm glad we can be honest with each other." She stood up and slumped back down on the sofa. "That should help you sleep."

He rolled over to one side and propped up on an elbow. "Thank you, Josie, but after a hard day of driving, I might need another one on the trip home."

"Or maybe I'll need one after a hard day of riding." Scarlet dotted her cheeks when a vision of him in a big hotel bed appeared in her mind.

"Just name the place and time." He shifted position until he was sitting up. His hand came across the two feet separating them and rested on her shoulder. The touch, the heat, the electricity, the sparks—all of it combined told her that there was definitely chemistry there, and on a dark Thursday night in Montana, she wished for more.

*   *   *

Deke's biceps bulged at the weight of the two big logs he carried to the fire. With that much burning power, they should stay toasty warm all through the night. He positioned them at the right angle to get the most heat out of them and then turned around just in time to see Josie crawling up the ladder to the top bunk. Her well-rounded butt made his hands itch for just a single touch. Her lips were still puffy from all the making out, and those blue eyes—Lord, he could dive right into them and drown.

"Good night, Deke," she said as she pulled the covers up to her chin. "I got to admit this has been kind of fun."

"It's been an adventure all right. Good night, Josie. Sleep tight." He stretched out on the bottom bunk. The mattress above him was all that separated her luscious body from his view but in reality all he had to do was shut his eyes and there she was in one of the two shirts that she'd worn all week. And there she was in her thermal knit shirt and flannel pajama pants that were simply too sexy for words. And there she was in his arms not half an hour ago, kissing him back and making him rethink his whole outlook on relationships.

"I wonder what Jud is going to say about us staying in a bunkhouse together for a whole week," he whispered.

"You talkin' to me or sayin' prayers?" Josie asked.

"Talkin' to myself. You going to tell Jud that we shared a bunkhouse?"

"Hell, no! And don't you, either. I'm professional at beating around a bush until it doesn't have a leaf left on it," she said.

"You might give me a head's up if he does find out so I can plan to be gone a day or two until he cools down." Deke chuckled.

"And you do the same," she said. "Good night again, Deke."

"'Nite, darlin'."

*   *   *

Josie opened one eye and without moving her head an inch, scanned the small room. Everything looked just fine. Deke and Rascal were both snoring in the bunk below her. But fear had wrapped itself around her like mummy rags. She couldn't move and could only breathe in short gasps.

That only happened when something was terribly wrong. She managed to sit up but her arms felt heavy. Had it been a nightmare? She frowned and tried to remember if she'd dreamed at all. She started to throw back the covers and saw the reason for her fear. A black furry spider wasn't an inch from her hand, and she was frozen.

She opened her mouth to scream but nothing came out. She tried to raise her other hand to slap at it or brush it off onto the floor but it was glued to her side. The spider stopped and backed up a couple of inches. Then with one hop it landed on her shirt.

"Deke," she whispered.

Nothing but soft snores.

"Deke." She managed to get out another word.

Still nothing.

"Deke!" She forced all the air from her lungs in one shrill scream.

He sat up so fast that he bumped his head, swore, and Rascal took off for the sofa. "What?" he asked gruffly.

"Help me." She couldn't take her eyes off the black thing, no bigger than a nickel and yet only slightly smaller than a grizzly bear.

"Josie?" His chin appeared over the top of the bunk rail. "What is it?"

"Spider," she whimpered.

"Don't move." He disappeared.

That wasn't helping. She couldn't move. She could barely speak, and that damned thing was crawling up her shirt toward her neck. If it touched her skin, she would die of sheer fright. Where was Deke?

His big hand came up over the top of the bunk and he grabbed the spider in a tissue, squeezed it in his fist, and then took it to the bathroom. When she heard the toilet flush, her arms worked again. They flailed at the place where the spider had been as she threw covers and pillow off onto the floor.

"Hey, come on down here and let's talk about this," Deke said.

She flew down the ladder at the end of the bed, grabbed the first thing she could find, and hurried to the bathroom. "I've got to get it off me."

"It's dead, Josie. I swear it's dead." Deke followed her.

She peeled her shirt over her head and tossed it in the corner. Next the pajama pants came down to her ankles and she kicked them in the direction that the shirt had landed. It wasn't until then that she realized she'd picked up Deke's western pearl snap shirt. She shoved her arms into the long sleeves, fastened the snaps, and rolled the sleeves up. It stopped right below her panties but she didn't care.

"Are you okay?" Deke asked from the other side of the door.

She swung the door open and picked up the pajama pants and shirt, holding them like a dead rat by the tail, not wanting to touch them but seeing no way else to take care of them. Brushing past him, she went straight to the fireplace and tossed both items into the blazing embers. They quickly ignited but the fire was short-lived.

Deke slipped one arm around her knees and another around her shoulders, picked her up, and started toward the sofa. "It's pretty cold in here. Should I build a fire?"

"No, we need sleep, but I'm not getting back into that bed, not ever."

"Want to trade beds?"

She shook her head. "Just let me sleep the rest of the night with you. You'll keep me safe."

He bypassed the sofa and went to his bunk, eased down onto the bed, and laid her on the bottom bunk. Then he crawled in beside her and pulled the covers up over them both and wrapped both arms tightly around her.

"It was a tarantula," she said.

"No, darlin', it was fuzzy and black but it wasn't a tarantula," he said.

"Not that one." She shivered. "But the one when I was eight years old was a tarantula. I woke up and it was sitting on my pillow, staring at me. I couldn't move or scream or do anything. And then it crawled right onto my forehead."

Deke hugged her even tighter to his chest. "Well, that explains a lot, but I'm here now and if you wake up again, you won't even have to call out to me. I'll know it so shut your pretty eyes and go to sleep."

She was stiff as a board for a long time, but finally she sighed and her body began to relax. Deke's strong arms around her body assured her that he wouldn't let anything harm her, but she couldn't sleep.

"Talk to me," she whispered.

"About what?"

"Tell me about your mama." She snuggled in closer to him.

"She was tall and had dark hair. She worked nights most of the time at the Seymour hospital. She read me bedtime stories and made the best apple dumplings in the whole world. I still miss her," he said softly.

"And your dad?"

"Granny said that as long as I was alive Jimmy Sullivan would never be dead," he said. "From the pictures, I'm pretty much the image of him except that I got Mama's eyes. I didn't miss him as much as I did Mama, but then I was younger and she made sure I had all the comforting I needed."

"I can't imagine losing my parents. Just thinking about not having them makes me sad."

He drew her even tighter to his side. "I can't imagine having parents that I could call or go visit. Don't ever take that for granted, Josie."

"After this week with no way to call them, I won't. Do you want a family, Deke?"

"Someday."

"Me too." She yawned.

Being there with him right next to her, their bodies touching from toes to cheeks, she felt safe and warm. She could have listened to him read the whole Bible to her, or even the phone book that night. His deep drawl chased away all the fears of spiders and everything else. She wanted to hear more of it.

"You mentioned a cousin who owned the Double Heart. Were y'all close?"

Deke chuckled. "Not one bit. He's a couple of years older than me and he was raised in Fort Worth. He only came to Dry Creek a couple of weeks in the summer, and he hated everything about ranching. One year they talked me into going to Fort Worth and spending a week with him. I hated it as much as he did ranchin' so I understood him better the next year."

"Why did he come back?" she asked, her eyes getting heavy, but she didn't want to go to sleep as long as he would talk to her.

"He inherited the ranch and I was already in the one across the road. He was between jobs and he'd gotten married. His wife didn't like country living so he put the place up for sale. I guess he thought he could lease the land, live in the house, and commute to work. But when he did find a job it was in Dallas and his wife declared that she wasn't going to be stuck on a ranch."

"Hmmm…" She tried hard to keep her eyes open.

"Go to sleep, darlin'. We've got lots of time to swap stories." He kissed her on the forehead. "If you have nightmares, just wake me up and we'll talk some more."

"Thanks, Deke," she murmured.

"Anytime." He took her hand in his and held it on his chest.

When she awoke, Deke was sitting beside the bottom bunk in one of the kitchen chairs. He held a cup of coffee in his hand and had a smile on his face.

"Good morning," she said as she sat up.

He put the cup in her hands. "Good morning to you. Rascal and I have done a thorough search of the whole place. There are no more varmints."

"Thank you." She smiled sheepishly. "I feel pretty stupid this morning."

"You shouldn't," Deke said. "That kind of childhood trauma would stay with someone forever. Did you finally sleep okay?"

She kept her eyes on the coffee, watching the steam spiral upward. "Yes, but poor old Rascal lost his bed."

"Hey, he had a choice. He could sleep on our feet or the sofa. He chose the sofa." Deke tipped her chin up and gazed into her eyes. "I loved having you in my bed last night, darlin'."

"So we are friends?" She smiled.

"We had our first sleepover last night so I'd say we're on the way to being..." He paused. "What is it the kids call it? BFTs?"

Josie laughed. "BFFs. Best friends forever."

"Well, we can't be that because Allie has that spot, but we can be BFFTs."

"And that means?"

"Best friends forever two." He grinned.

"What about Lizzy and Fiona?"

"They'll have to be number three and four. Ready to go have some breakfast? I'm surprised that Everett hasn't already been trying to raise us with the walkie-talkies."

"Thank you, Deke, for everything," she said seriously.

"Ahhh, shucks, ma'am. It wasn't nothing. But if a bear comes out of the woods and starts chasing me, I will call in the favor and expect you to shoot him."

"You are afraid of bears?"

"Nope but I am afraid of two tons of mean, hungry bear chasing me with the intent of having me for supper."

She put her hand on his knee. "I promise I will protect you from all bears. That's what friends are for."

"Breaker, breaker, you kids ready for breakfast?" Everett asked through the walkie-talkie.

Deke crossed the room and picked it up. "Be there in ten minutes."

Josie crawled out of bed and tugged at the bottom of Deke's shirt. "Mind if I use this again tonight?"

"Honey, it looks better on you than it does on me" He grinned. "Keep it until we get home."

She picked up her jeans, shirt, and bra for that day and disappeared into the bathroom. She brushed her teeth and stared at her reflection in the mirror. She'd slept in bed with Deke and would do it again that night or she'd sleep on the sofa because wild horses couldn't drag her up on that top bunk again. She could kill a grizzly bear with nothing but her pocketknife, but there could be a mate to that spider hiding somewhere in a crack and it would come out that night.

She hung Deke's shirt on the hook on the back of the door and got dressed, pulled her hair up into a high ponytail, and took another peek at herself in the mirror. She heard the front door open and figured Rascal was already on his way to the cabin, so she left the bathroom and went to the sofa. She turned her boots upside down and shook them to be sure no bugs were in them and then tugged on a pair of socks, jammed her feet into the boots, and looked up at Deke.

"I'm the spider buster. Stick close to me and I'll save you," he teased as he held her coat for her.

They didn't have to knock on the cabin door. Like usual, Everett swung it open. "Well, did you finally wake up?"

"It's only"—Deke looked across the room at the clock on the wall—"six o'clock. The sun isn't up yet."

"No, but it's a rising," Martha said.

Everett laughed so hard he had to hold his sides.

Deke wondered if the old guy had lost his mind.

Josie cocked her head to one side and frowned.

"Inside joke that you kids are too young to understand and is a little too risqué for me to repeat in mixed company." Martha blushed and went back to putting the finishing touches on breakfast. "Pull up a chair. It's going on the table in about five minutes. I'd say you got here at exactly the right time."

"I'm glad you guys decided to stay until tomorrow. Roads are pretty clear, but it is Friday the thirteenth." Martha brought a basket of biscuits to the table.

"We'll get the chores done and then we'll play some board games," Everett said. "Since this is a bad luck day, we'll make the most of it. Besides, this is our last day with y'all."

"But we'll see you before long," Josie said.

Four months! Where would she and Deke be in their friendship/relationship by then? Would this whole week just fade into the background or would it lead to something else? She glanced over at him, and he raised one shoulder.

So he was thinking the same thing and didn't have any more answers than she did. Amazing how that after such a short time, they could read each other's minds.

*   *   *

Deke threw himself back on the sofa that night and groaned loudly. "If I never see another Monopoly game in my life it will be too soon."

"If you die and make it to heaven"—Josie fell down beside him—"burn them all before I get there."

"Everett and Martha did have a good time," he said.

"They should have. They beat the socks off us twice." She sat straight up and her eyes narrowed into slits. "Do you think they cheated?"

"Hell, I don't know. I was so ready to get out of there that I would have helped them cheat if I'd seen a way." Deke moaned.

"Poor baby." Josie sat down close to him and planted a kiss on his cheek. "We lived through it and you know what they say about if it don't kill us..."

He picked up her hand and held it on his knee. "After today I should be ready to bench-press old Lucifer if that's the truth. Maybe I needed today so that I won't get all choked up when we leave tomorrow."

"Speaking of that." She squeezed his hand. "If that offer to ride home with you still stands, I'll take you up on it. I'd rather be moving in a truck than stuck in an airport because of ice or snow," she said.

"Long as you don't ask me to play Monopoly or even dominoes on the way home," he said. "The only thing I will consider is strip poker."

"Honey, I'm a damn fine poker player, so you might want to reconsider that," she teased.

Immediately she pictured him losing one piece of clothing at a time. First the shirt. The sound of the old striptease music played in her head. Then a boot and a sock. The music got louder.

"What are you thinking about? You've got an impish grin on your face." His voice brought her back to the present and the vision disappeared.

"Playin' poker with you," she said honestly.

Deke blushed scarlet. "Well, honey, when I get back to Dry Creek, I will definitely polish up on my game so we'll have a fair match."

"I'll be lookin' forward to it," she said.

After all that talk, she could not force herself to crawl into bed that night with Deke, but the sight of that spider wouldn't go away. She checked her bed three times to be sure there were no spiders and then stretched out for the final night in the bunkhouse. She shut her eyes, counted to a hundred, forward and then backward, tried the old sheep jumping over the fence thing, and nothing worked.

"Hey, wiggly britches, I can't sleep, either," Deke said from the bottom bunk. "What are you thinking about?"

"Going home, I guess," she said. "What about you?"

"Well, I got to admit, I like that you said going home and not going to Dry Creek. That means you are thinking about it as home and not a stopover on your way to somewhere else."

"It is home," she whispered.

She shut her eyes again and still she couldn't sleep. "Deke?"

"I know," he said as he crawled out of his bed, climbed up the ladder, and wedged himself between the wall and her body. He slipped an arm around her and with her back to his body, they got comfortable. "Better?" He yawned.

"Yes," she whispered.

He gently brushed her hair away from her face and kissed her on the cheek. "Now I believe I can sleep."

"Me too, but what if we break down this bed?"

"Then we'll sleep on a quilt in front of the fire. Shhh, darlin', go to sleep. We've got a long way to go tomorrow."

She slipped her hand under his. Yes, there were sparks and vibes and desire at his touch but there was something more that night, and it went much deeper than anything she'd ever known before.

And it felt so right.

Chapter Fifteen

This is a good day except for the good-bye crap." Josie sighed when she awoke the next morning. Deke was already up and scattering the last embers in the fireplace so they would go cold.

"Don't think of it as good-bye. Think of it as a time when Everett will get his business all straightened out and join us. Oh, I forgot about something. There's an animal shelter about five miles from here, and with the after-Christmas influx of animals, they've got a lot they're needing to find homes for. Think we should go by there and get a dog for Everett so he'll have some company?"

"If he's moving to Texas, does he need a cow dog now? Poor old thing would just have time to get used to this ranch and then be moved. Plus, remember, he'll be living in the hotel for a little while." Josie sat up and pushed the covers back.

Had Deke really slept with her all night or had she dreamed that he was there with her? She picked up the pillow and removed the case and a little scent of his shaving lotion wafted across the space to her nose. There was her answer.

"Not for a working dog but for something to keep him company. He's going to miss Rascal," Deke said. "And it could be a thank-you present for all he's done for us. It would only take an hour out of our day."

Josie crawled down the ladder, removed the sheets from both beds and piled them on the floor, then folded the quilts and laid them on the bottom bunk.

She went into the bathroom, hurriedly dressed, and started to lay his shirt on the sofa but changed her mind and shoved it into her suitcase. Rascal got up and moved toward the door when Deke zipped his duffel.

"We'll get this trip started in a minute, old boy," Deke told Rascal.

She picked up her small bag with one hand and the sheets with the other one. "Maybe we should stick around long enough to wash these and finish taking care of the fireplace."

"I doubt that Everett will— Hey, my phone is dinging." Deke pulled it from his hip pocket. "It's got a signal but needs charging. What about yours?"

She checked both her pockets and frowned. "Deke, I have no idea where it is."

He put a finger on her lips and she forgot all about cell phones. "Shhh...if mine needs charging, yours does too."

She strained her hearing until her ears ached and then she heard a faint sound coming from her suitcase. She found it in an outside pocket with her extra pair of socks and grabbed it up like a long-lost sister, hugging it to her chest.

Deke opened the door to a bright orange sliver rising up

over the mountain to the east. Rascal went out like a flash and disappeared into the cabin before Deke and Josie were halfway there.

"They must've been watching for us as usual," Josie said.

"I'm just real glad that Rascal talked me into letting him ride along on this trip. He's never been away from me for a whole week and he would have been lonely even with Allie checking on him every day," Deke answered.

The kitchen door flew open when they stepped up on the back porch. Martha motioned them inside and Everett sat on the floor in front of the fireplace with Rascal in his lap.

"You sure you don't want to let him stay with me? I promise I'll treat him right and bring him home to Texas safe," Everett asked.

"Better take him with me. The cattle are probably getting pretty feisty thinking their boss has left," Deke answered.

"Well, now, I hate good-byes and I know you two are eager to get on the road and get home. So I packed you a thermos of coffee, a couple of travel mugs, and a brown bag breakfast," Martha said. "Me and Everett made a couple of calls this morning and we're going to take your little car back to the rental place in Missoula." She bustled around, pouring coffee into the thermos and adding a muffin to each brown bag. "I know the lady who runs the place and she said that it's no problem to return the car at a different site. Plus, she'll write up these extra days as weather emergencies and it won't cost you any more than you already paid. So that's took care of. Do you need anything else?"

"Just a hug," Josie said hoarsely as she dropped the

sheets in front of the washing machine. "And thank you for taking care of my rental car, but how..."

Martha wrapped her arms around Josie. "I need to get out and do some shopping and so does Everett. I'm down to ten pounds of flour at my place and there's another storm coming down from the north. I'll drive his truck and he'll take that car. We'll shop and have dinner at our favorite little place up there and be home in time to do evening chores. And thank you," she whispered.

"For?" Josie said softly.

"This is the first time he's let me stay all night in this house. We're making progress toward me coming to Texas with him."

"I'll have a room ready for you," Josie whispered.

"Okay, Rascal, it's time—much as I hate to admit it. You hold down the fort until I get there." Everett stood up. "We ain't going to stand on the porch and wave at you kids until you disappear. It's too cold and I hate good-byes even worse than Martha. So y'all pick up your bags and get going. I'm going to pretend that you are out at the barn taking care of the bulls."

Deke laid a hand on Everett's shoulder. "Thank you for everything. We'll be looking for you and our bulls in a few weeks."

"You're welcome. Thank you for the company and the good biscuits every morning. I'll be down there soon as I settle everything here," Everett said. "Now go before Martha sees tears in my eyes and thinks I'm a wimp."

"You kids be safe now." Martha handed Josie the brown bags and the thermos.

"Yes, ma'am." Josie hugged her one more time and jogged out to the truck.

*   *   *

Deke picked up both Josie's suitcase and his duffel bag and opened the front door to find the ice and snow scraped from his windshield. He turned to thank Everett for that, but he couldn't get a word out past the lump in his throat. So he wrapped the small man up in his arms in a hug, patted him on the back several times, and then released him.

Everett clamped a hand on Deke's shoulder and nodded without saying a word while Rascal tore out across the yard and did a couple of laps around the truck before waiting for someone to let him inside.

Deke had trouble keeping the tears at bay as he waved over his shoulder and quickly strode toward the truck.

Josie climbed into the truck and grabbed a McDonald's napkin to wipe the tears away. Rascal jumped in with her and scrambled over the top to sit right behind Deke. She set the brown paper bag and thermos at her feet and waved at Martha, who had drawn back the curtain.

Deke tossed the luggage into the backseat beside Rascal and then rounded the front of the truck. Martha blew them a kiss and he sent one back to her before he settled into his seat, fastened the seat belt, and started up the engine.

"Home in two days?" Josie asked as she reached for another tissue.

"It might take until Monday or Tuesday. We'll watch the weather and sidestep all the storms."

"Hungry?" She glanced at the paper bag.

He shook his head. Swallowing food would be next to impossible. "Nope. But a cup of coffee would be good. First stop the dog shelter."

Josie brought out two travel mugs from the paper bags

and filled both with coffee, draining the last drop from the thermos. The coffee was gone by the time they reached the shelter, a tiny place on the outskirts of town, but there was plenty of parking. The lights were on and one truck was sitting out front.

The lady apologized for the smell as soon as Josie was inside. "I've been the only one who could get out this week and I'm doing the best I can. We always end up with a lot more animals after Christmas. Kids think they want a puppy or a kitten, but then they find out how much work a pet is and we wind up with them."

"We're looking for a dog that needs a good home," Deke said.

"Oh, Deke, look there's a redbone hound puppy." Josie stared longingly at a cage with a floppy-eared hound inside. "And look at those eyes."

"And right there is a whole bunch of kittens. I love kittens and so does Rascal. You think we can get half a dozen of those and that puppy all the way to Texas?" Deke poked his finger into the cage and a yellow-and-white kitten sniffed it.

"I do have a half Chihuahua and half teacup poodle puppy that I'd love to see placed. He's pretty lonely since his brother and sister were adopted." The lady went for a cage and brought out a little black ball of fur that wasn't any bigger than a softball. "He'll probably weigh about five pounds when he's grown. He was the runt, so I wouldn't be surprised if he's even smaller than that."

Deke took the puppy from her and held it up to his face and chuckled when it licked him from chin to nose. "He's so cute, Josie. I think Martha and Everett need this little boy."

"So do I," she agreed.

"Okay, then we'll adopt him. Fix up whatever papers there are and tell us how much we owe," Deke said.

"Are you talking about Everett over near Hall?" the lady asked. "If you are, then I'm going to waive all fees. I go to church with Martha, and I know she'll love this puppy."

"That's the one. What do we need to do then to take him home?" Josie asked.

"Walk out of here with him. Are you the kids who got snowbound over at his ranch, the ones that are going to buy his rodeo bulls?" she asked.

"How did you know that?" Deke asked.

"Honey, this place isn't a big city and everyone knows everyone else's business. Phone service has been back on in Hall and around here a couple of days." The woman smiled. "And we all have those old CB radios."

Deke tucked the puppy inside his coat. "Are you sure there's no adoption fees or anything? The police isn't going to come get us for dog nabbing, are they?"

"Puppy has a good home. That's what we strive for. You guys drive safe now. Wait a minute. You'll need a leash for him and some puppy food." She bent down and opened a couple of doors under the counter. "I've got an old one somewhere and you'll also need a pound of special food just for his size. Here they are!"

"Thank you so much." Josie took them when she handed them both up over the counter.

"I'll give you half an hour and then I'll call Martha and see how she and Everett like a new baby in their house," the lady said as she stood up.

"Thank you," Deke said.

They stepped out of the shelter and Deke slung his arm around Josie's shoulders. "And thank you for not saying that we could manage half a dozen cats and a new puppy on a long trip home."

"You were serious?" she asked.

"You bet I was. Don't tell me that puppy didn't steal your heart."

"It did for sure and we'd best get on out of here or I might go back in there and take him and your cats to Texas with us."

Rascal roused up from the backseat and sniffed the puppy when Deke showed it to him, and then he laid down and went back to sleep.

"Guess he's saying he doesn't want one of those things." Josie held out her hands.

Deke handed over the tiny little dog and she kissed it right on the nose. "If Everett doesn't want you, I will make you the official mascot of my new hotel." She talked to him the whole way back to the ranch. "And now we are going to take you inside to see what Everett and Martha think of having a baby in the house."

Rascal raised his head, peeked out the window, and crawled down into the floorboard.

"Looks like Rascal has had all of Montana he wants." Deke laughed.

"Me too, but I'm falling in love with this little boy pretty fast, so we'd better get him inside before I don't even give Everett a chance at him." Josie reached for the door handle and let herself out.

"What'd you forget?" Everett yelled from the open door.

"Nothing. We brought you something," Deke shouted as he made his way to the porch.

Martha poked her head out around Everett's shoulder. "What did you bring? I love surprises."

Josie held up the puppy. "Rascal thought it might help,

since he turned down your invitation. This little guy is half Chihuahua and half teacup poodle and he'll only get to be about five pounds."

Martha reached for him and cuddled him up under her chin. "Oh, Everett, we have a baby. What are we going to name him?"

A wide grin split Everett's face. "Don't reckon he'll be much use as a cow dog but he'll be real good at keepin' us entertained. You tell Rascal thank you for us. Now get on out of here before you make this tough old man cry."

"We should have asked first," Josie whispered as she hugged him again.

"I might have said no then, but..." His voice broke. "Go on now and call us when you stop tonight."

Deke clamped a hand on Everett's shoulder and then he and Josie went back out to the truck. It wasn't until they were back on the highway that Rascal found his way up onto the seat and looked out the window.

"That was worse than the first good-bye." Deke finally broke the five-minute silence.

"I know." Josie swiped a hand across her cheek.

Deke picked up his coffee cup. "Any more in the thermos?"

"Not a drop."

"Well, that didn't last long," he said.

"What? The pain or the coffee?"

"Coffee. The pain might be with us until they get to Dry Creek. Who would have thought we'd get so attached to a couple of old folks like we have?"

"Crazy, isn't it?" she said around the lump in her throat.

After another minute of quiet, Deke said, "Hey, the charger is in the console if you want to juice up your phone."

Josie set her travel mug in the holder, found the charger, plugged it into the cigarette lighter outlet, and then stuck the other end into her phone. The thought of being back in touch with the world should have lifted her heavy heart right out of her chest, but it didn't.

"So this is what it was like before cell phones and electricity," she said.

"And washing machines and electric coffeepots." He nodded. "Want to throw our phones out the window, turn around, and go back to Montana and settle down in a little cabin somewhere on a creek that will provide us with water?"

She shivered. "No, thank you. I like my hot showers and I really like pushing a button on the washing machine."

An hour later, just outside of Deer Lodge, the lump in Deke's throat had shrunk to the point he figured he could swallow, and his stomach had been grumbling for a while.

"What's in those bags?" he asked.

"I smelled bacon when I took the mugs out. Hungry now?"

"Starving," he answered.

She brought something wrapped in foil and opened it. "Smells like bacon and cheese and eggs. Looks like a muffin."

"I'm almost to the point that I would eat Rascal's dry dog food right now."

She handed it to him and he bit into it while she removed the foil from the same thing out of her sack. "How is it?"

"Terrible. You'll hate it, so I might as well eat it for you."

She took a small bite and slapped him on the shoulder. "This is amazing. Biscuit, bacon, cheese, jalapeño peppers, and eggs all in one muffin. Now, I wonder what's in those other three things all wrapped up in our bags."

"I wouldn't fuss if it was more of the same. Reckon you could call Martha later on and ask her for the recipe. You could make them by the dozens and I could pop them in the freezer and eat four every morning for breakfast," he said.

"Or you could call her and make them for me," she said.

"You make better biscuits than me," he protested. "Is there another one in my sack?"

She brought out two banana nut muffins but hit pay dirt on the third try when she found another breakfast muffin. "Eat slowly. You'll have to make do with dessert after this, but I do see a Ziploc bag full of chocolate chip cookies and whoa, another bag of those apple things that we made."

"Wouldn't by any chance be a pint jar of the 'shine in there, would there?" he asked.

"Nope, guess she didn't want us to get caught with an open container in the truck."

"They were probably thinking more of Rascal than us. Who'd take care of him if we had to sit in jail for a month?" Deke said. "Take a look behind you. I can see it in the rearview, but you'll have to turn around in the seat and look out the back window."

Her blue eyes bulged when she saw the bank of black clouds coming toward them. "Oh, no! Do you think Martha and Everett made it to Missoula? I'll feel horrible if they get stuck somewhere because of me."

"Call her and see. You do have her number, right?"

Josie pulled a notepad from her purse and punched the numbers into her phone. Martha answered on the second ring.

"We're fine. We returned the car and are headed back home now. We brought Bitsy with us and Everett babysat him while I ran into the grocery store and got a few staples. The weatherman says the storm is going to hit us right in the face in the next hour. We'll be back at Everett's and I'll just stay there until it passes through," she said without taking a breath. "Where are you kids?"

"The sign we passed a minute ago said we are ten miles out of Butte."

"That's good. You're outrunning it, but it will go right on down into Colorado, so stay to the west of it or you're going to be spending a lot of time in a motel," she said.

"Will do. Y'all be safe," Josie said.

"Oh, honey, we're so old we don't have to be safe anymore. We just have to enjoy it." Martha giggled.

"Martha!" Josie exclaimed.

"And anyway," she said, "we can't thank you enough for Bitsy, Josie. He's just what these two old folks need in their lives."

"I'm so glad you like him," Josie said.

"Call me when you are checked into a hotel for the night. Oh, and Everett says to tell you that the Western Inn in Spanish Fork, Utah, is pet friendly. He used to drive through there with his dog and he remembered that motel," Martha said.

"Thank you for the information, and the breakfast was delicious."

"Me and Everett took us a little sack breakfast with us to Missoula so we had the same thing you did. It was a fun adventure to get out and drive while we had breakfast. We pretended we were going on a long trip."

"And you might be real soon, so keep that recipe handy."

"One would sure hope so. Bye now."

Josie hit the END button and slid her phone into her shirt pocket. "Hand me yours and I'll get it charged up."

He worked his phone up out of his hip pocket and gave it to her. "Who are you going to call next?"

"No one right now. I'm going to concentrate on outrunning this storm so we don't have to spend a week in a hotel room," she said.

"That would be horrible, now wouldn't it?" he teased.

"Yes, it would."

He jerked his head around and asked, "You don't want to spend more time with me?"

"I did not say that."

"Yes, you did," he argued.

"Okay, so I did, but it wasn't because I don't want to spend time with you."

"Then what is it?"

"I plead the fifth."

"As in Jack Daniel's or the Constitution?"

"Probably both," she answered.

"Fair enough," he said. "I can already feel my shoulders tightening up again from that fall and this driving. Can I book a massage later tonight?"

"Deke Sullivan, you are wicked," she fussed at him.

"Well, thank you, lovely lady. Now tell me what Martha said that made you blush."

"She said that she and Everett were old enough they didn't have to be safe, they just had to enjoy it," Josie said honestly.

Deke felt the slow burn coming from his neck to his cheeks and there wasn't one thing he could do about it.

"You are blushing!" Josie said.

"Well, hell's bells, Josie. That's pretty damned bold for an old gal."

"Yep, it is, and before I forget, they named the puppy Bitsy. That sign says it is one mile to the I-15 exit. I vote we get out at the next gas station, get a coffee refill, and let Rascal water the frozen grass."

"Sounds like a plan to me," Deke said. "And it's pretty clear this isn't your first road trip."

"Not by a long shot."

He pulled off at a gas station. She snapped Rascal's leash to his collar and led him to an area with a sign that said it was the pet playground. He didn't waste any time wetting down a small bush and then he was ready to explore the area, digging around in the snow to make sure there was grass still down there somewhere. The gas pump dinged, but Deke was so involved admiring the swing of Josie's hips and the curve of her waist that he let fifty cents' worth of gas run out on the ground before he got it turned off.

"Get your head on straight, cowboy," he fussed aloud at himself.

Chapter Sixteen

The motel that Everett suggested in Utah had one room left, a king suite, and it was pet friendly. It was only six o'clock in the evening, but Josie felt as if she'd been riding for a week in the buckboard of a covered wagon.

"I could sleep standing up in a broom closet," she murmured.

Deke slung his duffel bag over his shoulder and rolled Josie's suitcase down the long hall to the last door on the right. "Guess that means no massage tonight."

"Depends on whether you are receiving or giving." She leaned against the doorjamb while he slipped the card into the slot. The room was big enough, warm enough, and she'd gladly take the sofa bed, since he'd dished out the money for the first night. But before that she wanted a long hot shower and his shirt.

Deke's hand shot out toward her. "Give me the leash. I'll take him outside. We passed a grocery store about a block up the road. I'll walk up there and get us some food for supper."

He was bone tired and she could hear it in his voice. Driving all day in anything from snowflakes to drizzling to pouring down rain took its toll on a man, no matter how tough he was.

"Better idea. You take Rascal out and I'll call in a couple of pizzas. They deliver them right to our door according to that card setting on the television. What kind do you and Rascal like?" she asked.

He reached for his wallet. "Meat lovers'."

She waved him away. "Let me get this, so I don't feel like a moocher."

He nodded, which proved just how worn-out he was. Deke Sullivan was an old-fashioned cowboy who did not let the women folks pay for anything. He'd proven that at noon when she'd tried to pay for their lunch.

She picked up the phone and dialed the number from the advertisement, put in an order for two large meat lovers' pizzas, an order of breadsticks with marina sauce, a bottle of Pepsi, and a six-pack of beer. The kid on the other end of the phone said to expect delivery within thirty minutes. That was long enough to take a long shower, so she rolled her suitcase into the bathroom and turned on the water.

Letting the water beat down on her stiff back muscles, she relived the whole day. They'd listened to at least twenty of the country music CDs in a case he kept on the back floorboard. She'd enjoyed every minute of it after a week with no music in her life, but at least one line in every song reminded her of Deke.

"At least we agree on country music. If he'd liked anything else, I might have started hitchhiking to the nearest bus station."

She heard noises in the room, which meant he was back

in the motel, so she quickly washed her hair and stepped out. It only took a few seconds to dry her body and get into his shirt. Rascal was curled up on the sofa. Deke was talking on the phone.

"Your turn when you're ready," she said softly.

"See you later, Allie. Thanks again for everything. I'll repay you double next time you and Blake want to take a trip," he said.

When he turned around his face was etched with weariness but he managed a smile. "Jud says if you don't call him, you are in big trouble. I'm going to take a shower and get comfy. After pizza, I may sleep until morning."

"I ordered Pepsi and a six-pack of beer, too," she said.

"Have I told you today that I love you?"

She shook her head.

"Well, for a good cold beer and half a pizza, I'll tell you again. I love you, Josie Dawson." He opened his duffel, brought out his sleep clothes, and disappeared into the bathroom.

Until that moment, she hadn't realized that he didn't sleep in underwear. The picture that popped into her head put high color into her cheeks, especially when she thought about how she'd slept in the same bed with him the past two nights.

She quickly slid her phone out of her purse and hit the speed dial for Jud. He answered on the first ring. "I've been waiting to hear from you all day. I've watched the weather and was hoping y'all got out before that second storm swept into the area. Where in the hell are you?"

"Place called Spanish Fork, Utah," she said.

"And?" Jud asked.

"And I'm too tired to give you details of this past week. I will tell you that Deke and I have formed a partnership with the rodeo stock and our first bulls will arrive with Everett, our new friend, sometime in May or June. He's going to stay at my hotel until he figures out if he likes Dry Creek. If so, he'll buy some property and build a house. If not, he'll go back to Montana before the winter snows hit," she said.

"I asked about you, not your new friend," Jud said.

She recognized that tone and never had liked it. "I'm fine. Rascal is fine. Deke is fine," she shot back at him.

"Hey, don't get hateful with me. I was worried," Jud said.

"Then don't use that tone on me. I'm not your daughter," Josie said.

"But you are my sister and I'm duty bound—"

She butted in before he could go on. "You are released from that duty."

"I don't want to fight with you, Josie," Jud said.

"Me either. I'm tired to the bone but glad I decided to ride with Deke because the Cheyenne airport is closed. We are all three worn-out from driving all day in the rain and snow and I expect we'll be just as worn-out tomorrow night. I will tell you everything when I get home, darlin' brother," she said. "And right now there's a knock on the door so my pizza and beer is here. Good night and I love you."

"I expect more than this when you get home," Jud said.

"And you will have it," Josie told him.

At least most of it, she thought as she told him good-bye and hit the END button. She hurried past a growling dog who did not like being wakened from his comfortable nap and gave the delivery guy her credit card. She signed the receipt that he produced, remembering to add a tip, while he carried the boxes, beer, and Pepsi into the room.

Rascal sniffed the air and whined when the kid left.

"In a few minutes. How about some of your dry food while you wait?" She removed his bowl from a bag and filled it about half full. "That should hold you until Deke is out of the shower. I'll fill up your water bowl. That might be what you want more than food."

While Rascal ate every bit of the food, drank some water from the bowl, and then went back to his warm spot on the sofa, Josie dialed Kasey.

"Hey, girl, Jud tells me you are off on a trip with Deke. I want details," Kasey answered.

"I'm so tired I can barely stand up so you'll have to wait for very many details. A spider got into bed with me—"

Kasey sucked air and then butted in. "Sweet Jesus! What happened?"

"Deke killed it."

"Marry him." Kasey giggled.

"You are crazy."

"Not as batshit crazy as you when you unloaded on Chance when he cheated on you with Liz." Kasey's laughter got louder.

"She was my friend," Josie said, defending herself. "And I don't want to talk about it."

"I'm sure he doesn't either and he probably won't ever cheat again."

"I hope not," Josie said. "He married that girl. And I did not touch his truck."

"No, you didn't, but that bucket of baseballs I was throwing to you hit the mark every single time," Kasey reminded her.

Josie didn't even have to shut her eyes to see those balls going through his pickup windows and dinging the sides of his truck. Or the expression on Liz's face when Josie marched into the karaoke bar that evening where the two of them were hugged up together in a slow dance. She went to the stage, plugged in a tape, and sang Miranda Lambert's "White Liar." It might have been off-key but Chance and Liz got the message loud and clear.

"Where are you right now?" Kasey's voice jerked her out of the past and into the present.

"Spanish Fork, Utah."

"I don't mean the town. Are you in your own room or..." She let the sentence hang.

"We have one room with a huge king-size bed and a pull-out sofa. And there are no spiders," Josie answered.

"Some days you just can't win." Kasey laughed. "Call me when you get home with a full report of what happens with that sexy cowboy. I'll make Jace or Brody watch the kids and we'll talk a couple of hours," Kasey said.

"The report won't be that long."

"Still got two days to go. You could write more into it," Kasey teased.

"Good night and good-bye," Josie said.

Drops of water still hung on Deke's hair and a day's worth of scruff had grown on his jaw. Soft brown chest hair peeked out from the top of the thermal shirt he wore at night. His upper arms strained the sleeves of the knit and his pajama pants hung low on his narrow hips. Knowing there was no undershorts between that flannel and his bare butt, as well as other things, made her fight back the second blush that evening.

"Jud?" he asked.

"I called him, but that was Kasey just now. Let's eat and see if we can find something on TV," she said.

He picked up the remote and flipped through the stations until he came to *NCIS*. "This all right?"

"It's great. I love Gibbs." She opened all the boxes and twisted the tops off two beers. "They're cold and so is the Pepsi. What we don't use right now, we can put in the refrigerator for later."

Deke picked up a slice. "Half an hour ago I wasn't sure I had the energy to chew, but the shower helped. I hope tomorrow is smoother sailing than today." He sat down on the sofa beside Rascal and fed the dog a bite before he started eating. "Rascal likes pizza, but his favorite fast food is tacos. He can eat six, lettuce, tomatoes and all."

"Won't that hurt him?" she asked.

"No, but he don't get to eat them when he's riding very far with me in the truck. Especially in the winter when it's raining and the windows have to be up," he said.

She smiled and nodded, understanding perfectly as she took the room in. Not much smaller than the bunkhouse, and a king-size bed took up most of one wall. The television sat on top of an entertainment unit that had a small refrigerator and microwave on shelves below it. A half wall separated the part with the sofa, flanked on both ends by small tables with lamps, from the bed area, so that must be why they could call it a suite. A coffee table with a glass top was placed about a foot from the front of the sofa.

Josie had spent the night in far fancier places and she'd spent even more nights on the rodeo rounds in some that would make this place look like a palace. At least it wasn't a broom closet. The television worked and there was beer and pizza—all in all, no complaints.

"I'll pull the sofa out for me," Deke said.

"Nonsense, that bed over there is plenty big enough for both of us. And Rascal too. The past two nights we've slept curled up together in a bunk bed. We'll have our clothes on and I've never spent a night on a comfortable sofa bed. If the bars under the mattress don't catch you right at shoulder level, you can bet your sexy ass they will get you on your lower back," she said. "Besides, you need a night of good solid sleep, since we have another full day of driving ahead of us."

"So you think my ass is sexy?" he asked.

"Yes, I do, and that is why Rascal will sleep between us." She reached for the pizza box, tossed in half a dozen breadsticks and a container of marinara, and sat down on the floor on the other side of the coffee table. She dipped a breadstick in the marinara, chewed and swallowed, and then downed a quarter of a bottle of beer.

"Damn, that tastes good," she said.

He picked up another slice. "I don't know which is better. The food, the beer, or being able to get out of the driving rain."

"All of the above," she said.

When they finished eating, she shut the pizza boxes and put them on top of the microwave. He put the beer and soda pop in the tiny refrigerator. She turned back the bed and he set a glass of water on each nightstand.

They crawled between the covers at the same time with what seemed like a city block of space between them. "This bed is bigger than the whole bunkhouse." She yawned.

Deke scooted over and brushed a soft kiss across her lips. "Not quite, but after a week in bunk beds, it feels like it would easily cover an acre of ground. Good night, Josie."

"'Nite, Deke."

Rascal hopped up on the bed and wiggled his way right in between them with his head resting on the middle pillow on the big bed.

"See, I told you." She smiled. "Good night, Rascal."

The dog thumped his tail against the comforter a couple of times and then shut his eyes. Suddenly, Josie felt alone. For the past two nights she'd had a warm body so close that they'd practically become one. She rolled over on the other side, but there was Rascal and she couldn't even see Deke. She flipped away from the dog's pizza breath and sighed. He was only a couple of feet from her, but it felt like a country mile, and she missed his big strong arms around her.

*   *   *

Deke figured when he propped two pillows against the headboard and started watching another episode of *NCIS* that he'd be out within ten minutes, but he was too damned tired to fall asleep. The last time he was this tired was when he'd driven all night from a rodeo out near El Paso so he'd be home in time to do chores the next morning.

Josie's blond hair made a halo around her face. Long, light brown lashes rested on high cheekbones and were topped off by perfectly arched brows. He had to fight the desire to kiss those plump, slightly open lips and run his fingertip down her jaw. A softness that Deke had never felt for any woman melted his heart. She'd proven that she cared about him with the massage, ordering pizza and beer so he didn't have to go to the store—a dozen little things that showed that he mattered to her.

He awoke at two o'clock in the morning with a start. Somehow he'd gotten under the covers and was facing the clock. He turned over to find only Josie's face and hair showing. The comforter was pulled up to her chin and old Rascal was still on top of the covers between them. Some sidekick he was. He found the remote beside Rascal and hit the POWER button to turn off an old episode of *Happy Days*.

He shut his eyes and went back to sleep, wishing that he was back in the bunk bed, where he had a reason to cuddle up next to Josie. The next time he awoke it was to Josie sliding out of the bed and tiptoeing to the bathroom. A glance told him that it was seven o'clock. He didn't hear rain, so that was a good sign.

Rascal opened his eyes, eased off the bed, and stood by the door. Deke dressed quickly and snapped the leash on the dog's collar. "Good boy. You didn't make me get up one time in the night and go outside with you. But I bet you are about to burst a bladder right now."

Josie yelled from the bathroom, "I took him out at midnight. You were snoring and so tired I hated to wake you."

"I do not snore," Deke declared.

"Yes, you do. Rascal and I made a trip out to the doggy place and then came right back inside. The stars were shining at midnight, but according to my phone, it's going to start snowing here by ten this morning." She came out of the bathroom, stopped in front of the sofa, and stretched, first raising her arms and then bending over to touch her toes.

Josie was curvy with that slim waist and those well-rounded hips. And her legs went on forever and ever. He imagined them wrapped around him, and suddenly a tent appeared under the sheet.

"Your turn in the bathroom. I'll get dressed and take Rascal out; then we can pack it up and be on our way." She picked up the leash and snapped it onto the dog's collar.

Thankful that she disappeared out the door, he hurried

to the bathroom and took a quick cold shower. When he returned to the room, her bag was packed and ready to go. Leftover pizza was all tucked away in one box, the four unopened beers and the Pepsi were in a plastic bag, and she was sitting on the sofa, waiting. This woman was one in a million, for sure.

"You'd do to ride the river with." He smiled.

"What does that mean?"

"It's something my grandpa used to say about my granny. I guess it means that you take care of things and if we were in the Old West, you'd make a good woman to journey through life with."

"Well, thank you. You paddle a pretty good boat yourself, Deke," she told him. "Are we ready? I checked the weather on the television. That storm has pushed all the way to Durango and is still going south. We should keep west of it through today, and if it drops into the panhandle of Texas we might have to go all the way down to Phoenix before we can go east."

"Damn!" He jerked on his boots. "Forget about getting home tonight, then. It will be at least tomorrow and maybe even Tuesday."

"No matter what, I'm sure we'll make do. And it still beats hanging out in the airport by myself."

"Well, now, darlin', havin' you along to keep me company sure beats travelin' alone too." He set the bag of dog food on top of the suitcase, popped up the handle, and grabbed his duffel with his other hand. "I'll take these out and come back for Rascal and the leftovers. We'll just keep listening to the weather and figure out our way as we go. It's the only thing we can do."

She wrapped Rascal's leash around her wrist and picked up the pizza box in that hand and the plastic bag in the other. "I can get this and we won't have to come back. You should get the receipt for your taxes, since this is a business trip."

"Man, you are as handy as the pocket on a man's shirt," he said.

"You trying to charm me again?"

"No, darlin', that is the gospel truth."

*   *   *

At noon they stopped at a steak house for a real meal and both ordered an eleven-ounce sirloin. Josie checked the weather and found that they were barely keeping ahead of the snowstorm.

"Check Flagstaff, Arizona, for a weather report." Deke had his phone out and was checking weather in surrounding states.

"Snow on Monday," she said.

"Now check Amarillo."

"Snow on Monday afternoon."

"And how about Vernon?"

"Snow Monday night."

"Then we'll go to Flagstaff and drive like a bat out of hell out on I-40," he said. "When we get past Amarillo, we'll start angling south and be home Monday night."

"We have a plan." She sighed.

"Yes, we do, and as long as the roads are dry we can drive until about eight tonight before we stop, if that's all right with you."

"That should put us in Gallup. Want me to check on pet-friendly hotels?"

"That'd be great," he said.

The waitress set their food in front of them and Josie

laid her phone to the side. "Lord, this looks good. I love steak."

"As much as pizza and beer when you are very tired?"

"Hell, no. Nothing could compare to that pizza last night," she said as she cut a chunk off and popped it into her mouth.

He added extra butter to an enormous baked potato. "You've said more cuss words the past thirty-six hours than I've heard you say since I've known you."

"Cussin' comes out when I'm tired or worried," she said.

"What are you worried about?" he asked.

"Not much, but I am pretty damned tired, and if I never see snow again, I'll be a happy woman."

"I could make you very, very happy." He grinned.

Oh, honey, I have no doubt in my mind that you could, she thought.

She cut another bite of steak. "Do women fall at your feet and lick your toes when you say things like that?"

The shiver started at his head and stopped at his toes. The snarl lasted longer than the shiver. "That is so gross."

"Then get the picture out of your mind." She laughed.

"I can't and it's ruining my appetite."

"Think about a big fat bologna sandwich with nothing but thick slices of onion and horseradish sauce," she said.

"Now my taste buds are rebelling. I'm going to think about you sitting across from me and you are wearing my shirt and your long legs are bare. There we go, my appetite is back and I can eat again." He cut off a bite of steak. When he'd swallowed he laid his hand on hers. "Seriously, I am very glad you are along on this trip. I like the comfortable silence that we share for miles on end. I love that we like the same music, and when we do talk, it's like we've known each other for years. I've never had that kind of thing with another woman, Josie."

"What did you talk about with the other women?"

"Not much," he answered.

Josie understood exactly what he *wasn't* saying, and a streak of jealousy shot up her spine.

"Something wrong?" Deke's long arm shot across the table to gently touch her cheek.

"What makes you think that?" she asked.

"You went kind of pale, like you were about to choke on something," he said.

She laid down her fork and knife and held his hand there, loving the tenderness and the care behind it. "I'm fine."

He brought her hand across the table and kissed each knuckle. "What were we talking about?"

"What you talked about with other women," she answered honestly.

"That's all in the foggy past, darlin'. I like talkin' about today and the future much better." He turned her hand over and kissed the palm.

Details.

That's what Kasey asked for, but Josie wasn't sure she wanted to share any of this with her cousin or anyone else. And a little voice inside her head said that this was only the tip of the iceberg compared to all that could happen on this trip.

Chapter Seventeen

Finding a pet-friendly hotel in Gallup was not difficult. Finding one with a room to rent was the big problem. Every single one that Josie had researched on her phone was flashing a NO VACANCY sign when they drove past it. So they drove on to Grants and once again snagged the last pet-friendly room in a hotel.

"So could you sleep in a broom closet tonight?" Deke asked.

"Standing on my head," she said with a nod.

"We got a king-size room but no sofa or refrigerator. Looks like a lot of truckers stay here from that lot around back. We've got an outside door. You comfortable with all that?" he asked as he parked the truck and trailer as close to the room as he could.

"I'm tough. If there's a bed big enough for the three of us and a decent shower with hot water, I'll be fine," she answered.

"Pizza again?" he asked.

"We finished our leftovers, but I bet we can find someplace around here to deliver." Josie snapped Rascal's leash to his collar and opened the back door to the truck.

He bailed out, sniffed the ground, and promptly hiked his leg on the truck tire then pulled against the leash until she walked around the parking lot with him twice. When they made it to the room, the shower was running. Steam escaped from under the door and Deke was singing "Firecracker" and be damned if his voice wasn't every bit as deep and sexy as Josh Turner's.

The lyrics talked about her being a blond bottle rocket in the middle of the night. Was that the way Deke saw her? Even after the big spider fiasco? Josie took the leash off Rascal and he headed straight for the bed, turned around three times, and plopped his head down on the middle pillow.

Deke again sang "Die a Happy Man" by Thomas Rhett. The words said that if all he ever got was her hand in his that he could die a happy man. Josie found a blast of new energy and danced around the room as he sang.

When the shower and the singing stopped, she threw herself backward on the bed. Deke had Josh Turner's voice, Luke Bryan's cute little dimple on one side, and that sexy smile that melted a woman's thong under britches. And Blake Shelton's height and muscles.

She reached for the remote and hit the POWER button for the television. It came on to the CMT channel and videos were playing. Carrie Underwood was belting out "Before He Cheats." That was a sobering video for sure. Deke Sullivan had no idea what a temper Josie had. If he did he wouldn't even glance at her because she'd proven that she didn't take well to cheating. The job that Carrie did on her cheating boyfriend was nothing compared to what she'd done.

When Deke came out of the bathroom, Pistol Annies were singing, "Hush, Hush." He sat down on the end of the bed and flashed one of those thong-melting smiles.

"I like this song. It's life all done up with a pretty bow. Life happens but by damn, it's all kept hush, hush and swept under the rug."

"You speakin' from experience?"

He chuckled. "Miranda looks like she'd be a real pistol even if she is wearing that cute little blue dress that makes her look like a Sunday school teacher. But, darlin', I bet she can't hold a candle to you."

As luck would have it, the very next video was "I Feel a Sin Comin' On," also by the Pistol Annies. The music reached right down into Josie's soul and wrapped around every desire in her body when the lyrics asked sweet Jesus not to hold it back. She had never wanted to get up and dance a striptease and she had to fight the desire to do one for Deke right there in the hotel room.

No beer for you tonight, girl, and you'd better turn off that television right now if it's going to put ideas in your head about things that should never happen.

She handed Deke the remote, careful not to touch his fingers. "I'm going to take a shower."

"Hey, did I say something wrong?" he yelled.

She opened the door an inch. "Not one thing. Those memories from the foggy past you talked about surfaced and I need to wash them away."

The music stopped and she could hear voices, which meant Deke had switched channels. Smart cowboy for finding something other than county music on the television—especially if the thump of that steel guitar did things to him like it did to her. She stood under the warm water, enjoying the way it beat down on her tired muscles for a long time, then hunger got the best of her. She quickly wrapped a towel around her wet hair, dried her body off, and dressed in panties and his shirt. When she left the bathroom she found an array of small bags of chips, sandwiches, fresh fruit in cups, individually wrapped pastries, and candy bars all spread out on the bed.

"I got dressed and ran on over to that convenience store about half a block up the road. There was nothing other than pizza that I could get delivered so we're having a backseat picnic," Deke explained.

"A what?" She bent over and towel dried her wet hair.

"That's what my folks called it when we were traveling and nothing but gas stations were open. They'd buy whatever they could, put it in a brown bag, and give it to me in the backseat of the truck and call it a picnic."

"Looks good to me." She hung her towel over the only chair in the room and took her place on the other side of the food.

Can I have half a dozen of your kisses for dessert?

No one, not even Kasey, who never, ever doubted Josie, was going to believe that she had spent ten days in a room with a cowboy like Deke Sullivan and did not have sex with him.

"I like you, Josie. We can talk about anything or nothing just like I can with your brother and cousins," he said between bites of a sandwich.

A smile tickled the corners of her mouth. "Does that mean I'm one of the boys? Do I get a special cowboy hat to prove it?"

"Oh, honey, you will never be one of the boys. You've

got too many curves for that and you are much prettier than any of those other Dawsons. But other than the Logan girls, I've never had a female friend. They're like sisters but you . . . hell, I'm talking in circles."

"I like you, too, Deke. I've had lots and lots of male friends but there's something special between us." She poked him on the shoulder with a forefinger. "I feel like we were destined to find each other and be best friends and partners."

"With benefits?" He grinned.

"In your dreams, cowboy," she smarted off.

*   *   *

"Well good morning, sleepyheads," Deke said, all cheerful and bright eyed as he stepped into the room the next morning. "Looks like Rascal is ready to hit the road. How about you, gorgeous lady?"

"Give me five minutes." She yawned. "And there is nothing pretty about me in the morning."

"In the eye of the beholder, darlin'." Deke smiled. "I'll take my baggage to the truck." He snapped Rascal's leash to his collar and slung the door open. "Dammit!"

Josie rolled her eyes and sighed at the snowflakes drifting down from gray skies. "I'll check the weather on the television and see what I can get up on my phone. We'd best get a move on."

"Thanks." She stepped outside and Deke eased the door shut.

Josie grabbed the remote and flipped through it until she got to the Weather Channel. She tossed it in the middle of the bed while she dressed in her last clean pair of jeans, a long-sleeved knit shirt, and then pulled a flannel shirt on over the top of that. She brushed her teeth, swept her blond hair up into a ponytail, forgot about makeup, and shoved everything that belonged to her into the suitcase.

When Deke and Rascal returned she was looking at disastrous news on her phone and hearing it on the television. "The storm has gone wild. The interstate is open to Clines Corners, but from there on out past Amarillo it's closed. We'll have to head south and go east when we hit Roswell. Weatherman says it will be noon by the time it gets to Roswell."

"We'll be through there by noon without a problem," Deke said. "You ready to go?"

She was busy packing all the leftover food into one bag. "I checked for places to get gas and refill the thermos. Looks like Clines Corners is the last stop before Roswell."

"You got it." His eyes looked worried. "We should have kept driving last night. We could have been home about now if we hadn't stopped to sleep."

"And we could have been dead if either of us had fallen asleep at the wheel." She shoved the partial bags of food into a bag. "We'll just stay out of the storm as much as possible and hopefully we'll be back in our own beds tonight."

"Oh, you mean me and Rascal don't get to sleep with you anymore?" He handed her the dog leash, picked up her suitcase and the groceries, and followed her out to the truck.

"You'll miss me?" she asked.

"Oh, honey, you have no idea," he answered.

*   *   *

Josie's first feeling was pure elation. But then a picture of Liz's smug grin when she told Josie that she and Chance had been screwing around behind her back flashed through her mind, right along with the anger…the anger she had felt when Chance broke up with her an hour later in a damned text instead of face-to-face.

What if that happened with her and Deke? He was Jud's friend and best friends with her sister-in-law and her two sisters.

"You are doing that again," Deke said.

"What?" she asked.

"That expression on your face says you are facing off with the foggy past. Want to talk about it?"

"Reality is a bitter pill. I was playing what if," she said.

"What if what?"

"Okay, I was in a very serious relationship with a guy about a year ago. He cheated on me with my good friend."

"Okay," Deke said slowly.

"Think about it, Deke. If whatever this is between us led to something serious and…"

"You sayin' I might cheat on you?" His voice was chilly.

"Would you?"

"I told you, Josie, I'm either in for the long haul or not at all. When I commit, it will be for life," he answered. "Do you still love him?"

She shook her head. "No, but sometimes I do miss my friend. We'd been roommates in college. Imagine the shit storm in Dry Creek if…"

He shook his head. "Don't go there. Let's just take this a day at a time and see where it goes but never worry about me cheatin'. What happened when you found out?"

She related the story of the baseballs and the song.

"Didn't he sue you for destroying his truck?"

"Luckily, we had a hailstorm that night. He wasn't about to admit what happened and why, and since Liz lived in south Texas, she didn't have much fallout. They got married last month."

Deke turned on the windshield wipers. "If she can take him from you, then someone else can take him from her."

"Paybacks are a bitch," Josie said with a grin.

He pulled into a convenience store. She snapped the leash on Rascal's collar, and Deke fueled up the truck and went inside. When he returned with ham and egg burritos and two large coffees, she made a quick trip to the bathroom. When she finished she saw that he'd loaded up on more snack food and added a flat of two dozen bottles of water.

She stared out the side window at the city getting more and more congested with the business rush hour at hand and then the traffic thinning out on the east side of town as they left it behind them. It was fifty-nine miles from there to Clines Corners and neither of them said a word the whole distance.

Is he thinking about my temper or what I said about the shit storm if things went south between us? I wish he'd say something. Anything. Hell, we can even talk about what we'd do if we did get stuck out here in this snowy wilderness. I should never have shared that story with him about Chance and Liz. What in the devil was I thinking?

The wind was coming down from the north at twenty miles an hour according to the radio DJ, but Josie figured he was downplaying the whole report. From her standpoint, it was gusting at sixty miles an hour, sticking to everything from the windshield to fence posts, barbed wire, and even the spines on cactus.

Nothing had ever looked so good as the big red sign shining through the snow announcing Clines Corners

Retail Center. Deke nosed the truck and trailer into one of the last parking spots reserved for bigger vehicles behind the big store and Josie bailed out before Deke could even get the leash on Rascal. She jogged into the store, brushed the snow from her shoulders, and quickly glanced around. There it was—a yellow sign with red lettering pointing her to the restrooms. Hoping it wasn't one of those bathrooms-for-one, she hurried that way.

It might not be her lucky day with Deke but it sure was when it came to the ladies' room. She did not have to wait. As she washed her hands and dried them, she vowed that she would not drink two huge cups of coffee between there and Roswell.

A sale rack of T-shirts caught her eye and she flipped through them in a hurry, draping three over her arm. If they had to spend another night on the road, she damn sure was not sleeping in his shirt again. On her way to the counter she picked up two foot-long subway sandwiches, two pints of milk, and a chew bone for Rascal.

Deke turned around with a plastic sack in his hands. "That looks like positive thinking to me."

She stepped around him and laid her items on the counter.

He held up his bag. "I've got pork rinds and candy bars. I'll share if you will."

"One of these is for you unless you want to swap with Rascal and take the chew bone," she teased, glad that they were back on familiar footing.

"Not a chance. Anything else we need or want before we get back on the road?"

"Nothing I can think of." She pulled out a credit card and paid for her purchases.

See there. You were worrying for nothing. He was

probably thinking about the weather, not that story you told him, the voice in her head said coldly.

"Hush," she said.

"Pardon me." The little dark-haired clerk raised an eyebrow.

"I'm sorry. I was thinking out loud."

"Sexy cowboys do that to you. Man, he's the finest lookin' thing I've seen in days." She winked as she rang up Josie's purchases. "I ain't seen a man that pretty since the last time I went to a Blake Shelton concert. You best hook him soon or he'll get off the line and you'll lose him for sure."

"We are only friends and today I'm not sure about that," Josie said.

"You are kiddin' yourself if you think y'all are only friends. He looks at you like he could have you for breakfast, dinner, and supper, and you look at him the same way. You'll figure it out but remember I told you first." She smiled as she put a pen and the receipt on the counter for Josie to sign. "Be careful out there, now. Roads are slick and it's a long way to another station."

"Thank you. We'll keep the speed down." Josie scribbled her name and picked up her bags.

She started to run from store to the truck, but halfway there, her feet went out from under her and she landed flat on her back, wet snow hitting the part of her face that wasn't covered by the T-shirt that had flown out of the bag and landed on her. There was no air in her lungs and she couldn't force herself to inhale.

"Josie!" Deke yelled loudly as he propped her up into a sitting position and jerked the shirt away from her face. "Are you okay? Did you break anything?"

She sucked in several lungfuls of air, but she still

couldn't speak, nod, or even blink. And his warm breath on her cheekbone wasn't helping one damn bit. She pushed at him and inhaled again, that time getting some relief from the tightness in her chest.

Deke had his phone out, punching in numbers. Why would he call Allie? Then it dawned on her that he'd hit three numbers instead of hitting a speed dial for his best friend.

"If you just called 911, end it right now," she said between gasps. "I'm fine. It knocked the wind out of me, but nothing is broken."

"Are you sure?" he asked and then spoke into the phone. "I'm sorry, ma'am. False alarm. I thought my friend couldn't breathe, but she's okay now."

"I might be sore a couple of days, but I'm okay," she said.

He quickly gathered up the items and put them back into the bag, hung it on his wrist, and picked her up like a bride. She snuggled closer to his chest as she took deep breaths and let them out slowly. Then she felt herself leaving his body and being placed in the passenger's seat. His strong arm grazed her breasts as he reached for the seat belt. Her flesh tingled even through layer and layers of clothing.

"I should have let you walk to be sure nothing was broken or sprained," he said.

"When I catch my breath, I'll be okay, Deke. Let's get on the road and put some miles between us and snow." She leaned against the headrest and shut her eyes.

"As still as you were, I was sure you'd hit your head and was dead," he said as he started the engine.

"I hate being tall," she murmured.

"Why would you say that, Josie?" He pulled out onto the highway. "You look like a runway model."

"Yeah, right!" She opened her eyes and straightened up. "When I was a little girl I was the tallest one in my class and I had this long, skinny neck. The kids called me a giraffe and used to ask me how the weather was up there."

"I got a lot of that, too, but I imagine it was worse for a girl," he said.

Rascal poked his head in between the two seats and licked her across the cheek.

"Sweet boy," she said as she scratched his ears. "Did his chew bone make it back in the sack?"

"Along with sandwiches and milk and some T-shirts."

She started to reach for the bag and flinched.

He tapped the brakes and slowed down. "We should stop at the Roswell hospital and have you checked. You could have fractured a bone in your wrist or your arm and not know it."

"It wasn't my arm, it was my shoulder and it's okay. Really, it is. I've fallen harder in the past and after a couple of days even the soreness went away. I've had broken bones, Deke. I know the difference," she protested.

She undid her seat belt and turned around in the seat. Sitting on her knees, she found the bag with Rascal's new bone and tried to unwrap it but couldn't get it out of the bubble wrap.

Deke inched his knife upward from the pocket of his jeans and handed it to her. "Give it back closed."

"I know the rules. Remember I am superstitious," she said.

"Just makin' sure. I don't want to have an accident on the way home because of bad luck."

"Always give a knife back the same way you got it." She repeated the old rule as she opened the package and offered the bone to Rascal.

He sniffed it and then gently latched onto it with his teeth, plopped down on the seat, and set about trying to chew the thing into nothing but shreds.

"I believe he likes it." She snapped the knife shut and handed it back to Deke.

"He loves those things. It might last him until we get halfway home. He can make short order of one," Deke said as he slowly made the exit onto the two-lane road headed toward Roswell. "It's going to be a long day. Let's play two truths and a lie."

"That sounds like fun. You go first," she said.

"Okay. Number one: I hate mushrooms. Two: I'm a sucker for a good dancer. Three: If someone offered me a million dollars to relocate to the center of Dallas, I would take it."

She didn't even hesitate. "Three is a lie. All the money in the world couldn't make you live in a big city. Two is easy. You love to dance. But one might have stumped me if three hadn't been so easy. I didn't know that you hated mushrooms."

"Your turn, and mushrooms are the only thing I really don't like. Do you eat them?"

"No!" She shivered. "They have very little flavor and feel like I'm chewing on sponge."

"That's good news. I won't have to pick them out of the spaghetti sauce when I cook for you," he said.

"You can cook?"

"I can and I shouldn't have told you that, since I could have used it." He grinned.

"Okay. Number one: I'm clumsy. Two: I've been to half of the states and have magnets for my refrigerator to prove it. Three: I did some barrel racing when I was in junior high school."

He could imagine her in the saddle on a fast-moving horse, maneuvering around big barrels set up in a corral. And dammit! She did look sexy in those tight jeans and cute little western shirt in the picture in his head.

He kept one hand on the steering wheel but rubbed his chin with the other. "You play tough. I don't think you are clumsy, even if you did fall a little while ago. There was that time in the barn when you got off balance but I wouldn't call that clumsy. I wouldn't be surprised if you have been to that many states, since your family likes to go to rodeos. And I don't have a bit of trouble picturing you as a barrel racer. So my guess is that number one is a lie. Why'd you stop barrel racing?"

She shrugged. "Truth is that Kasey was better than me and I was jealous."

"And what were you better at?" Deke asked.

"Chemistry. Math. All those things came easy for me, so I tutored Kasey to get her through high school."

"What about college?"

"She got married right out of high school and didn't barrel race again after that. I went on to college and got my degrees."

"More than one?"

"Double major in geology and agriculture."

"I'm impressed." He grinned. "Smart and beautiful."

"That's so sweet," she said and tapped the clock, which displayed 11:11, with her fingernail.

"I saw it first so I get to make a wish," she said.

"Have at it. I make my wishes when 12:34 pops up. What are you going to wish for?"

"I don't kiss and tell. What will you wish for if you see your magic number?"

"Same here. No kissing and telling, but I bet it doesn't

come true." He grinned. "Check the weather again and we'll see if there's even a possibility my wish will come true."

She touched the screen on her phone and groaned. "No service."

"What's the next town?"

"Duh...no service. No GPS. No Internet. Nothing but a blank screen," she said.

"Duh..." He picked up a road atlas that had been shoved down between his seat and the console. "Don't go anywhere without a map."

She flipped through the pages until she came to the New Mexico map and ran her finger across the major interstate and then down from Clines Corners to Vaughn and on down.

"Says it's Ramon, but the lettering is so small that I bet it's just a community instead of a town, and it's the only thing between us and Roswell."

"Good thing we've got plenty of gas and food."

And clean shirts, she thought but she didn't voice it out loud.

"And we are here," she said. "And that is it. One dilapidated old building with a few dead trees—"

"Holy mother of God!" Deke yelled and whipped the steering wheel to the left, taking the truck out across the road and barely coming to a stop before he plowed right into one of those trees.

Chapter Eighteen

W hat in the hell happened?" Josie asked.

"Didn't you see that car that lost control and slid right in front of us?"

She looked into the side mirror, and sure enough there was a gray compact car slammed against the old building not fifty yards behind them. "No, I was looking at the map. Oh my God, I hope no one is hurt."

"We'd better go see. Get out your phone and dial 911," he yelled above the wind as he was out of the truck in a flash and running toward the car.

"No service, remember?"

"Dammit!" he swore. "Stay right here. I don't want you to fall again."

She grabbed the keys, didn't bother to lock the door, and got to the old building seconds after he did. The two front doors of the vehicle were crumpled and wouldn't open, but the back driver's-side one gave Deke no problem.

"Are you okay, ma'am?" he yelled above the wind.

"I need to get to the hospital!" the lady screeched. "My baby is comin'. I swear to God it's comin'."

Josie opened the other door and crawled inside the car, over the seat, and sat down on the passenger side. The car was so old that it had a bench front seat and no console, so she inched closer to the woman and laid a comforting hand on her shoulder.

"My name is Josie Dawson. This is Deke Sullivan, and we'll help you however we can, but I have to know if you are all right before we move you."

"I'm fine. Oh God, it hurts and I want to push," she said.

"Can you move all your fingers and toes?" Josie asked.

"Yes. I'm fine. I hit my head on the steering wheel but the seat belt kept me . . . oh, Lord, did it hurt my baby?"

"What's your name?"

"I'm Maddie McKay, my husband is in Roswell waiting for me at the hospital." Each word came through clenched teeth.

"Okay, Maddie, I'm going to unfasten the seat belt and I want you to lie down on the seat and let me check you. Can you do that?" Josie said.

"I can do anything," she squealed, "if you will just help get this baby out of me and get us to Roswell."

Josie moved back over into the backseat and Maddie slid down until she was stretched out. Tears rolled down her cheeks and she wiped them away with the back of her hand.

"If she is going to have this baby right now, she can't do it in this car. There's not enough room," Deke said. "And you were supposed to stay in the truck."

"You don't have the right to tell me what to do," Josie said.

"Don't argue with me."

"Will y'all stop fighting and get this baby out of me!" Maddie screamed.

Josie shot a look at Deke, but it bounced off his worried face. "We'll help you, but you need to get over the seat so I can carry you to my truck. We'll drive like hell to Roswell to get you to the hospital. How far is it from here?" Deke said.

"Sixty miles. And I've got one minute between pains now so here goes." Maddie got to her knees and made it to the backseat before the next pain hit.

Josie got out and Deke reached inside, wrapped one arm around Maddie's shoulders and the other around the back of her knees and gently brought her out of the wrecked vehicle. He started for the truck and had no sooner taken two steps until Maddie sucked in a lungful of air and let out a screeching scream.

"Josie, put Rascal in the trailer," Deke said.

"Don't let my baby die," Maddie gasped. "Promise me, Deke. Promise on your mama's heart, you won't let my baby die out here in this damned cold weather."

"I'll do my best," Deke said. "Now I'm going to lay you down on this seat and Josie is going to see how you are doing. She's a ranchin' woman so you don't need to worry none."

"You ever delivered a baby?" Maddie panted.

"No, but I've pulled lots of calves, and I was right there in the room when my cousin had her third child about six months ago. I watched everything real close but I bet we can get to the hospital."

Josie knew exactly what folks meant now when they said they were "sweating bullets." Her hands shook as she gently lifted Maddie's dress tail, and sure enough the baby was crowning. No wonder the poor girl wrecked her car and wanted to push.

"Deke, you're going to have to help me," she said.

"What do I do?" he asked.

"Deliver this baby while I clean my pocketknife and find something to tie off the cord. Why didn't I bring my sneakers?"

The snow got harder as Josie hurried around the truck and dragged her suitcase and his duffel out onto the ground. She found nothing in hers, which was no surprise, but Deke's netted a gold mine in a hooded sweatshirt. She pulled the string from the hood and tucked the shirt up under her coat to keep it dry. One of her new T-shirts would do for padding and one of the plastic bags could carry the placenta to the hospital.

"Cold," Maddie said. "I'm so cold. My baby is going to freeze to death."

"No, it's not. We are going to make sure that you get to the hospital as soon as it's born and we get back on the road," Josie said in a soothing voice. Every nerve in her aching body was stretched to the limit. She quickly shut the door and carried the suitcases to the trailer on her way back to the other side of the truck. Forget about outrunning the storm. They'd be lucky if they made it to Roswell, the way the storm was shaping up.

"Messing up your truck," Maddie said between pants.

"Aw, don't you worry none about that. These leather seats clean easy. Push, Maddie, give it all you've got," Deke encouraged.

"I hate my husband!" she yelled.

"You'll love him tomorrow but right now it's okay to hate him," Josie said. "One more push, darlin', and this baby's head will be out."

"Promise. Oh. My. God. It hurts. I will never do this again." Maddie pushed and sure enough a little round head with lots of black hair was introduced into the world. "Is it over?" She gasped for breath.

"One more to get the shoulders," Deke answered. "Good girl. Give it all you've got. That's good. Real good."

A tiny little boy slid out into Deke's hands, and he quickly cleaned out the baby's mouth. The baby had a great set of lungs and he used them the moment his airways were cleared.

"I'm going to reach inside your pocket and get your knife to cut the cord. We can tie it off with this string I pulled from your sweatshirt and wrap the baby in this T-shirt to keep him warm," Josie said as she worked.

"Is it over?" Maddie asked.

"One or two more pushes and then it will be done and we'll get you and this little boy to the hospital," Deke said.

Deke wrapped the newborn in a bright red Christmas T-shirt and then again in his sweatshirt, drawing the sleeves around him twice to form a type of bundling. Before he handed the baby off to his mama's waiting arms, he stared down at the newborn. The expression on Deke's face was so beautiful that time stood still for Josie. She knew for certain in that moment that there was more to Deke Sullivan than chasing women in bars on weekends, more than running rodeo stock, and even more than ranching.

"Now you hold this precious baby boy close and stay very still. We'll get there as fast as we can," he said softly as he put the baby in Maddie's arms.

"He's beautiful but he was supposed to be a girl,"

Maddie whispered. She touched his face and his nose and traced his lips. "I want to unwrap him and see if he's got all his fingers and toes. Did you notice?"

"No, but there'll be plenty of time for that. We just need to keep him warm and you still until we get to the hospital and the doctors can take care of you," Deke said. "Let's get this wagon train moving." He slammed the open door and jogged around to the driver's side of the truck.

Josie eased into her seat and fastened the seat belt.

"Maddie, are you comfortable?" Josie asked.

"My bottom feels like I just birthed an elephant but that's not as bad as those pushin' pains," she said. "Thank you both. I don't know what I would have done if you hadn't come back for me."

Deke started the engine and turned on the heat. "Josie, keep your phone out and check it every few minutes. As soon as you get reception dial 911."

"Rascal!" Josie yelled.

"No, his name is not Rascal," Maddie said. "We thought we were having a girl and her name was going to be Emily, but since it's a boy, I don't know what his name is."

Deke braked. "Where are we going to put him?"

"In my lap. He'll freeze back there," Josie said.

Rascal had to be coaxed up into Josie's lap and then he wasn't so sure about the newcomers in the backseat.

"It's okay, boy. We're taking them to the hospital and then you can have your seat back," Josie whispered in his ear.

He plopped down with his butt in her lap and his paws and face on the console, where he kept an eye on the strangers. Josie kept petting his head and scratching his ears, reassuring him by her touch while Deke kept both hands on the wheel and his eyes on the little bit of yellow line that was visible through the snow.

"If I never see another snow in my life, I will not bitch," he said.

"Me either," Maddie said. "I wasn't driving fast because the roads were slick and then a pain hit and I grabbed my stomach and the car went into a spin, went right in front of your rig and I thought I was going to die."

"I just saw a flash of gray. Thought at first my eyes were playing tricks on me. They should never make cars that color. You can't see them in rain or snow," he said.

"I'll never drive anything but a red car from now on." Maddie yawned.

"Don't go to sleep," Josie said.

"Why?"

"You hit your head on the steering wheel. I couldn't find a knot anywhere. If the swelling went inside, you could have a concussion."

Deke glanced into the rearview and then back at the road. "And with all that pushing, it could cause a bleed, so that's why you need to be very still."

"Now I'm scared," she said.

"It's only a little over an hour to the hospital and they'll do tests, which will probably prove that you are fine but it doesn't hurt to stay awake and be still. Is the baby all right?" Deke deftly changed the subject.

"He's chewing on a fist. Do you think I should offer him the breast?"

Deke's cheeks turned crimson. Still yet another layer peeled back from that rugged charming exterior.

"I'd wait until we get to the hospital." Josie's stomach grumbled, but everything was in the trailer. Sandwiches were probably frozen by now, along with everything else she'd thrown back there. Besides, she couldn't drag out food with a dog in her lap and a young woman who shouldn't have anything until the doctors examined her.

"We've come forty miles," he said. "That's more than halfway, Maddie."

"I'm doing fine," she said. "But my poor little boy has to go home to a pink room with lace curtains and my old doll collection displayed on a bookcase."

"It won't take you long to redo that room," Josie assured her.

Maddie whimpered. "He can't go home in a pink gown with lace around the hem."

"I'm sure his daddy and all your family and friends will find something perfect for him before you even leave the hospital," Deke reassured her.

Jodie checked her phone and shouted, "Hallelujah!"

"Service?" Deke asked.

"Yes!"

She punched in 911 and immediately a female voice answered.

"Thank you, Lord." Maddie groaned.

"Hang on. The snow is letting up a little. We're only fifteen minutes from Roswell." Deke accelerated another five miles an hour.

Josie held the phone away from her ear. "She's going to stay on the line and talk us to the emergency room doors. She's got someone on the other line with the hospital staff and they're going to be waiting with a team of doctors and Maddie's husband."

"Just a little bit more, then? I'm so tired, Josie," Maddie said.

"What's your husband's name?" Josie asked.

"His name is Bobby Ray. He's going to be surprised that

the baby is a boy. I could call him now that we have reception. Oh, no! I left my purse in the car and I don't have my insurance cards or…" She started to cry. "They told me it was a girl and we've been getting ready for a girl for months."

"I'm sure there will still be plenty of things you could use or return. Or maybe you'll have a little girl next time," Josie said.

"Oh, no! I'm never having another baby. Not ever. Bobby Ray said he wants four but I'm tellin' him the only way that's going to happen is if he has the next one," she said stoically.

Josie's laughter startled Rascal and caused Deke to tap the brakes.

"You scared me. I thought you were crying for a minute there," Deke said.

Josie wiped her eyes with the back of her hand. "I agree, Maddie. If our men had to go through half an hour of labor for every child they fathered, the population explosion would take care of itself."

"Amen, sister," Maddie mumbled.

"Don't shut your eyes. Stay with me. It's only five more miles until we make the first turn and from there it's only a mile to the hospital. Bobby Ray is waiting. Do not go to sleep," Josie said sternly.

Maddie's eyes popped open. "You sound like my granny." Deke chuckled.

"What?" Josie glared at him.

"Nothing."

"I bet he just now pictured you with gray hair but don't worry, he'll still love you even then," Maddie said. "How long have y'all been married? Not long enough for a kid but long enough for a dog, evidently. Some folks start off that way but I got pregnant early in our relationship so we bypassed the dog stuff."

"The lady on the phone says turn right onto Fifth Street and then the second left onto Pennsylvania Avenue and the hospital is on the right," Josie said.

Deke eased around the first right and slowed to a crawl. He made the second left with no problem and pulled right up to the emergency room doors, where a whole team of medical staff rushed out to his truck. In a blur Maddie and the baby disappeared through the big double doors.

Chapter Nineteen

I can't leave until I know she's going to be all right," Josie said. "I know it's crazy. We need to get home and it's another ten hours of driving in good conditions, which means we won't get there until midnight."

Deke laid a hand on her shoulder. "I'll find a parking spot and take Rascal for a walk. He'll be all right in the truck for an hour, and Josie, there's no way we're going to get home tonight. My arms are aching from hanging on to that steering wheel and you have to be getting sore from that fall and being all tensed up over this baby. We'll drive a few more miles and get a room for the night."

"You'll get no argument from me. After all that tension, we both need a place to crash while the adrenaline rush settles down."

She picked up her purse and headed inside the hospital. There was a gift shop on the bottom floor, so she stopped and bought a little boy's outfit, a blanket, and a big helium balloon showing everyone that a baby boy had entered the world that day. She found out where the waiting room on the OB/GYN floor was located and sat down beside a nervous young man with blond hair and the clearest blue eyes she'd seen on anyone other than her brother, Jud.

"My wife had our baby a month early out there on the road. She wrecked her car and she could have been killed," he blurted out. "And it's a boy and they told us it was a girl and we don't have a thing for a boy."

"Are you Bobby Ray?" she asked.

"Yes, ma'am."

"I'm Josie Dawson. Deke Sullivan and I were the ones who brought your wife in a few minutes ago. Your baby boy was breathing good and Maddie was awake and talking to us when we arrived. But she did bump her head on the steering wheel when the car crashed so I'm sure they need to check her for a concussion. Maddie might have a few bruises on her knees and where the seat belt kept her from flying through the windshield, though."

Bobby Ray nodded seriously. "Thank you, ma'am, for taking care of her. They couldn't tell me anything at all and I've been worried that my son was dead."

She wrapped her arms around him. "He was eating his fists last time I saw him. They'll come out here and talk to you as soon as they figure everything out, I'm sure. And Bobby Ray." She passed the gift bag with the little boy things over to him. "You take this in to her. She's worried about all that pink and lace too."

"Are you sure? I can pay you back for it. I just was so afraid that our baby didn't make it that I didn't even think of this kind of thing," he said.

"I'm very sure, and consider it a gift. We were happy to help."

"We'll never be able to repay you," he said.

"Invite us to your fiftieth wedding anniversary." She smiled.

Bobby Ray managed a weak smile. "I'd be honored but I might not live that long. Maddie scared forty years off my life today. I'm sorry I wasn't there for her."

Josie patted him on the shoulder. "There's more to a baby boy's life than the first hour."

"That's right, Bobby Ray," Deke said from the doorway into the waiting room.

"This is Deke Sullivan. He delivered your son," Josie said.

The young man jumped to his feet and stuck out his hand. "Thank you, sir, for all you've done."

Deke pumped his hand up and down a few times before he dropped it. "I'm glad that this woman here"—he nodded toward Josie—"took so long at that Clines Corners place or we'd have missed the wreck altogether. It's amazing how things like that work."

"Me? It was you who was dragging your feet," Josie protested.

"You been married long?" Bobby Ray asked.

"We are not married!" Josie and Deke said in unison.

"Well, you sure act like you are," Bobby Ray said.

"Maddie McKay's family?" A nurse stepped into the doorway.

"Yes!" He turned so fast that Deke had to catch him to keep him from falling on his face at the nurse's toes.

"You can see your wife now."

Bobby Ray picked up the balloon and gift bag and headed for the door. Halfway there, he turned back and motioned for them to follow him. "You should come with me, both of you."

"Is that all right?" Deke asked the nurse.

"Maddie is asking for Josie and Deke. Would that be you?" the nurse said.

Deke draped his arm around Josie's shoulder on the way down the hall. "We should have you checked out while we are here."

She shook her head. "Not necessary. But I won't argue about a hotel room as soon as it's time to check into one. A long, hot bath would be wonderful."

"I bet you feel like I did when I played football." Deke smiled.

They waited at the door while Bobby Ray rushed to his wife's bedside. He dropped the balloon and the gift on the floor inside the door. The balloon stopped floating when it hit the ceiling, so Deke grabbed the string and tied it to the doorknob.

Maddie put the baby in his arms. "Josie, look at him since they've got him all cleaned up. Isn't he beautiful? I never thought babies were pretty. They all looked like wrinkled prunes, but not our boy. He's too gorgeous for words."

Josie looked over Bobby Ray's shoulder. "Yes, he is and he'll grow up to be a heartbreaker for sure."

I want a whole bunch of those, she thought. *I don't care if they are boys or girls or a mixture of both, but I want to feel like Maddie does right now.*

Maddie went on, "They said I don't have a concussion but I will have a bruise where the seat belt held me in, but the baby wasn't hurt."

"That's great," Josie said and then grabbed Deke by the arm. "Look at him, Deke. He's going to have dark hair."

Deke peered down at the baby and whispered, "I love babies."

The doctor poked his head in the door. "Are you the folks who delivered this baby?"

"Yes, sir," Josie answered.

"Good job." He gave them a thumbs-up. "He's only five pounds and eight ounces and he's early but his lungs are developed. We'll keep Mama and baby a couple of days to be sure everything is fine after a traumatic birth out in a snowstorm but I don't foresee any problems."

Bobby Ray carried the baby across the room and sat down on the edge of the bed. "I was so scared when they called me and then you didn't get here when you should have. I love you, Maddie."

His tone, his body language, and his eyes backed up his words.

I want that, too, Josie thought. *I want my husband to be that much in love with me when we have every one of our children. That's what life and living is all about.*

Deke crossed the room and touched the baby's tiny hand and immediately he grasped Deke's hand in a firm hold.

"I believe I just got the first handshake from this cowboy. What are y'all going to name him?" Deke asked.

Josie's heart melted at the sight of the wee little hand wrapped around Deke's huge finger and even more at the expression on Deke's face. Someday that big old cowboy was going to make a wonderful father, and whoever was the mother of his children was going to know that she was loved.

"We don't even have a name picked out," Bobby Ray said. "They were so sure it was a girl. What do you think, Maddie? Before we knew, we talked about Derrick."

"And we also thought about Eli," she said. "What do you think, Josie?"

"Is your name really Bobby Ray?" It wasn't easy to take her eyes from the baby but she glanced up at the father.

"No, it's Robert Rayford. I was named after my grandpa and Rayford is my mama's maiden name," he answered.

"I always liked the name Ford," Josie said.

"Oh, I love it," Maddie said. "We could name him Robert Rayford Junior. And call him Ford," Maddie said.

"I like that." Josie bent and gave the newborn a kiss on the forehead. "It's a good strong name. Are you on Facebook, Maddie?"

She nodded. "I sure am and I'd love to have you for a friend."

"Me too," Josie said. "I'd like to keep up with Ford and see his pictures."

"Josie Dawson, right? I will friend you as soon as I get my tablet back from that wrecked car," she said.

"We should be going, Deke. We've got a long way to go."

He slung an arm around her shoulders. "I guess we should."

"Thanks again," Bobby Ray and Maddie said at the same time.

Josie smiled at Maddie. "Take good care of that precious baby."

"And post lots of pictures," Deke said as he ushered Josie out of the room.

Sparks from his touch sent heat through her body. But what really warmed her heart was Deke's expression when that tiny little hand wrapped around his finger.

Chapter Twenty

Well, dammit," Deke swore when they were outside the hospital. "Looks like the storm caught up with us."

Josie tucked her chin down to keep the blowing snow from her eyes. Deke moved his arm from her shoulders and laced his fingers in hers. *Not a good idea*, she thought. *If I fall you'll go down with me. And I can slip on a single snowflake.*

"Let's find a motel right here in Roswell rather than trying to go any farther. I feel like a rubber band that's stretched so tight that it's about to pop," he said.

"Even though we're less than six hours to home?"

"With this weather it could take ten or twelve. As much as I wish I were Iron Man, I need some food and rest." He dropped her hand and opened the truck door for her.

Rascal roused up from his blanket and sat up straight, his eyes glued to the driver's side of the truck until Deke was inside. Then he stuck his head between the two seats for a bit of petting.

"You were pretty damned heroic back there, delivering that little baby."

*   *   *

The hotel parking lot was already full and several trucks were parked out behind, but there was room for one more, so Deke nosed into the slot and pointed next door. "That's a steak house right there. If we can get a room, I'll walk over there and get takeout so we don't have to leave Rascal in the room alone."

Josie agreed with a quick nod, the adrenaline rush from the whole day wearing off and hunger setting in. She thought of the sandwiches she'd thrown in the trailer. Probably smashed and frozen, and there was nothing worse than soggy tomatoes and lettuce.

She pulled her coat tighter across her chest and watched the snow cover the windshield. Ten minutes passed and he still hadn't returned. Her imagination went crazy, sending her a visual of Deke lying in a pool of blood inside the lobby. He had slipped and fallen and hit his head on the corner of a table holding the coffee machine and died instantly.

An ambulance siren sounded in the distance and got closer and closer. She unfastened her seat belt and whipped around in the seat, but all she could see was the big trailer behind the truck. Before she could get out and start toward the lobby to see what was happening, the driver's-side door swung open and Deke held up a key card.

"I snagged the last room, which was not pet friendly, but the sweet little lady made an exception when I assured her that Rascal was a good boy," he said. "I'll get the luggage and the food bags if you'll snap the leash on Rascal and bring him inside."

Josie had no doubt that Deke's charm was what got them the key to that last room and that Rascal had little to do with it. Her suspicions were confirmed when she and Rascal reached the lobby right behind Deke. The clerk wasn't a day over nineteen and her gaze followed Deke all the way across the floor.

When they were in the elevator, Deke hit the number three button. "Remind me to never listen to weathermen again."

"Remind me to never think that I can fly into Montana and trust that I can get out before a storm hits. My granny says everything happens for a reason and she's always been right. I guess I'll have to wait a while to figure out what the reason was for this, though."

The light flashed that they were on the second floor and the elevator groaned. Josie crossed her legs and her fingers. But it did go on up and the doors opened. Rascal was the first one out and tugged at the leash for her to follow him.

"Number three-two-five." Deke manhandled the luggage and two bags of food into the long hallway. He handed her the card when they reached the room and she tapped it against the lock. A green light flashed and she opened the door to find not a room but a full-fledged suite with a Jacuzzi.

"Oh. My. Lord!" She gasped.

"The clerk gave me a discount, since it was the last one and now she can turn on the no-vacancy lights." He grinned.

It was on the tip of her tongue to say, *I bet she'd give the room to you free for an hour with you naked in that Jacuzzi.* But she smiled and said, "Well, aren't we the lucky ones today?"

"Yes, ma'am, we are." Deke dropped the bags in the middle of the sitting area. "I'm going next door for takeout before I take off my coat and boots. How do you like your steak and what sides do you want?"

"Medium rare, loaded baked potato, and you choose the rest and we'll share," she said.

She was still staring at the round Jacuzzi tub when Deke left. If only she had a bathing suit, she'd get into that right then. But no one packs a bikini when going to Montana in the winter. She headed for the bathroom and found a huge vanity with two sinks, a shower above a tub, and big thick towels.

In addition to that gorgeous tub, the sitting area offered a television, closet, sofa that made out into a bed, a coffee table, minikitchen with a sink, microfridge, and a coffeemaker, plus a basket filled with extra coffee, an assortment of teas, and two bags of popcorn.

The bedroom wasn't an area but a nice big room with a king-size bed, end tables with lamps, a second television, and a door that closed it off from the sitting room. Rascal had claimed the sofa and whimpered when she came back.

"Poor old boy." She stopped to pet him. "I bet you are thirsty and hungry too."

She dug through the plastic food bags until she found his bowls, filled one with food and the other with water, and set them on the tile around the base of the Jacuzzi. He was more thirsty than hungry and quickly drank all the water in the bowl.

"I don't need a bathing suit. I've got a T-shirt, and my underpants cover more than a bikini." She went back to the bags and brought out one of the new Christmas shirts. As she undressed down to her panties, she made her way to the tub and adjusted the water until it was warm enough. Jeans, bra, socks, boots, and coat were all piled up on the other end of the sofa from Rascal's spot when she eased down into only two inches of water and leaned back.

The tub was full and the jets running so she didn't hear Deke when he returned. With closed eyes she was enjoying every single little blast and all those sweet little bubbles working magic on her tired muscles. It wasn't until she caught a whiff of grilled meat that her eyes popped open to find Deke sitting not six inches from her on the edge of the tub.

"If we're having a wet T-shirt contest, you are the winner." He grinned.

There was that wicked cowboy charm again, complete with a twinkle in his eyes and a raised eyebrow. She flipped the switch for the jets to the off position and eased up to the top of three steps leading down into the huge tub. Before she could swing her long legs out over the side, Deke had crossed the room, thrown open the closet, and brought her a fluffy white robe.

"No need to get dressed to eat. This will keep you warm and then we can both hop back in that tub." He held the robe for her and then went to the coffee table and started pulling boxes out of the plastic bags.

She cinched the belt around her waist and imagined a naked Deke in the tub. She whipped around so fast that the room did a couple of spins and she felt herself swaying. Finally, she got control and eased down on the sofa.

"Well, crap!" he said. "All we have is plastic knifes."

"We both have a pocketknife," she reminded him.

"I'm so hungry that I forgot about that." He worked his knife up out of his pocket and carried it to the sink to wash it.

Josie picked up the plastic knife they'd sent with the meal.

"I've got another one in my duffel bag. I'll drag it out and you can use it."

"Always carry a spare?" Josie asked.

"Most of the time," he answered.

"I'm glad you do. I couldn't bring mine since I didn't check my luggage."

He found the second knife, washed it and handed it off to her. His fingers brushed against hers in the transfer and the chemistry between them was so strong that it flat out took her breath away.

"Open it," he said.

"What?"

"Your knife so I can hand it back to you opened when I get it washed. That way it'll be ready to use," he answered.

"Oh, the knife."

"What did you think I was talking about? The front of that robe?" he teased.

"I'm so hungry that my brain isn't working right." She started opening one box after another. "Good Lord, Deke! Did you get every side order they had?"

"Almost. Everything looked good so I bought it. Besides, we've got a refrigerator and microwave and we can have leftovers after a while," he answered.

He sat on the floor on the other side of the coffee table and handed her knife back to her. He popped open the larger two boxes to reveal huge steaks and baked potatoes, and surprising still steaming hot. The smaller containers contained slaw, baked beans, okra, and corn on the cob.

She cut into the steak and popped a bite into her mouth. "Amazing." She dragged out the word.

He sat down on the sofa across from her and used a plastic fork to dig down into a potato for his first bite. "Well, it has been a long time since breakfast, so I imagine shoe leather would taste pretty good right now."

Rascal leaned over as far as he could without getting his nose right in the food. He licked his lips and whimpered. Deke cut around the T-bone, leaving a quarter inch of meat around it and then tossed it over next to the Jacuzzi beside his bowls. Rascal wasted no time getting from the sofa to the bone.

Josie patted the sofa. "You can move to a more comfortable place now."

"I'm fine right here. Soon as I get finished I'm getting in that tub. The warm water and jets might help get some of this tightness out of my arms and back."

"I'll take a shower and a nap while you—" she started.

He held up a palm. "You see the size of that thing. We can both get in it and not even touch each other. I've got a pair of sleep shorts that..."

Crimson filled her cheeks instantly.

"Well, Miz Dawson, from that blush, I do believe that you thought I was going to get in it butt naked, didn't you?"

"The thought did cross my mind," she said.

"And?"

"And I was being polite and offering to let you have a turn," she answered.

"Well, I do have something to wear that can keep me decent so that we can both get in together unless you don't trust yourself with me." There was that brilliant smile and one dark eyebrow shooting a dare toward her.

"I've been sleeping with you for two nights and in the same room with you for a week. I haven't torn your clothes off and attacked you yet, have I?"

He chuckled. "I keep watching the clock for 12:34 and

making wishes. Maybe one of them will come true before we get home."

"You are incorrigible," she said.

"That's a big word to use on an old rough cowboy like me."

"It's the truth. You will never change."

Deke grinned. "Never say never."

*   *   *

The water had cooled by the time they finished their midafternoon meal, so Josie drained half of it and turned on the hot water. She left her robe hanging on a desk chair and slid into the water again. Full stomach, warm water—she'd have to be careful or she would fall asleep.

Bracing her neck on the edge of the tub, she stretched her legs out and hit the switch for the jets. Deke had taken his suitcase to the bedroom and soon he came out wearing nothing but a pair of baggy red basketball shorts that came to his knees. Dark hair covered his broad chest and legs. Josie's fingers itched to touch it—just to see if it was as soft as it looked.

He didn't use the three steps down into the water but rather slung a leg over the side and slipped down into the water like a sleek otter. "Sweet darlin'," he moaned. "A good steak and now this? I would have given that girl at the desk my bank account if I'd known how good this would feel."

"Never been in a Jacuzzi before?" she asked.

"Hell yes, but never after a day like we just had," he answered.

"Want to go into details about when and where?" she asked.

Never ask a question that you do not want to hear the answer to, the voice in her head said bluntly.

"Do you?" he fired right back as he stretched his legs out to the other side, brushing against hers as he brought them to rest right next to hers.

"Hell, no!"

She wasn't sure if she was answering his question or telling him not to touch her, but either way, he did not move the leg one inch. His toes were right next to the elastic in her underpants and he wouldn't be still. He fidgeted, moving his foot around in the water and then bringing it back to rest on her upper thigh.

They started at the same time.

"Josie..."

"Deke..."

"Beauty before brawn," he said.

She moved over to his side to sit beside him. "I... well..." she stammered.

He turned toward her, cupped her face in his hands, and leaned toward her lips. Already wet from the water, she didn't even need to moisten them but her tongue flicked out anyway. Then his mouth was on hers and his tongue teased its way into her mouth, deepening the kisses even more. She shifted her position so she could wrap her arms around his neck. He pulled her to his chest without stopping the string of kisses so hot that it was a wonder the water didn't hit a boil.

"I've wanted to do that all day," he whispered.

A thin, wet T-shirt was all that separated her aching breasts from his bare chest and she wanted to feel skin on skin. She leaned back enough to whip it up over her head, and with a hop, she was sitting in his lap. The kisses got hotter and hotter as his hands roamed over her back and down under the elastic of her hipster underpants to massage her bottom.

She slipped her hand down past the band of his shorts and circled his hardened erection with her hand. He was ready; she was damn sure ready. And yet, something inside her head said not to do it.

"God, Josie," he groaned. "I've wanted you for weeks. Please don't stop."

She tugged at his shorts and he wiggled free of them. She tossed them and her underpants out onto the tile and eased herself down onto him until he was planted firmly inside. But before she could begin an underwater rhythm, he flipped her over and took the job upon himself.

"Condoms," he groaned.

"Don't need 'em," she panted. "I'm on the pill."

He kissed her eyelids, the tip of her nose, her ears, and then came back to her mouth. Their tempo sped up until she was built right up to the top of a high cliff. As if he could sense her climax and wanted to prolong her pleasure, Deke slowed down, but the kisses—oh sweet Lord, they kept her at just below the boiling point the whole time.

"Deke, I'm so ready." She groaned as she dug her nails into his back.

That time when she was panting so hard she could scarcely breathe and, ready to fall into the abyss called afterglow, he hoarsely whispered her name and with one final thrust they came together.

She had to hang on to Deke with both hands to keep from dying from pure ecstasy right there with jet bubbles beating against their bodies.

"My God," she whispered when she could inhale.

"I knew it would be that good," he said hoarsely. "And that is not a line, Josie."

"Oh, yeah?"

"Promise. Confession. This is my first water sex."

She brushed a soft kiss across his lips. "Mine too. Want to compare it to bed sex and see which one is best?"

"Oh, darlin'." He nodded.

He slid away from her and rose up, water sluicing off his tall, dark, sexy and sleek body. He stepped out of the tub and picked up one of the towels folded on the side of the tub. She stood up and locked gazes with him. He hurriedly finished drying off and reached for another towel without blinking.

Every fiber of Josie's body reacted to his touch as he gently dried her body and then scooped her up and carried her to the bedroom. He shut the door with his bare foot, set her on the end of the bed, and then threw back the covers.

"Like this," he said.

"That's what I had in mind," she told him.

He gathered her up again and gently laid her on the sheets. His lips found hers and Josie was lost all over again. Hot kisses, excitement building with each touch of new territory until finally he moved over the top of her. She wrapped her legs around him, drawing him into her with one hand while the other tangled itself into his hair.

It might be crazy. Hell, she might regret it, but right now she wanted Deke, whether he had a reputation or not. Everything disappeared just like it had in the water. There was no one else on the face of the earth, maybe in the whole universe but Deke and Josie, and they needed each other.

Josie hadn't really thought he could take her to the same heights again, but she was wrong. The water sex was not a bit better than plain old bed sex, and when it was over, a warm afterglow wrapped itself around them like a cocoon. He pulled the covers up over them and held her tightly, her fingers splayed out on his chest as she used his arm for a pillow.

"That was a first," he whispered.

"Deke, you can't tell me that you were a virgin," she said.

"No, but I've never had sex without a condom and wow, just wow," he murmured.

"Well, I have and still wow, just wow," she said.

He kissed her on the forehead. "You are amazing, Josie Dawson."

"It was a first for me, too," she said.

"Water sex?"

"No, afterglow. And I really like it."

Chapter Twenty-one

Deke awoke to the sound of Rascal scratching on the door and in that time between dreams and fully awake, he thought he was in his own bedroom. It must have been a fabulous night because a naked woman was in his arms. Then suddenly his eyes were fully open and everything came back to him in a flash.

Jud Dawson was going to kill him. Blake and Toby Dawson would help Jud drag Deke's cold, dead body to the Brazos River. In fifty years they would find a male skeleton chained to a couple of concrete building blocks and some forensic scientist would finally figure out what happened to Deke Sullivan.

Rascal scratched again and Deke glanced at the clock on the nightstand. Six thirty—but was that in the evening, or had he and Josie slept all night and it was morning? He eased away from Josie and out of bed, padded naked across the carpet and carefully opened the door.

"Give me time to get dressed," he whispered to Rascal.

The dog sat down and stared at the door.

"Cross your legs. I'm hurrying," Deke murmured as he dressed.

When they finally made it outside to the pet area, Rascal had to smell every shrub before he could find a place to hike his leg. Deke shivered against the cold north wind, but at least the stars were shining and half a moon hung in the dark sky. When Rascal finished he wanted to amble around and check out every snowflake that had fallen. Deke gave him plenty of leash to explore for a few minutes while he tried to sort out what in the hell he was going to say to Josie when she awoke.

He was so deep in his own head, he didn't even hear his phone ring until the third time and then he dug around in his coat pockets until the fifth ring before he answered it.

"Hey, are y'all going to make it home tonight?" Jud asked. "And where is my sister? I tried to call her three times before I gave up and called your number."

"She's asleep. We had a rough day and it was snowing really hard so we decided to stop in Roswell, New Mexico. With any luck, we'll be in Dry Creek before dark tomorrow." Deke was amazed that his voice sounded normal.

"Rough day?" Jud asked.

"I'll let her tell you about it. It's quite a story, but we're fine. I'm out with Rascal in about eight inches of snow," Deke answered.

"Tell Josie to call me soon as she wakes up. I can't wait to hear this big story." Jud chuckled.

"What's the weather like there?"

"Roads are clear. No rain in sight and today it was fifty degrees. Leave that cold weather and snow behind you. We don't want it. Wouldn't mind a few days of rain but that's all," Jud said.

"Will do my best not to let it cross the border into Texas. I've seen enough snow to last me a lifetime. See y'all tomorrow. Will you tell Allie what's going on?"

"I sure will and be safe," Jud said.

Deke's breath was a fog when he exhaled. He'd never been able to keep much of anything from Allie, so he sure didn't want to talk to her. Not that Monday evening or anytime in the near future. She would be the first one to welcome him home, so he'd have to face her tomorrow but that gave him almost twenty-four hours to figure things out.

*   *   *

Still feeling the effects of the afterglow, Josie awoke slowly and hugged herself as she relived each delicious moment that she'd spent with Deke that afternoon. She rolled over to slip her arms around him, but all she got was a pillow. Sitting up quickly, she glanced around the room.

The bedroom door was open and the suite was eerily quiet. She pushed back the covers and got out of bed. Rascal and Deke were gone and somewhere over there on the sofa a phone was ringing. She rushed in that direction and dug around in the pile of clothing until she came up with it. Biting back a groan when Jud's smiling face appeared on the screen, she took a deep breath and answered it.

"Hey, Jud."

"Did I wake you? Well, if I did, I'm not sorry because it's too late to take a nap. You'll never be able to sleep tonight," Jud said.

I rather spend more time in bed with Deke than sleep anyway, she thought.

"Darlin' brother, after the day Deke and I had I could sleep for a week," she said.

"I talked to him. He's outside with Rascal and says the snow has stopped."

She padded naked to the window and looked outside. Stars shone brightly in the sky. "Looks like it. Maybe we'll have dry roads the rest of the way."

"Deke says you have something to tell me," Jud said.

Sweet Lord, what has he said?

"Well, we did deliver a baby today," she said.

"A real baby or a calf?"

She exhaled slowly. "A real one."

Please God, let this be what Deke was talking about.

"Are you joking with me?"

"Nope." She picked up the robe and put it on as she talked and kept looking out the window. "This car came out of nowhere, flew across the road in front of us, and slammed into an old bar building up in Ramon."

Deke and Rascal came in as Josie told her brother the rest of the story, but she kept her eyes on the stars. She could not turn around until she finished talking to Jud. She didn't want her brother to hear a change in her voice.

"Right now, though, I'm starving. Can we talk more about this when I get home tomorrow?" she asked.

"Sure thing. Ever since we were kids, you always woke up from our naps hungry. Y'all be careful," Jud said and ended the call.

She slipped the phone into the pocket of her robe and turned around slowly. Deke's arms were open wide and she walked right into them.

"What are we going to do about us now?" he asked.

"Think about it later," she answered. "Right now I'm going to take a long, hot shower."

"Josie, this...what we did...it's not like..." he stammered.

He tipped up her chin and she expected a kiss but his eyes locked with hers. "I don't know where this is going when we get home, but that was not a one-night stand."

Her arms went around his neck and she pulled his lips to hers for a long, lingering kiss. When it ended she stepped out of his embrace and touched his cheek. "I know it wasn't, Deke, but we both need to think about where this could or will go and the consequences."

"I'll run us another Jacuzzi," he said.

"I wouldn't trust myself in that big tub with you again."

She went straight to the bathroom, shut the door, and adjusted the water in the shower. The robe went on a hook, her phone on the counter, and Josie stepped into the tub. She'd barely gotten wet when the curtain slid back and there was Deke wearing nothing but a smile.

He got in with her, soaped up a cloth and pulled her hair up with his free hand so he could wash her back from the nape of her neck all the way down to her legs. Somewhere in the middle of the job, he dropped the washcloth and finished the job with soapy hands.

She flattened her hands against the shower wall to keep her knees from buckling. The sensation of his touch was surreal. Nothing had ever felt so good or created such beautiful multicolored sparks.

"Feel good?" he drawled.

"Absolutely amazing," she said as she turned, wrapped her arms around his neck, and, with a little hop, locked her legs around him. "Deke, we can't do this when we get home."

"We're not home yet," he said hoarsely.

She slid her hand between them and guided him inside

her. Bracing her on the back shower wall, he started out at a slow pace but after that back washing, she'd had enough foreplay. She rocked with him with the shower beating down on his back until they were both panting. Words weren't necessary; they weren't even possible. All she could do was groan when they both reached the edge together. He slid down into the tub to a sitting position with her in his lap.

Her ear was plastered against his chest, listening to his heart racing in unison with hers. By shutting her eyes, she could imagine that the warm shower was rain and they'd just made wild, passionate love beneath a willow tree in the springtime. Suddenly, she hoped that she and Deke were still together when the willow trees were leafed out and when there was a soft drizzle coming from the sky.

"Penny for your thoughts," he said softly.

"I was thinking about sex in the rain," she answered honestly.

"I was thinking"—he inhaled deeply—"about making love to you in a hayloft."

"Just so long as it's not in three feet of snow."

He chuckled. "We might have a real problem with that much cold."

She wiggled backward until her back was at the other end of the tub. "Deke, this is beyond amazing, but is it wise?"

He picked up one of her feet and started to massage it. "Today let's live in this little bubble with only me and you inside it."

Pulling her foot back from his big hands took every bit of willpower that she could muster up. "Okay, but let's leave this part of the bubble and get out the leftovers. I've worked up a hellacious appetite."

"Me too, Josie."

*   *   *

Jud was wrong when he said that she wouldn't sleep after a late nap. She slept like a baby all night curled up in Deke's arms. Sunrays coming through the window awoke her the next morning. The sound of Deke singing "Make Me Wanna," with the music coming from his phone.

The lyrics talked about her sliding over closer to him in his old truck so he could tell her everything. Josie raised her arms and stretched, rolling the kinks from her neck before she got out of bed. Today, finally, she was going home. She'd been eager to get there all week and now she wished she could stay in the hotel one more day, maybe one more week.

She only needed to pull on a shirt when Deke came out of the bathroom. He kissed her softly and pointed to the coffeepot. "It's ready. I thought we'd get everything ready, take it down with us, have breakfast, and then go."

"Weather report?"

"Storm stopped right about the Texas line, but the highway has been cleared. Two hours and we'll be back in the state and about four after that we should be home," he answered.

She sipped at a disposable cup of coffee. "It's not as good as what we had in the bunkhouse."

"I doubt we'll ever get any that good again." He laid a hand on her shoulder and brushed another kiss across her lips. "I'm going to take Rascal on out, then put him in the truck."

"Honeymoon is over," she teased.

"Darlin', the honeymoon would never be over for us.

We might burn down the world with the heat but the honeymoon would last forever."

"Yeah, right." She smiled.

She carried her coffee with her to the luggage on the sofa. Deke's shirt—the one she'd slept in after the spider incident—was right there on the top of his folded clothing. She slipped it over into her bag and added the one remaining Christmas shirt she'd bought at Clines Corners. A quick trip to the bathroom to brush her hair and teeth and she returned with her cosmetic bag, added it to the suitcase, and zipped it shut. She sorted through the food bags, keeping only a few things and tossing the rest in the trash can. Rascal's dishes went into a plastic bag along with what little food was left.

One glance around the room to be sure nothing was left behind and she was ready to go. *Nothing but some scorching-hot memories*, she thought. *Every time it snows I will remember this hotel, that tub, and all that happened here. I'll close my eyes and feel the heat and his kisses.*

"Ready?" Deke poked his head into the door. "They've got a fantastic breakfast laid out down there. Sausage gravy and biscuits, eggs, a waffle maker."

"Hungry, are you?" she asked.

"Honey, after all the energy we went through last night, it may take days to build me back up." He zipped his duffel, threw it over his shoulder, and hung the two plastic bags over the pop-up handle on her suitcase.

"And here I thought you were this big playboy who could go all night and half the next day." She followed him out into the hall.

"I can but not with you," he said.

"Oh? And what makes me so different?"

"It would take a year and a whole ream of paper just to start listing all the things that make you different, and I love every one of them."

"Now that, Deke Sullivan, is a good pickup line."

*　　*　　*

They arrived in Dry Creek in the middle of the afternoon. Deke pulled the truck and trailer up in front of Jud and Fiona's place, and Deke carried Josie's case inside for her. They'd listened to the radio and talked very little on the way home. Roads were clear so they didn't even have to discuss highways or where to turn. It was almost a straight shot from Roswell to Throckmorton and then only a few miles to Dry Creek.

"Josie!" Fiona came from the kitchen and hugged Josie. "Y'all made it home. We've been watching the Weather Channel constantly. You both look tired."

"We are, believe me. It's been quite a journey and if I ever say anything about going to Montana in the winter again, just shoot me," Deke said.

Fiona moved from Josie to hug Deke. "I made a chocolate cake." She peeked over Josie's shoulder.

"Save me a piece. I'll be by later or tomorrow to collect it. I should be getting on home right now. Allie is tired of doing my chores, and tell the truth, I'm eager to see what's going on at my place," Deke said.

"And I bet Rascal is ready to get out on his own property without a leash on his collar," Josie said. "I'll walk you to the truck."

"No need. Your bag is right here." He tipped his cowboy hat at the ladies and was gone without giving Josie a hug or even a pat on the back.

"Never knew him to turn down chocolate cake for anything," Fiona said.

"He's just worn-out from this trip. Did Jud tell you that we had to deliver a baby in a blizzard?" Josie asked.

"No, but you can tell me while we have some cake and coffee. The guys are all out doing chores but I'm sure the whole family will be here later." Fiona headed for the kitchen.

Josie would have rather gone home with Deke, but she followed her sister-in-law.

"Brody might be stopping by later," Fiona said. "He's on his way to somewhere in the eastern part of the state to deliver a bull. I've never met him but Jud is all excited about getting to see his cousin."

"Hey, I hear my sister made it back in one piece and just in time so she can see Brody." Jud's big booming voice filled the lobby and kitchen. He breezed into the room and swept Josie off her feet, twirling her around twice before he set her back down.

"I missed you, too, Jud, and hog-tie me and throw me in the cellar if I ever talk about going to Montana in the winter again." She laughed.

"That's almost exactly what Deke said." Fiona smiled. "I think they've both learned a lesson."

That first initial meeting with her brother was over. Now she could breathe easy and enjoy that slab of chocolate cake that Fiona had dished up for her.

Josie heard a slight ping in her hip pocket. She took out her phone and read the text from Deke: *I miss you already. Jud is on the way.*

She quickly typed in: *He's here and everything is fine and rightbackatcha.*

Another message appeared: *Call me later?*

She hit the keys again: *Yes*.

Jud chuckled. "I've got so many things to tell you that I don't know where to begin, Josie."

"Can we drill next week?" she asked.

"No, but the report on the environmental stuff is coming right along. We might be able to start in late March or early April."

She clapped her hands. "Now that's good news and I've got more." She took a deep breath. "We got a fantastic deal on the bulls. And—" She hesitated but only for a moment. "Deke and I are going to be partners. The rancher we bought them from is moving to Dry Creek in early summer and bringing them to us then."

"Partners, huh?" Fiona said.

Josie nodded.

Jud grinned. "So I guess y'all will keep the new stock over at Deke's place?"

"That's the plan, but it'll be a few months before they arrive."

"Oil and bulls can wait. Jud says you've got a fantastic story about a baby," Fiona said.

"Yup, but right now I hear a truck pulling up outside. Brody is here," Jud said.

He and Josie both headed toward the front door, pushing and shoving like they were teenagers. He slung open the door just as Brody reached up to knock.

"Come in! Come in! I'm so glad to see you." Josie grabbed his arm and pulled him inside the house into a fierce hug. "How are things at Hope Springs and what's going on in Happy? Is Kasey adjusting to ranch life?"

Jud clamped a hand on his shoulder. "Welcome to Dry Creek and the Lucky Penny. Want a cup of coffee?"

"No, answer my questions first," Josie said.

"Yes, to the coffee. And one question at a time." Brody grinned.

He removed his jacket and hat and hung them on the hall tree. He raked his fingers through his dark hair in an effort to get rid of the hat mark but it didn't work. His light blue eyes scanned the living room as they passed through it.

"Nice place y'all got here," he said.

"It was an old brothel and then a hotel," Jud told him. "Fiona, darlin', come meet Brody Dawson."

"Hello. We are glad you could stop by. Want some cake and ice cream with that cup of coffee that Jud offered?"

"I'd love that and it's a pleasure to meet you," Brody said.

He could only stay half an hour but he answered all Josie's questions in that time and told Jud that it looked to him like he had a great ranch from the little he could see of it. They were standing on the porch waving when Josie's phone pinged.

She pulled it out of her hip pocket and checked the message: *Rascal is happy to be home, but he misses you too.*

Her thumbs flew over the keyboard: *Will call later.*

One more message appeared: *I'll leave a candle in the window if you want to come over tonight.*

"Important message?" Jud cocked his head to one side.

Josie knew that look. It was the big-brother-stepping-into-your-business look.

"Martha and Everett made me promise to let them know when we were home safe. Did I tell you that we took them a Chihuahua puppy before we left?"

Chapter Twenty-two

Josie hunched her shoulders inside her heavy coat and crammed her gloved hands deeper in the pockets. Standing on her property with nothing but a locked gate separating her from Deke's ranch, she could see the light that he'd said he'd leave on for her. The warmth beckoned, drawing her toward it like a lover. She shouldn't succumb to its summons or to Deke's charm, but she wanted his arms around her and she wanted to cuddle up to his naked body after passionate sex.

She shouldn't give in to desire. She should go home and go to bed.

Alone.

That thought was chillier than the north wind whipping around the legs of her jeans and finding its way up under her coat to make shivers slide down her spine. She tugged at it and fought with that unwanted voice in her head another minute before she pulled a hand free from her pocket, braced it on the fence post, and jumped over. Clumsiness took over the minute her feet were on the ground and she had to do some fancy footwork to keep from falling on her butt.

Once her mind was made up there was no going back. She fixed her eyes on the light and headed in that direction. Smoke spiraled up from the top of a chimney, which meant a warm fire waited. Nostalgia for the old bunkhouse fireplace made her walk faster. When she built her house she would have a fireplace, maybe one in the living room and the master bedroom.

"With a big cowhide rug in the front of it," she murmured.

An enormous pecan tree, its bare limbs shining against what was left of a waning moon, stood just inside the white rail fence separating the pasture from the yard. She was about to open the gate beside the tree when she heard a vehicle coming down the lane.

"Dammit!" she swore, and stepped back to hide behind the massive trunk of the tree.

Thinking it might be Blake or Toby—or worse yet, Jud—she kept her hood up and planned her escape back to the barbed wire fence and to her own property. No matter who it was, it was a sign that she should not see Deke that night. And if she could get past the first night, then she could do so the second and all those in the future.

A bright red car came to a stop right outside the gate. "Well, it isn't my cousins or my brother," she whispered.

A light popped on inside the vehicle and a woman leaned forward to apply lipstick in the rearview mirror. She fluffed up her long, blond hair and smiled at her reflection before she opened the door and slung her legs out. Tight-fitting jeans tucked down into cowboy boots and a leather jacket hugged her body like a glove. And that hip-swaying gait said the woman was there for a purpose.

She raised her hand to knock, but before she could, Deke's tall, sexy body was silhouetted against the light flowing from the house. The woman didn't give him time to wipe the smile off his face or invite her inside. She wrapped one leg around his knees, both arms around his neck, and planted a kiss on his lips that went on forever.

Deke took a couple of steps back and kicked the door shut with his bare foot. That was the last sign Josie needed for one evening. She turned around and jogged back to the gate. Hardly even breaking stride, she slapped a hand on the post, jumped over with the grace of a deer, and didn't stop running until she was in the car. Covering her face with her hands, she gave herself a lecture that would have fried the hair off Lucifer's horns.

"Idiot! Idiot!" she chided herself as she finally threw her head back and stared at the sky. "He applied the charm at the right time. I fell for it, but it will damn sure not happen again."

*　　　*　　　*

Deke had sent Josie a text and was about to push the SEND button when he heard the crunch of tires on the gravel. He laid the phone aside and heard the gate hinges squeak, boots walking up the steps and across the porch as he hurried across the floor. He swung the door open and a blur with blond hair was suddenly wrapped around him like a rattlesnake.

He tasted beer and cigarettes and knew immediately this was not Josie. He took two steps back and shut the door with his foot so that he could see the woman plainly.

"Nicole." He frowned.

"I missed seeing you on New Year's Eve so I thought we'd celebrate tonight." She flashed a smile and removed her jacket to reveal nothing but a black lace bra and lots of skin. "I came by twice this week but you were gone." She sat down on the edge of the sofa and removed one boot.

Deke folded his arms over his chest. "Stop right there and put your coat back on. This is not a good time."

Nicole giggled. "Are you sick? You've never turned down a good time, Deke Sullivan."

"I'm expecting company," he said.

She sighed as she tugged her boot back on and picked up her jacket. "Maybe another time, darlin'." When she'd zipped her jacket, she paused to kiss him on the cheek. "Please don't tell me that you've fallen in love. I don't mind sharing, but to never have you around for a booty call, that would make me cry."

"Never say never." Deke smiled.

"Tell whoever is on her way that she is one lucky woman." Nicole blew him a kiss as she left.

Deke threw himself back on the sofa and picked up his phone and edited his note: *The lights are still on and the fire is almost as hot as you are.*

His heart jacked in an extra beat as he hit the button to send the text.

Nothing came right back.

Fifteen minutes later, still nothing.

An hour later, he gave up and went to bed—alone.

When his phone rang the next morning, he sat straight up in bed, quickly grabbed it, and without even checking to see who was calling said, "Are you all right? Why didn't you—"

"Deke, it's Jud. Of course I'm okay," he said.

"You woke me from a dead sleep. I must've been dreaming," Deke said.

"It's seven o'clock and we're about to have breakfast. The rest of the family is here, so I wondered if you wanted to come over and eat with us," he said.

"Be there in ten minutes." Deke yawned.

"Drag your feet and you might not get any bacon." He laughed.

He fed Rascal and dressed while the dog gobbled down a can of food and half a bowl of dry feed. When Deke stepped outside, Rascal rushed to the yard, sniffed the air, and headed off in the direction of the barn. He looked back when he crawled under the fence.

"I'll be gone an hour. You check things out and if there's anything that needs taking care of, I'll do it when I get back. Until then you are the boss and don't let those cows tell you otherwise," Deke said.

Rascal squared up his shoulders and continued his journey. Deke took a moment to suck in a lungful of the fresh morning air, to look out across the pasture sprouting the first sprigs of winter wheat. That meant in two weeks he could turn his cattle out to feed on fresh green grass. A robin startled him as it flew from the top of the gate to the yard and pulled an earthworm from the ground.

Deke brought out his phone to take a picture of the pasture and sent it on to Everett. It wasn't anything that would win a prize, but maybe it would spur him and Martha on to get out of that cold country and come on to Texas, where spring arrived a hell of a lot earlier than it did in Montana.

Deke had started the engine of the truck when his phone pinged. Hoping it was Josie telling him that she'd fallen asleep and hadn't gotten his messages until morning, maybe even teasing him about his pickup lines and charm, he checked the message. It was from Everett saying that he and Martha could sit and look at that picture all day and that they just might have to bring those bulls to Texas a little earlier than planned.

Still nothing from Josie. He drove from his place out to the road, made a turn, and, in less than two minutes, made another one down the lane to Jud and Fiona's place.

He whistled as he parked, hummed a country music tune by Josh Turner as he went from truck to house and knocked on the door. He didn't wait for someone to answer but poked his head inside and yelled, "Anybody home?"

"In the kitchen," Allie yelled. "Come on in."

He hung his coat and cowboy hat on the hall tree and glanced up the staircase. He'd love to run up there and wake Josie up with a kiss, maybe even cuddle with her a few minutes before they went down to breakfast together.

Fiona poked her head out of the kitchen and crooked a finger at him. "You sure are a slowpoke this morning. Are you getting old, or did that trip wear you plumb out? We're already around the table and passing the food."

"All of the above." Deke wasted no time getting from the living room to the dining room and quickly sat down in the only remaining seat at the far end of the table. He took two biscuits from the basket that Toby handed off to him.

"Where's Josie?" he asked.

"She was already up, loaded, and ready to go when we got to the kitchen this morning," Fiona answered. "She and Allie have gone up to Wichita Falls for supplies. Allie has a job and said she would be callin' you to see if you're free to help her put a roof on a house next week."

"What's this I hear about your late-night visitor?" Lizzy asked.

"How did you know about that?" Deke asked.

"She's friends with Sharlene, remember?" Fiona said.

"I wouldn't say that we're friends but she called this morning to tell me all about it," Lizzy told them.

"Then the whole family knows?" Deke frowned.

His favorite breakfast suddenly tasted like sawdust mixed with sand. Had they told Josie? Was that why she wasn't returning any of his texts?

"Knows what?" Blake came through the back door.

"Nicole went to see Deke last night," Lizzy answered. "She pays Deke a booty call at least every three months. She tells Sharlene everything and Sharlene loves to spread gossip, so she called me, looking for Allie. She wanted Allie to get the particulars, since Allie is your best friend."

Deke's heart was a heavy stone. He needed to talk to Josie—right now!

"She was there less than five minutes. I sent her away. Can we talk about something else?" he said as he scooped scrambled eggs onto his plate. "Good biscuits, Fiona. Is this Granny's recipe?"

"Glad to be home?" Toby asked.

"You'll never know how good my place looked yesterday or how big the house seemed after that little bitty bunkhouse," Deke said.

Holy smokin' hell! Why did he have to bring that up? Now Jud would picture him and Josie in a tiny place, constantly bumping into each other.

Lizzy took her phone from her pocket and read a message. Deke held his breath until his chest ached while she typed something back and laid the phone beside her plate.

"That was Lucy Taylor. She says the church is planning

a potluck on the Sunday before Valentine's Day and we're all supposed to bring a dessert and a cowboy with us."

"I don't have a cowboy to take with me. Reckon they'd be offended if I bring Rascal," Deke teased.

"I reckon." Lizzy pointed down the table at him. "That Nicole would make three fancy desserts if you'd ask her to go with you to the potluck."

"Ain't damn likely," Deke murmured.

"What? That she'd make the desserts or that you'd ask her?"

"Neither one. Both. All of the above. I ain't never taken a woman to a church social and I'm not starting now."

*   *   *

"You're awfully quiet this morning," Allie said as she drove toward Wichita Falls that morning.

"Just glad to be home where there's no snow," Josie answered. She couldn't tell Allie what had happened the night before without explaining why she was outside Deke's house.

"I love a pretty snow," Allie said, "but I also love to see it melt in a few days. I can't imagine what you and poor old Deke had to endure. He's an outside cowboy and not one to be cooped up, so he'll be glad to help me put a roof on Ruby's house this next week."

Josie nodded. "Probably so."

"Hey, and before I forget, thanks a bunch for coming along with me today. We haven't gotten to spend any one-on-one time together," Allie said.

"I need to pick up more paint for the hotel, so I'm glad for the ride and the company," Josie answered.

And more than happy to be away from Deke for a few

hours so I can figure out what to do. We talked about cheating. I told him what I'd done to Chance and Liz. I wonder what that bimbo's name is.

That hateful voice in her head argued with her. *What difference does it make? And you were as much to blame for that night of sex as Deke was. You don't change a leopard's spots, and you should know that, Josie Dawson.*

Chapter Twenty-three

Josie and Allie walked into Dry Creek's little day care, and Sharlene looked up from the floor, where she was surrounded by four small preschoolers. She had a big story book turned around so they could see the pictures as she read. Behind the book she had a script with the words and a note telling her when to turn the pages.

"Hey, Allie, Audrey has been an angel all morning. She's such a cuddle bug that I could sit and rock her all day. You can leave her with me anytime you need a sitter for a few hours," Sharlene said. "Hey, you're Josie Dawson, right? Kids, let's take a break. Y'all can play with the blocks for a few minutes."

"Yes, Miz Sharlene," a little guy said.

Sharlene rose up on her knees and then stood up. Her blond hair was pulled back in a ponytail at the nape of her neck. Her face was slightly round and she wore a lot of makeup for a woman who ran a day care, but then Sharlene Tucker had quite a reputation in Dry Creek. Josie had heard about her from Blake and then from Toby and then from Jud. She was a wild one on Saturday night, and yet Josie could see something sweet natured in her when she'd been reading to the children.

"Yes, I'm Josie Dawson." She held out her hand.

Sharlene's shake was firm and her smile sincere. What a woman did on her own time was her business, and Josie doubted that Sharlene had done anything that she couldn't match—not after that hotel in Roswell. "I hear you leased the hotel to house your oil crew when it gets here. You really think there's oil on the Lucky Penny?"

"I sure hope so," Josie answered.

"You should run it as a hotel. I'd stay in it." The tall blonde who'd been in Deke's arms the night before came into the room from the kitchen, and she had Audrey in her arms.

Josie felt like all the air had been sucked clean out of her lungs and she was withering up into nothing but a bag of bones and skin. She never wanted to knock a woman square on her ass before, but she did right then. She doubled up her fists, reminded herself to breathe deeply, and squared up her shoulders.

"This is Nicole and this is Josie." Sharlene made the introductions.

Nicole put Audrey into Allie's outstretched arms. "She just woke up. I thought I might have some time to rock her for a spell. I do love babies."

Josie unclenched her fists. Hitting the woman wouldn't do a bit of good. She wasn't at fault here. She was simply doing what she and Deke probably did all the time—enjoying a booty call after he'd been on a trip.

"I'm leaving, Sharlene. See you Saturday night at the

Rusty Spur?" Nicole picked up the same jacket she'd been wearing the night before from a row of hooks.

"I'll be there. Don't steal all the cowboys out from under me." Sharlene grinned.

"Oh, honey, there's only one cowboy I want." Nicole winked.

"He's a catch all right, and he ain't been roped yet, so you might have your work cut out for you," Sharlene said.

"Oh, I know how to work a cowboy," Nicole said as she eased outside and gently closed the door behind her.

"Okay, then." Sharlene laughed as she turned back to Josie and Allie. "So what happened with Deke?"

It was on the tip of Josie's tongue to tell her that it wasn't a damn bit of her business but she smiled and kept quiet.

"What about Deke?" Allie asked.

"I was talking to Josie. I wondered what it was like to be snowed in with him?" Sharlene said.

"Well." Josie leaned forward. "He likes good food. He's a hard worker and I hope a good partner because we bought four bulls for rodeo stock together and we plan to expand our business as we can."

"That's not what I was talking about. How on earth did you live in a little bitty bunkhouse with him for a week and not...you know." She whispered so the kids couldn't hear her.

"I'm one strong woman. I'm going to unload my paint at the hotel, Allie." Josie darted outside before Sharlene could say another word.

"Just a minute, Allie," Sharlene said loudly, but Josie kept going.

The wind always blows in Texas, right up until July Fourth and then a person can't beg, borrow, buy, or steal a hint of a breeze until after Labor Day. Old-timers said it was because it was so hot that it would melt the shell off an armadillo if it blustered around like it did in the winter months.

Josie kept her eyes down until she reached the hotel. She had her hand on the door handle when she recognized Deke's truck sitting not ten feet away, and there was Nicole, leaning in the open window, kissing him on the cheek.

Somewhere in the middle of the distance separating them, their gazes locked in a heated, fierce battle that needed no words. And then Josie unlocked the door and slipped inside.

*   *   *

Deke opened the door so quickly that Nicole had to do some fancy footwork to keep from falling on her rear end. Leaving the door hanging open, he rushed across the sidewalk and knocked on the hotel door. When no one answered, he tried to open it, but the damned thing was locked.

Nicole stormed across the walk and screamed at him, "Is that woman the reason you are throwing me away?"

"Just go away and don't come back around my place," he said.

"Oh, I'm going away, and when it comes to me, cowboy, don't call, don't text, and don't even look at me next time you are at the Rusty Spur." Her boots sounded like drum rolls as she marched out to her car and sped away.

He went back to his truck and called Josie, but after five rings, he gave up and sent a text: *We need to talk.*

One came back: *No need.*

His big thumbs flew over the tiny keyboard: *What did Sharlene tell you?*

His phone rang and when he saw the call was from Josie, he answered it before it hit the second ring tone. "Josie, talk to me. Nothing happened. I promise."

"Why did you ask what Sharlene told me? I don't rely on gossip, but I also can't erase the picture in my head of Nicole kissing you."

Deke leaned back against the headrest and pressed his thumb and forefinger on the bridge of his nose. "How did you know if Sharlene didn't talk?"

"I was there, Deke. I was on the way to see you when that hussy drove up and you opened the door for her, kissed her, and shut the door with your foot. I saw it all," she said.

"Did you stick around long enough to see her leave five minutes later? Or hear me tell her that I didn't want to see her?"

The long silence lasted for an eternity plus three days.

"Deke, who are we kidding?" she asked.

"Just let me in or come out here and talk to me," he said. "I want you to see my eyes when I tell you that nothing happened, other than what you saw. And she kissed me. I did not kiss her."

"We're both going to be very busy this next week, so maybe it's best if we cool off a few days before we talk face-to-face," she said coolly.

"But, Josie, that trip and our time together made me see things in a new light."

"Show me. Don't tell me," she said.

Chapter Twenty-four

Thursday morning brought one of those glorious sunrises to Dry Creek that belonged on a postcard or in an art gallery if a camera could have captured the brilliant shades of orange and pink. Standing in her bedroom at Fiona and Jud's place, Josie pulled back the curtains and was mesmerized by the sight before her. It reminded her of the colors swirling around in her heart and soul when the first afterglow had wrapped her and Deke in its warmth after that bout of Jacuzzi sex.

"Don't think about that," she said. "Don't dwell on the disappointments."

The aroma of coffee preceded the gentle knock on her bedroom door. She whipped around, ready to go to war with Deke again. Her heart sank when she realized that he wouldn't be bringing coffee. They were not in the bunkhouse or even in a hotel—not that day and most likely never again.

"Come on in. I'm awake," she called out.

"You need to open it. My hands are full," Fiona said.

Josie quickly crossed the floor and found Fiona on the other side with two big mugs of coffee in her hands. She handed one off to Josie and then sat down in the rocking chair pulled over beside the window.

"Are you okay? Jud says something is eating on you," Fiona asked.

Josie sat down on the edge of the bed and sipped her coffee. She couldn't tell Fiona what was really wrong with her because words couldn't begin to describe the emptiness in her heart.

"It's Deke, isn't it?" Fiona asked. "Y'all had an argument. He's a good man, like a brother to all three of us Logan sisters, but he does love to joke around. Did he hurt your feelings?"

"I'm fine." Josie smiled. "Just really tired from the trip and painting walls at the hotel until late last night."

"I can't imagine being cooped up with Deke for a whole week. What did happen in Montana?"

"Not one thing," Josie answered honestly.

But please don't ask me what happened in New Mexico.

*   *   *

On Sunday morning, Deke awoke to the sound of drizzling rain. He rolled over to suggest that he and Josie skip church and stay in bed all day and then he realized that he had been dreaming. Josie was not in his bed and he hadn't seen her since Tuesday evening.

He picked up his phone, but there were no messages or missed calls. Deke figured five days was long enough, so he sent a text: *Good morning, beautiful.*

And he got one right back: *Is that your best pickup line?*

He grinned and fired one back: *It is the truth. It is a good morning and you are beautiful.*

He checked the phone every few minutes all morning but nothing more. Still he'd gotten one line and that was a beginning. He and Rascal did the morning feeding chores and checked the green grass growing in his pasture.

All the goats were romping around in the rain like children let out of school at the end of the day. Deke had never liked goats, but watching the two new sets of twin kids carrying on head butting each other and playing chase around the pen made him glad he'd taken them when he bought Truman O'Dell's cattle right before Christmas.

"Josie likes goats," Deke told Rascal.

The dog's ears perked up at her name.

"I'm going to win her back. I've just got to prove to her that she can trust me, Rascal. I miss everything about her. I reach for her at night and she's not there. I wake up ready to see her sleepy smile and there's a hole in my heart." Deke headed back to the old work truck with Rascal at his heels.

The devil was surely in the details that morning. Halfway to the house a tire went flat and went into a long, greasy slide in the mud. Deke finally got it stopped with some powerful yelling and cussing. But when he got out, the tire that had blown was sitting in a gopher hole surrounded by water and mud.

Changing a tire didn't take long. He could take care of it and still make it to church on time. He got out the jack and checked to be sure the spare had air in it. With Rascal watching from the passenger window, he slipped the jack up under the frame and started pumping. When the tire was off the ground, he loosened the lug bolts and went back to working the jack.

He'd just gotten the lug nuts off and was about to pull the tire when the jack let go, setting him flat on his ass with a blast of mud blowing up all around him. What goes up in a wide splatter must come down, and it did, all over poor old Deke. He wiped enough from his eyes to see that the jack had slipped into another gopher hole. He jumped up, kicked the good tire on the passenger's side, and it immediately hissed and went flat, too, leaving the truck leaning to the right. Rascal's nose was pressed against the window, and when Deke opened the door, the dog tried to get traction but couldn't and wound up in a puddle on his left side. He got to his feet, did one of those dog wiggles from head to toe, and slung even more mud onto Deke.

"Looks like we're both going to need a bath." Deke groaned.

If he made it to church before the opening hymn that morning, it would be a miracle. He had to go because Josie would probably be there, and besides, they were having a big Sunday dinner at Fiona and Jud's afterward, and there was no way Josie could get out of that.

He raced into the house, leaving tracks and dirty clothing in his wake as he stripped off his boots, socks, and coveralls and ran a bath for Rascal. The old boy loved baths, so he gave Deke no trouble when Deke set him down in the warm water and lathered him up with dog shampoo. Rascal would have loved a good brushing after the towel rubdown but Deke didn't have time for that.

"Go lie by the fire until you get good and dry," Deke said as he shoved him out the door, drained the tub, and adjusted the water for a shower.

Thirty minutes later Deke slid into the Logan family pew and reached for a hymnal only to find they were all in use. The congregation was already on the second verse of

"Abide with Me," and he could hear Granny Irene down on the other end singing at the top of her lungs.

He realized he was sitting beside Josie when she nudged him and nodded toward her hymnbook. Flat tires, mud baths, hurrying through a dog bath, washing an acre of dirt down the drain when he took a shower, and driving more than ninety miles an hour to church—all that had nothing to do with the adrenaline rushing through his veins. That was because his shoulder and hip were touching Josie and his hand was covering hers to hold the hymnbook steady so they could share it.

Deke wished the whole service would be one song after another but after the song ended, the preacher took his place and cleared his throat. "Good morning, we're glad to see Irene Miller out this morning."

Granny waved and broke out into the first few lines of "I'll Fly Away." Deke immediately joined in with her, and before she'd finished the second line, everyone in church, including the preacher, was singing.

"Thank you, Irene," the preacher said when the last chorus ended. "God must've laid that on your heart today and what God tells us to do we shouldn't back down from. Before I begin, Lucy Taylor wants me to announce that three weeks from today the ladies are hosting a Valentine's Day potluck after church. Get in touch with her for the particulars. She needs a decorating crew to help with the fellowship hall."

He went right into his sermon at that time, but Deke didn't hear a word of it. He argued with himself about asking Josie out on a real date. Should he talk to Jud first?

No, you are nearly twenty-seven years old and Josie has to be about the same age. You are both adults. Would she go ask Allie if she could go out with you?

Deke grinned at the picture that popped into his head. He was acting and thinking like a teenager, not a grown cowboy, but then Deke had no experience with relationships. He could swagger into a bar, pick out the best-looking woman in the place and sweet-talk her into a one-night stand—that he could do standing on his head and cross-eyed. But he was sailing in uncharted waters when it came to the real-deal stuff.

Just like Blake, Toby, and Jud.

For the first time, he truly felt their boots pinching his toes as he walked a mile in their shoes. He glanced over at Josie and his chest tightened. Blond hair floating on her shoulders, big blue eyes looking straight ahead and one long leg crossed over the other. That morning she wore a sweater the color of a summer sky and a cute little denim skirt that skimmed the tops of her black cowboy boots.

In his imagination, he was busy taking off her outfit, one piece at a time, when she poked him in the ribs with her elbow. Holy hell! Could she read minds as well as run a ranch and go into the oil business?

"Benediction. The preacher called on you," she whispered from the side of her mouth.

Deke stood up so fast that it gave him a head rush, but he steadied himself on the pew in front of him. "Dear heavenly father," he drawled and hoped that something came to him to thank God for that Sunday.

He managed to stumble through a couple of sentences and ended with the appropriate amen. Irene shouted, "Amen!" and then said in a loud voice, "Thank you, Jesus, for letting Deke say the prayer. He always says a short one and I'm hungry."

Muffled chuckles floated toward the ceiling as everyone began to put on their coats and jackets. Josie slowly rose to her feet, her body so close to Deke's that he could have leaned slightly and brushed a kiss across her lips. He wanted to—God only knew how badly he wanted to—but the look in her eyes said that was way too soon.

"So are you coming to Fiona and Jud's for dinner?" she asked.

"I never turn down a good home-cooked meal. Did you make hot rolls?"

"I made a cherry pie. Katy made the hot rolls," she said.

She was talking to him. That had to be a step, even if it was a baby one, in the right direction. He started to say something but Jud clapped a hand on his shoulder. "I want to talk to you after dinner."

Deke swallowed hard. "What about?"

"You offered to help clear some land for our road. I want your opinion on where we should put it so it won't be an eyesore, but we'll talk more after dinner," Jud answered.

"Sure thing." Deke nodded.

"Did you think he was going to call you out with pistols?" Josie whispered.

"Do I need to get his permission to take you out on a date sometime this week before I ask?" Deke shot right back at her.

"I don't need anyone's say-so. I'm quite capable of making my own decisions," she said.

"Then?"

"You'll have to ask me to find out."

"Hey, Deke." Irene threw her bony arms around him. "Who is this lovely lady? I been tellin' you for years you'll come closer to finding a woman in church than in them damned bars."

"Mama," Katy scolded. "You don't cuss in church."

Irene let go of Deke and whipped around to narrow her

eyes at Katy. "I've got the forgetting disease so I have trouble remembering where I can cuss and where I can get a little nip of Jack Daniel's."

"Are you having Sunday dinner with us?" Deke asked.

"You bet your cowboy ass, I am," Irene whispered. "*Ass* is not cussin' and it's in the Bible."

"That's right. Can I sit beside you?" Deke asked as he looped her arm into his.

"If you help me keep things straight, you can." Irene giggled.

"Maybe you'll need to help me keep things straight," Deke teased.

"Oh, darlin'." Irene flashed a flirty smile. "I'm not the person for that job. But this good churchgoin' girl just might be the one to straighten you right up." She removed her arm from his and replaced it with Josie's.

"But…" he stammered.

"What's your name, honey?"

"Josie Dawson," she answered.

"Well, Deke, this here is Josie Dawson. I bet she's related to those Dawson boys who married my granddaughters and they are good people. So now you've met her and you can sit between me and her and the dinner table."

Josie started to remove her arm but Irene shook her head. "You hang on to him real tight or some of these hussies that are only here to pray for last night's sins might get him."

"You better listen to Granny." Allie laughed.

"Pretend. Maybe it'll keep her mind on the present for a little while," Lizzy whispered.

"Yes, ma'am," Josie said. "I'll do my best to keep him in line."

*   *   *

His shoulder touching hers, his thigh against hers, the scent of his shaving lotion, that tiny bit of dirt stuck on the upper part of his ear—it had all kept her from hearing a word the preacher said, and now they were walking out of church like a real couple.

Sharlene's expression said it all for everyone in the church.

Absolute shock.

Normally Josie didn't give a tiny rat's whisker what anyone thought of her, but she was going to settle down in Dry Creek, and she did not want a reputation like Sharlene had or that hussy Nicole or, for that matter, Deke Sullivan.

"Did you drive yourself?" Deke asked as they made their way to the church doors to shake hands with the preacher.

"I rode with Jud and Fiona."

"Ride home with me? We need to talk," he said.

She nodded and extended her hand to the preacher.

"Glad to have you join our congregation, Miss Dawson. We'll hope to see you every week." He smiled.

"Thank you. I'll try to be here."

The rain had stopped and the sun peeked out intermittently from behind wispy clouds but the gravel parking lot was far from dried out. Josie tried to pull her arm free, but Deke kept a firm hold on it as they headed toward his truck. He'd been the last one there and all the closer parking spots were taken, which meant they had to walk past everyone who was still getting into their vehicles.

Deke stopped to talk to several elderly couples, introducing her to so many people that she'd never remember their names. He opened the truck door and she finally slipped her arm free.

"I guess we are a couple now." He grinned.

"You might be guessing wrong," she fired back.

"Are we breaking up so soon after we have made it official? We used the same hymnbook. You hung on to me all the way out of the church and I'm taking you to Sunday dinner. In small-town Texas that's pretty much setting things in stone," he said as he fired up the engine and turned on the heater. "Everyone is already talking about what happened between us in Montana. What do you plan to tell them?"

"The truth," she said.

He hit the brakes so hard that she was glad she had her seat belt on and barely came to a stop before rear-ending the car in front of him. "For real?" he asked.

"Yes, every detail. From the books we read to the snow."

"And the spider?"

"Especially the spider and how you let me sleep on your bunk and were a perfect gentleman," she said.

He shook his head. "They'll never believe it. What about the Jacuzzi?"

"That, Mr. Sullivan, did not happen in Montana. It happened in New Mexico, and if I'm asked, I'll tell them in detail about how we worked together to bring a baby into the world in a blizzard. I'll bore them to tears with my stories."

"And if they ask about the hotel?" He took his foot off the brake and kept his eyes, at least one of them, on the road.

"I will tell them not to be so nosy. Now, Deke, what are we going to do about us, or is there even an us?"

"Josie, you know I party on weekends. If I have work

to do at the ranch, that comes first, but most of the time I manage to get at least one night a week to go barhopping and chasing women. Last night I stayed home with Rascal and tried to figure out a way to get you to talk to me."

"What did you want to talk about?"

"It didn't matter what the subject was. It could be about bulls, about books, about biscuits and yeast rolls, about mucking out stables or how much feed to give the horses. I don't give a damn what we talked about. Just hearing your voice and being able to see you was enough."

"That might be the best line I've ever heard."

"Does that mean if I ask you to go out to dinner with me tomorrow night that you will go?"

"Ask and find out," she said.

He inhaled deeply and let it out slowly. "Will you go out with me for dinner tomorrow night?"

"Why not a movie?"

"Because I don't want to sit in a dark movie with you. I want to see your face and talk to you," he said.

"How about next Friday night?" she said.

"I'll pick you up at six."

"That sounds great." Josie smiled.

He parked the truck beside all the other vehicles already in the yard, and once he helped her out, he looped her arm into his again. "For Granny." He grinned.

No one even raised an eyebrow when they entered the house. Blake was sitting in a rocking chair with Audrey in his arms. Toby was somewhere in the kitchen, because Josie could hear his deep laughter. Deke helped Josie out of her coat and then removed his leather jacket and cowboy hat and hung them all on the hall tree right inside the door.

"A normal Sunday dinner," she murmured.

"Oh, here he is." Granny Irene came from the kitchen

wearing a bibbed apron over her blue dress. She had a wooden spoon in one hand and a hot roll in the other. "Deke, you need to bring your new bride in the kitchen and introduce her to the rest of the family. I've been telling them how pretty she is and that she's a God-fearin' woman and not one of those hussies you are usually drawn to."

"Play along," Deke whispered. "If this is her only slip into darkness today, then we'll all be happy."

Irene led the way out of the living room, nibbling on the hot roll the whole way. "Folks, Deke has something to say so stop yakking and listen."

"I would like you ladies to meet my wife, Josie Dawson Sullivan." He winked at Allie.

"See, I told you that he got married while he was off gallivantin' around looking for a fancy bull. I might forget things but I remember the important stuff." She raised her chin and looked down her nose at the whole lot of them.

"Congratulations and welcome to the family, Josie," Katy said, crossing the room to give her a hug.

"Now, Deke, you can let go of her and go on in the living room and play with the kids. We'll take good care of her," Irene said.

Deke nodded and turned to walk away.

Irene shook the wooden spoon at him. "Well, hell's bells. That ain't no way to treat a new bride. At least give her a kiss. You're about to leave her with the in-laws, and they can be brutal."

"Granny, we are not mean," Lizzy said.

"You'd better not be," Irene said. "Well, Deke?"

Pure fiery heat started on Josie's neck and crawled right up to her face. Before she could say a single word, Deke had cupped his hands on her hot little cheeks and brushed the softest of kisses across her lips.

"Just right." Irene grinned. "That's the way a new groom should kiss his bride in public. Now go play with the kids so we can talk to her."

"I'm so sorry," Allie whispered. "But thank you."

"Okay, now, let's get this dinner on the table. I'm starving plumb to death," Irene said and then frowned. "Allie, who is this woman? Is it one of your friends?"

"Don't you remember, Granny? This is Deke's wife," Allie said gently.

"Don't tease me like that. Deke won't ever get married. Katy, did we go to church? Seems like I remember singing but…" Her voice trailed off. "I'm going to go in the living room and watch television. Did we have dinner yet?"

"No, but we are putting it on the table right now. You said you wanted to sit by Deke, remember?" Katy said.

Irene shook her head and the lights slowly went out in her eyes. She glanced around and then looked back at Katy. "Will you show me where to sit?"

"Yes, I will. You just come on with me and we'll talk while these girls get the food in the bowls and put on the table." Katy slipped an arm around her mother's shoulders and led her away.

"It's a scary disease, but we all do the best we can," Fiona said. "Hey, on a lighter note, what was that like?"

"What?" Josie raised a perfectly arched eyebrow.

"Kissing Deke. I always wondered if he was as good as his reputation."

"From that kiss, I'd say he's had plenty of experience," Josie said.

"Did it make your toes curl?" Lizzy asked.

"Slightly," Josie said. "He asked me out on a date next Friday night."

"Does Jud know?" Fiona asked.

"Not yet. You want to tell him for me?"

"Hell, no!" she said. "But I want you to do it at dinner so I can see his face. He fretted when y'all were in Montana. You know Deke has a reputation that makes the Dawsons all look like altar boys?"

"I know," Josie said. "But I'm a big girl and I make my own decisions."

"Said like a true Dawson," Jud said right behind her. "Deke says y'all are going out to dinner Friday night."

Josie turned around slowly. "Yes, we are."

"It'll take a lot to tame that cowboy."

"Hell, Jud! It's dinner, not a wedding. And I figured you'd throw a hissy, maybe even drag out the pistols for one of those standoffs like in the old western movies."

"Where'd you get such a crazy notion?" Jud asked. "I learned a long time ago to give you my advice and then stand back and laugh at you when you fell flat on your ass."

"Spoken like a true sassy Dawson and a brother who has learned a few lessons." Fiona pushed past them with a basket of piping hot rolls right from the oven.

"Amen! And, Jud, I could tame a wild bull with a toothache. The question is, do I want to?" Josie said.

"Well done," Fiona whispered.

"I wish I'd said I'd go out with him tomorrow instead of Friday night. Now I'm going to have to listen to advice all week from the whole lot of them." Josie groaned.

Chapter Twenty-five

According to Blake and Toby, the Dairy Queen was not a place to take a woman on a first date. Deke gave them the same argument that he'd presented to Josie: It was a place to get a burger and talk over malts and then maybe coffee as long as they wanted. But by Monday morning, he doubted himself and wanted something that Josie would remember forever. Surely he could come up with an idea that would knock her socks off.

"If only it was spring or summer," he told Rascal that morning as they fed the goats and watched the kids chase each other through mud puddles. "But in January the weather is as predictable as..." He paused, remembering the old hunting cabin sitting in a copse of scrub oaks all the way to the back of his property.

Could he get it ready in only four days? If he really worked at it, he thought he just might. The cabin hadn't been used in years and would take some real elbow grease, but Josie was worth it.

He took his phone from his shirt pocket and sent Josie a text: *Date night has changed. I have a surprise for you.*

One came right back: *I love surprises. Fancy dress or casual?*

He grinned: *Jeans and boots will be fine…and maybe my shirt that you stole in Roswell.*

She replied: *Do I have to give it back?*

His thumbs did double time: *It's yours now, darlin'.*

He read the next one out loud and chuckled: *Do I get a hint?*

His last one was: *Every day I'll send you one little hint.*

His phone rang right after he finished texting, and he answered without even checking to see who was calling. "I'm not telling you any more than that."

"Oh, and what did you already tell me?" Everett laughed.

"Everett! I was expecting the call to be from someone else."

"I guess you were. I'm just checking in. Bulls are fine. Bitsy is like a baby for me and Martha. And guess what? I'm going to bring her with me when we come to Texas. I've got a buyer for the ranch and they want to take over the place that last week in May. Will the hotel be ready for us by then?"

"I'm sure it will be, and if it's not I've got a guest bedroom you can use," Deke said. "You are welcome anytime you want to visit. Come on down for a few days and check out the place anytime you'd like."

"I might take you up on that," Everett said. "How are things with you and Josie?"

"We're working on it," Deke answered.

"It takes a lot of work." Everett laughed. "Keep at it, son. She's worth all the effort. Martha sends love. Bye."

Deke slipped the phone back into his pocket and put on his coat. "Come on, Rascal. We've got to go to the back corner of the ranch and check out Grandpa's old cabin. Did I ever tell you about the time me and Grandpa spent a week in the hot summer up there? It took Granny that long to cool down after Grandpa bought a tractor without asking her about it."

Rascal followed him outside and hopped in the truck when Deke opened the door. "Yes, sir, she was one angry granny. Not because he bought the tractor but because he borrowed the money to do it. That's when he told me to never, ever buy something I didn't have the money for and to never do anything without talking to the wife first."

Deke turned on the radio and kept time to the country music with his thumb on the steering wheel as he slowly drove around cattle in a pasture. He got out twice to open gates, drive through and then shut the gate, before he reached an old scrub oak–lined lane that was barely wide enough for his truck to get through. The rickety wooden bridge over Dry Creek held as he drove over it and then there was the cabin. It was even smaller than he remembered it, but with the little creek flowing in front and the sun setting about chimney level, it would be a sweet little sight.

"Sun sets right about six, not seven," he told Rascal.

He quickly sent a text: *Friday night. Five forty-five?*

His phone pinged when he was inside the cabin. The message was one word: *Sure.*

*   *   *

When Josie ran into the convenience store for a cup of coffee on Tuesday morning, Fiona handed her a candle that smelled like honeysuckle. *Hint Number One* was written on the note attached to the bright red ribbon tied around it.

"Deke turned down supper at Allie's last night. He's got something up his sleeve about this date y'all have on Friday," Fiona said.

"It's a big secret, but I get a hint a day. This is number one."

"A candle in a fruit jar?" Fiona frowned.

Josie sniffed the candle. "Not much of a hint, but I do like wildflowers."

She held the candle at chest level so she could get a whiff of the honeysuckle scent. Maybe he was taking her to dinner where there would be candles on the table like this one.

*   *   *

On Wednesday Sharlene showed up at the hotel with a strange, little, rustic-looking centerpiece. A short stick of firewood had three holes drilled into the top. Each opening held a small glass vial with tiny little snow flowers and daffodils. Again a note was attached to a red ribbon tied around the middle vial: *Hint Number Two*.

"Deke brought this by and told me to give it to you. You must have some powerful bewitching powers, girl. Women all over Texas have been chasing that cowboy for years. And I'm one of them. He said y'all have a date on Friday night?" Sharlene said.

Josie nodded. "Is that a big deal?"

"Oh, honey." Sharlene sighed. "You have no idea. The last time Deke went on anything that could remotely be thought of as a date was probably his junior prom in high school. He took Lisa Wilson."

Josie's curiosity was piqued. "And what happened?"

"Nothing that I know about. They went to the prom. He took her home and didn't even kiss her good night and the next week she started dating some boy from Throckmorton. Last I heard she was married to him and they had three kids," Sharlene answered. "So where are you going?"

"Have no idea. He says it's a surprise. This is a hint."

"So 'fess up. You've got a date with him. He's sending little inside personal hints. So tell me, what happened in Montana?" Sharlene asked. "These hints are connected to that, I'm sure of it. Bets are being placed as to whether there will even be a second date after this one. Deke's never been interested in real romance."

"I'll say it one more time. Nothing happened in Montana except lots of hard work and long hours of dealing with a blizzard and snow," Josie answered.

A vision of the bunkhouse came to mind when she looked down at the strange little arrangement in her hands. When they had been talking about their favorite things, she'd told him that she liked wildflowers.

*   *   *

On Thursday evening Jud brought a pint jar filled with candy kisses. A bright red ribbon was tied around the top and the note read: *Hint Number Three.*

"I'm not sure what's going on here, Sis, but Deke is so damned jittery, it's unreal. I'm glad that we aren't starting to gravel the road to the drill site until next week. I wouldn't trust him on a four-wheeler right now, much less a bulldozer. Allie says she's never seen him like this," Jud said.

"How much money do you have on the date? And which way are you betting?" Josie asked bluntly.

"Ten bucks on this being a flash in the pan. You've got a good head on your shoulders, Josie. I trust your judgment to realize that we've got too much work ahead of us for you to get tangled up with a relationship."

"Well, thank you, Jud, but I believe that is the pot calling the kettle black, since you got more than involved in a relationship. You got married." She twisted the top off the jar and took out a candy Kiss, unwrapped it, put it in her mouth, and held the jar out to Jud. "Want one?"

"No thank you. I'll let you keep Deke's kisses." He grinned.

Fiona came into the room and held out her hand. "I won't be so nice. I want a chocolate. And, Jud, you should remember one thing in all this. You changed. So don't be judging. And one other thing while I'm up here on my soapbox. Josie is your sister, not your daughter, so you don't get to tell her who to fall in love with."

"Love? Who said anything about love?" Josie asked.

Fiona stuck up her free hand and Josie did a high five.

*　　*　　*

Friday morning Josie opened her eyes to a cute little floral arrangement and two jars, one with a candle, the other with Kisses, on the bedside table not three feet from her.

"It's the bunkhouse. That's where the hints are leading, but Deke doesn't have a bunkhouse on his ranch and what does that have to do with our date?" She rubbed her eyes but couldn't figure out a thing.

There were four texts on her phone that morning. All of them from were Deke. Short and sweet. One simply read:

Will you be my Valentine? Asking early to beat out the other cowboys.

What other cowboys? She grinned as she typed.

Say yes and you won't have to find out.

She waited thirty seconds before she answered.

Let's talk about those other cowboys first.

It was a full minute before anything came back to her. *Not one of them is worthy of your second glance, darlin'.*

She giggled as she hit the keys. *Well, then*

She hit SEND and then typed, *I guess*

Sent that and waited.

Yes, I will be your Valentine.

His message was a red heart emoji.

She was getting dressed to go out to the drill site with Jud when the jitters hit her. Tonight was the night. Deke had made sure the entire town knew they had a date, but she hadn't seen him since last Sunday. She had to work hard all morning to keep her mind on oil wells and equipment but the excitement of the date overruled anything to do with business. She had lunch with Jud at his house and they spent the afternoon in his office with charts and soil sample results that had come in that morning.

Still no environmental reports, but they weren't expecting those until every bug, skunk, and mole in Throckmorton County had been studied. She left at five o'clock and hurried back to the hotel.

Fiona met her at the door with a frown. "You've got thirty minutes, and since this is the biggest thing that's happened in Dry Creek in years, you will need every bit of it to get ready. I'm surprised they aren't having a parade the way folks are keeping the phone lines hot. I'm surprised the cell phone towers between us and Throckmorton aren't smoking." She fussed from the bottom of the stairs as Josie took the steps two at a time.

Josie took a quick shower, washed her hair and dried it, slipped into a pair of skinny jeans and boots, and put on the shirt that she had stolen from him in Roswell. It had been washed and ironed but she imagined that she could still smell him on it when she stuck her nose in the collar. She rolled up the sleeves and tied the front in a knot at waist level and made it down the steps five minutes early.

"You are wearing that on your first date?" Fiona crossed her arms over her chest. "I'm going to lose the money I bet on you having a second date and I was going to gloat when I made twenty bucks from my sisters. Now I may have to shell out ten to each of them."

Josie threw an arm around Fiona. "This is Deke's shirt. I borrowed it when...well, I didn't have anything to sleep in one night in the bunkhouse. He asked me to wear it tonight. Oh, I think this might be the last hint."

"Well." Fiona's face lit up in a smile. "Then I'll put ten bucks on a third date."

The clock on the wall clicked to five thirty at the exact same time Deke knocked on the door. Josie opened it and her pulse kicked in an extra beat. There he was, black hat in hand, hair smoothed back away from his freshly shaven face, and wearing jeans and a dark green T-shirt under a chambray work shirt.

"You look amazing." He grinned and held out a heart-shaped box of chocolates. "It's a little early, but since everyone in town appears to be interested in our business, maybe they'll all get the hint that we're together."

"At least until Valentine's Day." She took them from him and wasn't a bit surprised at the bright sparks that flashed between them when his hand grazed hers.

"Who knows? Maybe I'll bring you an Easter bunny or maybe an Easter goat on our second date just to make sure everyone understands."

"Neither one unless it's chocolate." She draped her coat over one arm and laced her fingers in his.

"I'll have the princess home by midnight," Deke threw over his shoulder as he escorted her out to his truck.

"I'm not a princess, Deke," she said as she fastened the seat belt.

"No, you are the queen." He started the engine.

"So where are we going on this date that everyone in town is making bets on?" she asked.

"Look behind us." He glanced in the rearview mirror as he drove out of town. "I guess they've sent at least three spies out to follow us."

"I feel like a teenager." She laughed.

"It's Dry Creek. It's been a whole month since Fiona and Jud got married and the gossip vines are near death. Besides, folks around here are very serious about their betting, whether it's a checkers or a poker game or how many times we are going to have a date."

"Did you bet?" she asked.

"No, ma'am. I'm just hoping this is the first of many and that something comes along to take all their attention away from us. I saw 12:34 pop up on the dashboard clock today and that was my wish."

He crossed the cattle guard onto his ranch and stopped the truck, got out, and pulled a gate from one side to the other with a homemade sign on it written in big letters: PRAYER IS THE BEST WAY TO MEET THE LORD. TRESPASSING TONIGHT IS A FASTER WAY.

She was still giggling when he returned to the truck. "I wonder how many of them will think you are going to try to sweet-talk me into bed, since we are going to your house for our date. Which I don't mind at all. I've missed Rascal this week."

"Sorry, darlin', we aren't going to the house, but you can see Rascal Sunday afternoon when we go four-wheeling," he said.

"Oh, is that our second date, then?" she asked.

"No, ma'am. I'm going to ask you to go dancing with me at the Rusty Spur tomorrow night for our second date. Sunday will be our third one," he answered. "But I won't ask until after this one to give you time to think about it."

"Do you need time to think about it, Deke?"

He shook his head and brushed a sweet kiss across her lips. "No, darlin', I do not. I want to spend as much time as I can with you."

"Deke, I..." she stammered.

He reached across the console and laid a finger on her lips. "Don't say a word. I've got a lot of showing to do before you should say anything. Just enjoy the evening and say yes when I ask you to go dancing with me."

She wrapped her fingers around his wrist and kissed his finger. She would say yes to a second date, to the Sunday afternoon four-wheeler date, and to one every day next week but right then she was so stunned she couldn't say a word.

Sunsets in Texas are glorious on a poor day but on that Friday night, there were a few wispy clouds to give even more color to the sky. As he drove through the pastures she watched the sun sink lower and lower. It was only a rim of orange, throwing off brilliant shades of every color in the rainbow when he drove slowly down a rutted lane and parked on the side of a small creek.

"Where are we?" she asked.

"At the site of our first date." He quickly got out and rounded the front of the truck, opened her door, and helped her to the ground. "I want us to walk over that bridge together as the sun sets behind that cabin right there." He took her hand in his, and side by side they went to the center of the bridge.

It had no rails and was probably built back in the horse and buggy days but the wood was still sturdy. The small creek that ran under it didn't have a lot of water but that evening it was bubbling over the rocks, making a sweet sound that Josie could easily fall asleep to—in Deke's arms.

Deke squeezed her hand as the sun dropped behind the cabin. "What do you think?"

"There are no words to describe this, Deke. It's gorgeous, peaceful, almost like a bit of heaven has fallen just for us," she said. "Can we go inside the cabin?"

He dropped her hand and ran his own down her cheek. The chemistry between them was so full of passion and electricity that it made her knees weak. But not as much as the kiss that followed. It started off sweet and slow and then intensified and deepened with so much heat that she was sure the bridge would burn beneath them.

When he finally broke the string of kisses, he drew her close with an arm around her shoulder and walked beside her to the cabin. "This is the location of our date. The charcoal is hot but not as hot as your kisses, and the table is set for dinner. All I have to do is slap the steaks on the grill and we will be ready to eat."

He slung open the door into a place about the side of the bunkhouse but not nearly as well put together. A square room not any bigger than the hotel lobby, it had a set of bunk beds on one side, a table in the middle, and a sofa in front of the fireplace that had just enough blaze in it to be romantic. Candles and oil lamps were set in strategic places to give enough light for a romantic dinner. A fruit jar filled with red and white daisies sat in the middle of a table set for two with mismatched plates and cutlery.

"Deke, it is perfect," she gasped.

The grin that covered his face told her that he'd been worried that she'd be disappointed. She pulled him around to face her and her lips found his in another series of lingering kisses that had them both panting at the end.

"Maybe you'd better put the steaks on now or we'll skip the main course and go straight to dessert," she whispered.

"That sounds tempting, but not tonight, darlin'. Sex is not a first-date thing. In real dating, it's saved for later," he said.

"Who told you that?"

"I read it in one of those romance books in Montana." He chuckled. "The grill is set up right outside the door so you can talk to me while I cook and still stay warm. I missed you so much, Josie." After one more hug, and another kiss on the forehead this time, he crossed the small room and brought two huge rib eye steaks from a cooler and slapped them down onto a platter.

"Texting isn't the same as talking, even on the phone. I missed talking to you." She followed him to the tiny front porch.

"I was afraid to call because if you asked me about the date—well, I'm not sure I could keep things from you. It's been the longest week of my life."

The steaks sizzled when they hit the hot grill. "Deke, this is really great, but why? I can see that you've worked hard getting it ready. The whole place smells fresh and clean."

"When I stopped and really thought about it, what I wanted for you on this date was to make it special for us. The selfish side of me wanted to have you all alone without anyone interfering with our evening. Not any of the Dry Creek folks who might stop by the Dairy Queen for ice cream tonight or any of the women I've been with who might be there and come by our booth or table," he said honestly.

"Well, it's the best date I've ever been on and that includes first, second, third, and tenth dates," she said.

"It's the best for me because it is really my first date ever," he said.

"Deke Sullivan! You went to the junior prom. Sharlene told me so."

He shrugged. "I asked her because she was the only girl left in our class who didn't have a date. It could hardly be called a date. Grandpa let me borrow his pickup because mine didn't have an air conditioner and the passenger-side window wouldn't roll up."

"But…" she argued.

He flipped the steaks to the other side. "I can dance. I can flirt. I can pick up women. But I've never asked one out to dinner or on a date. It wasn't necessary and I didn't like any of them well enough."

"Well, that's honest enough," she said.

"Did Jud tell you that I'm helping him and Blake and Toby start building the road back to the site on Monday and that I'm helping Allie put a roof on a house pretty soon? And I heard from Everett and he and Martha might come for a visit before the big actual move?" He stuck a thermometer in one of the steaks. "Medium rare, right?"

She nodded. She didn't care if he talked about roads or

roofs, roads or steaks. Hearing his deep drawl was enough for her.

He carried the steaks into the cabin and shut the door with his boot heel. "It can work and only cost half as much. Look at us, Josie. Our first date and we're talking about a crazy oil well and a roof. I should be telling you how beautiful you are and recitin' poetry to you."

He set the platter on the table and unzipped a container holding two huge baked potatoes and a bowl of fried okra. After setting those beside the steaks he brought out a bowl of salad and two bottles of dressing. A final touch was two longneck bottles of beer.

"I believe that just about covers a steak dinner." She smiled.

He seated her and said, "I will say grace. Would you please hold my hand?"

She stretched her arm out across the small table and he covered her hand with his, bowed his head, and said, "Father, I thank you for Josie. Amen."

When she opened her eyes he kept his head bowed a moment longer. Tears stung her eyes as she looked up to find him gazing into her face. She wondered if he was praying about hope for something more emotional than whether or not the groundhog saw his shadow.

"I do not tease when I talk to God," he whispered. "And that is not a line. It's the pure gospel truth. Now which one of these steaks do you want?"

Josie pointed at one but she could have forgone supper altogether and gone straight to the bottom bunk. Surely he wasn't serious about no sex on the first date. Every hormone in her body hummed in excitement. She wanted to feel his body next to hers, to snuggle up in the warm afterglow after beautiful sex.

Josie had never been with any man like Deke. She was falling in love with him and maybe someday in the near future she could say the words, but that evening she just wanted to be with him. Like he said, to talk and to spend a whole evening together without family around—or even a sweet little granny who got mixed up and thought Josie was a new bride like all the Logan girls were.

It didn't take much stretch in the imagination to see herself married to Deke, but then this was his first date. He might be in love with her, but then he might want to explore all the possibilities around central Texas before he made a commitment like that.

What was she thinking? She might be ready for an exclusive dating commitment-type relationship, but not marriage. She had business to take care of, Kasey to worry about, and Everett and Martha were coming soon.

"So do you think Everett and Martha will like it here?" Deke asked.

The man could read minds. Maybe that's the way he got all those women to fall backward into bed and pull him down on top of them.

"Martha called me. She says soon after you talked to Everett, he got antsy and wants them to have a road trip, maybe stay two or three days just to look at our area," she said.

"I'm not surprised that he's getting stir-crazy. Next Thursday is Groundhog Day."

"What does that have to do with Everett?"

"It's hard to explain. But after a winter like he's had, he's probably hoping that the groundhog does not see his shadow and that the spring thaw is on the way. That gives a rancher hope that winter is over," Deke answered. "How are we going to celebrate the holiday?"

"Valentine's?"

"No. Groundhog Day?" He grinned.

"Maybe we could have a fourth date right here. I'll bring a picnic and a chocolate cake." She smiled.

"Will you wear that shirt again?"

"I can do that," she said. "But I'm not wearing it tomorrow night when we go dancing."

"Then you are saying yes you will go on a second date with me?"

She nodded. "I am."

"Good. I'm glad that's settled. I was afraid you would say no."

"I'm looking forward to dancing all night with you," she said.

Besides, Jud had put a seed of doubt in her mind that she needed to think about. Being together, alone, in a cabin like this was awesome, but how would Deke react to a bar full of sexy women? Could he keep his eyes and hands off them?

Chapter Twenty-six

The Rusty Spur looked like any one of a dozen country bars. A jukebox in one corner, a dance floor, a bar along one side, tables with mismatched chairs pushed against the back wall.

"Drink first or dance?" Deke asked.

"Dance," she answered. That should let everyone in the place know that they'd arrived together and he was taken for the evening.

Without a word, he led her out into the middle of the floor and picked up her hands. He put them around his neck and put his on the small of her back, pulling her so close to him that there was no space. He kept his eyes glued to hers as Luke Bryan sang "I Don't Want This Night to End."

"I don't want any night I'm with you to end," he whispered in her ear.

The next song was Tim McGraw's "Top of the World." It was fast enough that Deke started a swing dance, twirling her out and bringing her back to his chest as he sang with the lyrics that said it didn't matter where they were, because if they were together they would be sitting on top of the world.

"For real?" she asked. "Does it really not matter if we have nothing or everything?"

"As long as I've got you in my arms, nothing else matters," Deke said. "Fate must've known we would walk in the door at this time because I already recognize this next song."

She nodded as they began a fast two-step around the dance floor to "Already Callin' You Mine," by Parmalee. "Me too."

"I'd like to do just what the words say and get out of here with you, but darlin' we came to dance and have a few beers and that's what we'll do. When this one ends do you want to claim a table?" he asked.

"Sure. Can you grab me a double shot of whiskey with a beer chaser?" she said.

"You got it." He grinned.

As soon as the song ended someone plugged money into the machine and "Cotton-Eye Joe" started. Two lines formed on the floor and boot tapping sounded like drumbeats on the old wooden floor.

Deke wove in between them with their drinks. Several women reached out to touch his arm and say a few words, but he brushed them away with a nod and kept walking.

Jud was wrong.

Deke could walk through fire without getting burned.

He set the tray with two mugs of beer and the shot of whiskey on the table and then kissed her softly on the lips. "All the cowboys in this place better know you're mine tonight."

"And all those women eyeballing you?" She sipped at

the whiskey, letting the warmth of it lie on her tongue a moment before she swallowed it.

"I didn't realize there was another woman in the place."

"Deke, you really are a charmer." She laughed.

"I can't change who I am, but I can change what I do." He pulled a chair up so close to hers that when he sat down his shoulder and thigh pressed tightly against hers.

The heat of his arm thrown around her shoulders generated so much electricity that she could almost hear the static above another line-dancing song that had dancers stomping and yelling "yee-haw."

Five songs later they'd finished their beers and Faith Hill's "Just to Hear You Say That You Love Me" sent the line dancers to the bar for drinks. The floor was completely empty when Deke stood up and held out his hand. Josie put hers in it and he put it on his shoulder. Other than the sound of their boots, the beating of their hearts in unison, and Faith's voice, the bar was quieter than church on Sunday morning. When the last high note ended, the song started all over again.

"I didn't play this but I'm glad someone did." Deke breathed into her ear.

She took a step back but he pulled her into his arms and began to move around the dance floor again.

"Deke, how do you run the Double Heart all by yourself?"

He laid a finger over her lips. "Shhh, darlin'. Tonight is all about us, not ranchin' or oil or even buyin' bulls."

She laid her head on his chest and looped her arms around his neck. He rested his chin in her hair and held her close with one hand on her lower back. With the other hand he combed back her hair with his fingertips and tenderly kept his palm on her cheek. His heart beat steady and true, as if keeping time with the music. His touch on her scalp and her cheekbone was so intimate, so personal, that she forgot all about being in a bar full of other people. Warmth flowed from her lower back, creating an afterglow right there in the middle of the dance floor that no one else could see or feel.

*   *   *

The second date was a test, not for her but for Deke. Could he go to his favorite old stomping grounds and still feel the same way about her that he did when they were standing on the bridge watching the sunset?

As he two-stepped around the dance floor, he pictured the night before in the little cabin. The way Josie's eyes lit up when she noticed every little thing he'd planned made him feel like the cowboy king of a million-acre spread. He'd fallen in love and he liked the way it felt just fine. It wasn't scary and didn't make him want to run for the hills but filled his whole body with happiness. He tightened his grip around her waist and moved his other hand to cup her chin and tip her face up. The song ended, but a melody still played in his mind as he got lost in those big blue eyes.

Boots on the wooden floor sounded like drumrolls as folks headed for the bar for a beer or a drink, but Josie lingered in Deke's arms. Thirst for his body next to hers far outweighed a shot of whiskey or a cold beer. She recognized the next song, "Cowboys and Angels," and brushed a quick kiss across his lips.

"This is our song for sure," he whispered in her ear. "I do have boots and you have wings." His hand moved from her lower back to her shoulders. "I feel them sproutin'."

"Like it says, your touch is my temptation," she said huskily.

"And your kiss is my salvation," he said softly.

"You are right," Josie said. "This is definitely our song."

Deke kissed her on the forehead. He would always remember that first date. But tonight would always be branded into his heart and soul. That Saturday night when he went into the bar, he was Deke, the cowboy who was known for his love of a good time. When he left, he was Deke, the cowboy in love with one woman.

It might take six months or maybe a whole year to convince Josie that he was serious about her, but he was willing to wait. She was right about texts not being the same as talking. He loved the soft lilt in her voice, her laughter, the passion in her eyes when she talked about rodeo stock or oil wells. Hell, she could read the phone book to him and he'd sit there enthralled at every name that came from her lips.

Someone plugged the jukebox full of fast songs for line dancing after that one ended. When the first one ended with a loud "yee-haw" from the dancers and the second one began, Deke finished his beer and leaned across the table so Josie could hear him above the noise. "You ready to get out of here?"

She nodded, pushed back her empty bottle, and stood up. He laced his fingers in hers and led her outside, through a fog of smokers and to the truck.

"Look at that." He pointed to the clock on the dash as he started the engine. "Eleven eleven, you get to make a wish. Want to tell me what it is?"

She shut her eyes tightly and then popped them open. "My wish is that there will be a third date because they say the third is the charm."

"Charm for what?" he asked.

"Whatever it is supposed to be. Maybe we'll fight and figure out we were living in a bubble on these first two dates. Maybe we'll fall into bed and learn that what we had in Roswell was a one-time thing and will never happen again. Or maybe all the stars will align and we'll figure out we belong in a relationship. We'll have to wait and see if there is a third date to know," she answered. "But right now, Deke, I'm glad we left before they closed down the bar. I kind of like having you all to myself, whether it's in a cabin, a bunkhouse, or the cab of this truck."

"Me too," Deke said quietly. He paused for a moment. "I love to dance with you, but I'd like it even more in my living room or out at the cabin where it's just the two of us."

"Amen," she said.

Deke took a CD by Dustin Lynch out of the console and slipped it into the slot on the dashboard before he drove out of the lot. "I think we ought to listen to our song again."

"I'm really not an angel, Deke."

"Depends on who you ask." He grinned.

By the time the CD had played through they were back in Dry Creek and he'd parked outside Fiona and Jud's dark house. He got out of the truck, walked her to the door, and drew her close to him as if they were still on the dance floor. Humming the tune to "Cowboys and Angels," he held her tightly and moved around the porch floor for one more dance. When the dance ended, his lips found hers in a hungry kiss that blended two hearts together right there under the twinkling stars.

"Wow!" She panted when the kiss ended.

He lowered his mouth to hers again. When the kiss ended, he stepped back and tipped his hat. "Good night, Josie. The past two nights have been amazing."

She touched her lips to find that they were cool instead of burning up. "Yes, they have. Good night, Deke."

He made it to the porch before he turned around. "How about a four-wheeling date tomorrow after church?"

"Love it." She smiled.

He whistled the tune to their new song all the way to the truck.

Chapter Twenty-seven

Josie thought she'd be driving a four-wheeler, not crammed behind Deke on a seat made for one person. Not that she was complaining—no, sir! Her breasts were pressed to his back and her arms were wrapped around his chest. A soft springlike breeze whipped her hair away from her face as they made their way around the perimeter of the Double Heart Ranch.

"Hey." She leaned around so that she could talk straight into Deke's ear. "You really do need to get a sign up above the cattle guard so folks know the name of your ranch."

"Now that I've decided to keep the name, I'll have a new sign made. I'm thinking a good metal one this time instead of a wooden one."

"And it will squeak when the wind blows." She smiled.

He braked and brought the machine to a stop in front of the bridge over Dry Creek. It looked different in the daylight than it did with the sun setting behind it, but even with the stark dead mesquite and knobby old scrub oak still surrounding it, the place was serene and peaceful. He slung his long legs onto the ground and held out his hand to her. Without hesitation, she clasped it, and together they walked to the middle of the bridge.

"I used to think that the name of the ranch was kind of sissy, but here lately I'm realizing that it takes putting the heart and soul into anything that is worthwhile," he said.

"Why, Deke, you aren't just a flirt; you are a romantic," she said.

He let go of her hand and slipped his arm around her shoulders. "You bring out that side of me."

"Spoken with true cowboy charm." She leaned over and kissed him on the cheek. "Looking at that cabin makes me want a cup of campfire coffee."

"It can be arranged. There's an old pot in there, a fire-place, and some coffee left over from our first date night," he said.

With a tug on her hand, they both stood up at the same time. He pulled her to his chest and his lips closed on hers, his tongue teasing its way into her mouth to flirt and do a mating dance with hers.

"I've wanted to kiss you all day. Couldn't keep my mind on the hymns or the sermon in church," he said.

"Have you ever kissed a girl in church?" she asked.

He chuckled as he led her across the bridge toward the cabin. "Not me, darlin'. I might walk with the devil on Friday and Saturday nights but on Sunday morning, I do not tempt God. Have you ever kissed a boy in church?"

"No, sir. Maybe out in the car after church but not once inside the doors. If God didn't fry me with lightning bolts then Mama would with her lecturing. And believe me, God might shut his eyes to some things, but Mama never did." Josie went inside when he opened the door for her.

The cabin was chilly, so Deke set about making a small fire. She watched his biceps strain the seams of his jacket when he picked up two huge logs from the wood box and laid them in the fireplace. He blew on the first spark of fire and she touched her neck, remembering all those times when he walked up behind her and said something so soft that his warm breath kissed that soft spot right below her ear.

"And now to get the coffee ready," he said as he headed toward the table with the old red pump in the middle. A shiver of desire went through her as she watched his back and shoulder muscles working the pump until water gushed out into the dishpan below it. She'd felt his back and shoulders tighten when she dug her fingertips into them at the height of sex, felt them relax after they'd both reached the top of the climax together.

She removed her jacket and tried to slow her breathing. Neither one did much good when it came to cooling her down. He hung the poker back on its hook above the blaze and then sat down on the sofa with her.

"It'll be ready in a few minutes. This is where I first learned to drink coffee," he said.

"When you came back here with your grandpa that time when Grandma got angry?" Maybe if she talked, she'd get past the urge to crawl into his lap and undress him.

"No, before that when he brought me here to hunt deer one fall. Do you eat venison?"

She nodded. "I also hunt when I have the time. Does that make you want to run in the other direction?"

"I bet you look sexy as hell in camo and face paint." He

grinned. "Shall we come to the cabin next November and see if we can bag some winter steaks and roasts?"

"I was thinking about summer sausage." She slid over next to him.

"And maybe some jerky?"

"Oh, yeah, but I can make that myself. I've got a real good rub that gives it a little bit of heat," she said.

"Kind of like what is between us?"

"Oh, honey, there isn't a rub in the world that hot," she whispered.

With one swift move, his hands went around her waist and he shifted her onto his lap. "Think we could keep the heat going between us for a lifetime?"

"It would be worth a try." Her lips found his.

She pushed his jacket off his shoulders without opening her eyes. He quickly shed it and raised her knit shirt up over her head. She did the same with his. They ended the kiss for a millisecond to get them over their heads and then they were stretched out on the sofa, her chest to his. His arms were tightly around her so that she wouldn't slip off onto the floor and her hands were tangled up in his hair, steadying his head for round after round of long, hard kisses.

"The bunk bed is a little wider and a lot longer," she whispered.

She wasn't sure how he did it but suddenly she was in his arms like a new bride. He carried her to the bottom bunk, expertly slid her onto the bed, and stretched out beside her.

"I want you," he groaned. "But this is..."

She put her finger over his lips. "Don't talk. Don't think. Just make love to me."

"Well, darlin', I can damn sure give you that."

He started to undress her slowly, but hot passion overcame them both. He removed her boots and tugged her jeans off and she undid his belt buckle, unzipped his jeans, and jerked them down only to find he still had his boots on. He managed to get them off without ending the steamy kisses.

"God, Josie! I wanted to take it slow and make love but I've been thinking about touching you for days. The way the fire lit up your hair and I need to be inside you," he said breathlessly.

"I want you right now," she gasped as she wrapped her long legs around his body.

In one thrust, they were rocking together, giving and taking from each other as the whole world disappeared into a haze. Time didn't matter. Breathing didn't matter. The driving force was satisfaction and the only person in the whole world who could bring her to the end of the road was Deke. Then in an intense moment when she was sure her soul floated out of her body, they came together. He didn't roll to one side but after a couple of long, lingering kisses started all over again.

"Oh, Deke." She moaned.

"This time will be better," he whispered softly as he nibbled on her earlobe.

"I don't know how, but I'm willing to see," she said.

He took her right up to the edge of an amazing climax and then slowed down, prolonging the fever between them. Glad that the cabin was remote, she gave way to every emotion in her body and moaned loudly. In the middle of the second ride to a climax she squirmed against him, tightening her legs and digging into his skin with her fingernails. She needed the release or she was going to go up in flames from the inside out.

"Now?" he asked.

"Three minutes ago," she answered.

For the second time, they came together. He rolled to one side but kept her tightly hugged next to his body. "Josie, that was—you are—" He groaned.

"I know." She forced enough air from her lungs to say two words.

Afterglow was so bright and so warm as it slipped them into its cocoon that words weren't necessary. She was in love and she wanted to shout it to the whole world.

Chapter Twenty-eight

Josie got a call on Monday morning as she was leaving the hotel. She'd just finished painting the last room. She checked the caller ID and saw a new picture of Martha holding the puppy up close to her face.

"Hey, Martha," she answered.

"Hello!" Martha's excitement came through with the greeting. "Were y'all serious about us coming down there for a visit? We're getting real antsy and we could drive down in two days, stay a couple of days, and then come back. That way Everett would know if he really wants to do this before the buyer starts the paperwork."

"Of course we're serious. There's lots of room at the Fiona and Jud's house and we'd just love to have you," Josie answered.

"Okay, then, we thought we might be there on Friday evening, stay the weekend, and come back home on Monday. Will that work for you?"

"We'll have a room ready for you and a hug waiting."

"I'm as excited as a teenager," Martha said. "See you then."

Josie drove home and noticed that Fiona's car was in the driveway but Jud's truck was nowhere in sight.

"Fiona, I'm home!" she called out.

"I'm in the kitchen," Fiona yelled.

Josie hung her jacket on the coatrack. Fiona was busy stirring up a pan of corn bread for supper.

"I invited Deke to join us tonight. He'll be here in about thirty minutes. We are having ham, beans, and fried potatoes. And I made a double batch of brownies," she said.

A slow burn started at the base of Josie's neck and traveled to her cheeks. Every time she thought about him, she got a flash of the previous day in that cabin. She quickly went to the sink and splashed her face with cold water.

"You can set the table," Fiona said.

"I did something without clearing it with you and Jud." Josie dried her face and hands. "I told Everett and Martha they could stay here from the time they arrive on Friday evening until Monday. I hope that's all right."

"This is your home for as long as you want and there's plenty of room. You don't have to ask permission for guests, and besides, they gave you room and board for a week. I'd never refuse them."

Her phone rang again and the call this time was from Kasey.

"I'll be right back to take care of the table," she told Fiona. "Hey, Kasey, what's going on in Happy, Texas?" she said as she moved into the living room and got comfortable on the sofa.

"Don't know about the whole town of Happy, but things

on the ranch are beginning to get into spring mode. What's going on with your sexy cowboy?"

"I'm in love with him." Just admitting it out loud lifted a load from her chest.

"You just figure that out? Hell, girl, I heard that in your voice when you were on your way home from Montana. When's the wedding, and can I be the maid of honor?"

Josie laughed. "You're crazy."

"Maybe not as crazy as you think..." Kasey answered. "Sometimes when you know, you just know. And remember, I know you very well."

*   *   *

Josie was unloading supplies from her truck to the house when she got the call from Martha on Friday. She and Everett were in Throckmorton and would be there in half an hour.

"Josie! It's already spring in this part of the world!" Martha squealed as she bailed out of the truck and hurried toward the porch where Josie waited.

"Not yet, but it's on the way." Josie bent to hug the short woman. "How did Bitsy make the trip?"

"Bitsy is absolutely spoiled, as you'll soon see. Lord, I'm already in love with this place. We left Montana in below zero temperatures, but here there's green pastures and it got all the way up to forty-nine! I might not ever go home." Martha talked nonstop.

"Well, that would suit me just fine."

Josie looked up to see a wide grin splitting Deke's handsome face as he crawled out of his truck. "I wanted to welcome y'all to Texas."

Everett bypassed Deke's outstretched hand and hugged

Deke like a son. "I'm waiting on my hug from you, Josie."

She embraced him and then kissed him on the cheek. "Let's go inside and get you settled in. I'm frying chicken tonight for supper, and, Martha, if you aren't too tired, would you whip up one of those quick cobblers for us?"

"I've missed being in the kitchen, honey. Everett, you get Bitsy out and let him run a bit and then bring in our stuff. Don't forget his playpen and his toys." Martha looped her arm through Josie's. "Now let's me and you catch up over a cookstove. Tomorrow me and Everett want to take a look at your hotel and see the whole town."

Deke got her attention and winked. With company there would be no way they'd have a repeat of the previous weekend. Josie smiled and barely nodded as she and Martha went inside the house.

* * *

On Sunday morning, Josie awoke to find a text message from Deke: *I'm running late. Save me a seat at church.*

She wished that she were back in the New Mexico hotel waking up in bed with Deke, or at least waking up to his singing in the bathroom. But that morning she was alone in her bedroom with no one on the entire second floor but Martha and Everett. Since it was already seven o'clock, she'd bet that they were both in the kitchen, Martha helping with breakfast, and Everett and Jud deep in conversation about ranching business.

The trip had been an eye-opener for both Martha and Everett and had set their decision in stone. Come May, they'd be moving to Dry Creek. Jud and Fiona had extended an invitation for them to stay at their house until they found a place of their own. Everett had looked seriously already at the O'Dell place next to the Double Heart Ranch, but it was too big for what he wanted in his retirement. He had found a small sixty-acre hobby farm north of town that he and Martha both liked, but they were going to think about it before jumping in with both feet.

Josie unbuttoned Deke's plaid shirt and hung it on the bedpost. Then she dressed in the same jeans and shirt she'd taken off the night before "Good morning," she said when she made it to the kitchen.

"Mornin'," Martha said. "Me and Everett, we got a proposition for you."

"Well, you might go into it easy like and not just jump out there before she even gets her coffee," Everett scolded.

Martha shook a finger at him. "Me and Josie understand each other. We don't need no pussyfooting around, do we, Josie?"

"No, ma'am," Josie said.

"It's like this," Everett said. "We like it here a lot and we like that hotel and the little town of Dry Creek, but we just flat out can't make up our minds about that little chunk of land we been looking at."

"And," Martha butted in, "we want to buy this hotel. We'll give you a real good deal for your oil crew when that time comes. But when you don't need rooms for them, then we'll just have guests like any hotel. I know bookkeeping and I'm told Fiona can take care of the major books if we ask her."

"We'll make you a right fine deal." Everett smiled. "Blake told us that you'd put a lot of money into it and we'll reimburse you for that. Jud tells us that the oil crew might be here just about the same time that we are ready to move, so things would work out real good. Martha's got a house full of furniture and lots more in storage, so we could fill the place with what we already have plus buy what else we need."

"Are you sure about this? That's a big undertaking," Josie said.

"It feels right. I'll have enough to live on for the rest of my life from the sale, but me and Martha want to try something different for a spell. If we get tired of it, we'll offer to sell it to you first, but I don't think we will. Maybe if we have a little hotel here that serves up a good breakfast, it will attract some more folks in, and pretty soon all the rest of those empty buildings will be filled up," Everett told her.

"So what do you say?" Martha asked.

Everett had given them a fantastic deal on the bulls and now he was offering to do this for her. Josie was absolutely speechless for several seconds then she hugged both Everett and Martha.

"I say it's a wonderful idea. Thank you. That is an amazing offer."

Martha patted her on the back. "And it's an awesome adventure for me and Everett and Bitsy."

*   *   *

Deke waited at the church doors for her that morning. He'd thought with the extra stock and the fact that he'd overslept half an hour that he'd be a little late that morning, but luck was with him and he arrived five minutes before Josie.

God, she was beautiful in that straight denim skirt and matching jacket with a black suede collar. He'd love to take her home with him and take his time undoing every one of those cute little buttons down the side of the skirt.

He tipped his black hat and smiled. "Good morning. I need to make a trip to Wichita Falls right after church today. Do you think you could go with me?"

"Everett and Martha," she whispered. "It's their last day."

"Lucy has invited them to stay to the potluck after church and then go over to her and Herman's place for the afternoon. We could be back by suppertime so we can have a last meal with them before they leave tomorrow morning." He leaned in and brushed a soft kiss across her cheek.

"Then yes. What are we going to Wichita Falls for?" she asked as they entered the church together.

"I need to do a little furniture shopping and wanted your input," he said.

Deke missed Granny Irene sitting at the end of the pew. It was like the end of an era and he wasn't sure any of them were big enough to fill her shoes. Maybe like the song that kept playing through his mind about cowboys and angels, God had sent Josie, to sit with him in church so he wouldn't miss Irene so much.

Don't you tell her that, he thought immediately. *She definitely would not want to be a replacement for an old lady with dementia.*

He sang when he was supposed to, tried his best to listen to the preacher but finally gave up and let his mind wander to the times he and Josie had spent in the old cabin. And sighed when the preacher asked the longest-winded old guy in the congregation to deliver the benediction.

"So why are y'all going to Wichita Falls?" Jud asked Josie on the way out of church that morning.

"I need to do some shopping for some new furniture," Deke answered.

"Don't tell me you are replacing that sofa." Jud chuckled. "Rascal might divorce you if you throw out his favorite sleeping place."

"Never know. I might find something that I like better. Been lookin' at one of those fancy new things with the recliner on both ends."

Jud shook his head. "Rascal won't like it. Trust me."

"Well, you two have a good time. We'll take care of Everett and Martha. I feel like they're family already and they are so excited about buying that hotel," Fiona said.

"Buy the hotel?" Deke asked when they were outside. "When did this come up?"

"They asked me about it this morning," Josie said. "It's a good deal. They'll reimburse me for all I've spent. They want to run it like a real hotel and they'll give me special rates for my oil crew," she explained. "So you think I made the right decision?"

He kissed her on the cheek as he helped her into the truck. "That, darlin', is up to you. Let's go get some dinner and then hit a furniture store."

"We're really shopping for a new sofa?" she asked.

He got inside the truck and fastened his seat belt. "Not today, but Jud can think that. We are shopping for a new bed."

"Is yours worn out?"

"No, ma'am. It's perfectly good, but I'm tired of making love to you on a bunk bed and..." He paused. "Josie, there have been other women on that bed and you deserve better."

"That is the sweetest thing you've done yet," she said.

*   *   *

On Monday night after Martha and Everett said tearful good-byes that morning, Josie spent the first full night at Deke's place. She turned down the new bed he'd bought. He refreshed a couple of water glasses on the nightstands. They crawled into bed together.

"I missed this so much," he said.

"I liked our bunkhouse and traveling routines." She cuddled up next to him and yawned.

"I never, ever want to wake up in an empty house again without you. Will you move in here with me?" Deke asked.

It wasn't a proposal, but then maybe it wasn't time for that. *Baby steps*, she reminded herself. This was a commitment that she'd never been willing to embrace before, but right then she couldn't wait to say yes.

"Is that too soon?" he asked.

She propped up on an elbow and kissed him. "Yes, I will move in with you, and no, it's not too soon. I haven't slept well since we got home. I keep waking up and reaching for you."

"Same here." He pulled her closer and closed his eyes. In seconds he was asleep. She had looked forward to a night of wild sex again. But though it had been a whole week since they'd last had a chance to be together, just being there with him was enough for that night.

*   *   *

On the Monday before Valentine's Day, Deke made a run for another square of shingles to finish the job he was doing for Allie. While he was in Wichita Falls he stopped by a jewelry store to pick out something special for Josie.

The last time he'd given a girl a Valentine had been in

sixth grade, and in those days it was a card with a picture on the front and maybe a lollipop stuck on the back with a piece of tape. That brought back memories of the first time he met Josie and she'd had a red lollipop in her mouth.

That gave him an idea and he was on the way out of the store when a necklace caught his eye. It was a double heart with a single diamond in the middle. He stopped in his tracks and stared at it for a long time before he finally asked the jeweler to let him have a closer look.

"Can you wrap this for me?" he asked.

"I can, but it comes in a lovely red velvet box with a pretty white ribbon tied around it," the jeweler answered.

"That's great," Deke said as he handed him his credit card.

He left the store with a new spring in his step and went straight to a party store where he found a package of a dozen red lollipops tied with a red ribbon. He purchased those along with a cute little stuffed dog that resembled a redbone hound dog.

That evening he arrived home to find Josie in the kitchen. An apron was tied around her slim waist and the scent of something Italian wafted through the house along with the aroma of yeast bread and cinnamon. He picked her up and did a couple of swirls around the room with her before putting her feet back on the floor. She giggled and pulled his face to hers in a series of long, scorching-hot kisses.

"I missed you today," she said.

"I miss you every minute we aren't together," he said.

She pushed his chest. "Go get washed up. Supper in five minutes."

"That was a change of climate." He grinned.

"Has to be or the lasagna will get cold and the cinnamon

rolls will burn. One more kiss like that last one and we're going to forget about everything but going to bed together or stripping each other down and having a fling on the kitchen table."

He glanced across the room at the beautifully set table. "That would be a shame to waste that food, but hold that idea for later."

Supper was amazing, but he couldn't keep his eyes off Josie. The little red box, the stuffed animal, and the lollipops were lying on her pillow and he could hardly wait to get her to the bedroom that evening.

They'd fallen into a routine the past week. If she had time to cook, then he helped with dishes. If she didn't, then they shared the responsibility or ate over at Jud's or Blake's place when they were invited. She cleaned off the table. He put the leftovers away. She washed and he dried the dishes.

When they finished that evening he flipped the ends of the towel around her neck and drew her to him for a kiss. "Thank you for the great Valentine's supper. You know I could eat a wheelbarrow full of your cinnamon rolls."

"That's not Valentine's supper, darlin'." She grinned. "That comes tomorrow night when you take me out. But I do have something for you. Want it now or tomorrow?"

"Right now!" Deke said without hesitation.

She took him by the hand and led him down the hallway, stopping in front of a closed guest room door. "Close your eyes and don't open them until I tell you that you can."

He shut them tightly and let her lead him into the room. "Okay, now open." Her voice was filled with excitement.

It took a moment to focus and then he chuckled. Right there in the middle of the bed was a gallon jar filled with nothing but orange lollipops with a card propped up beside it.

"I remembered that you like orange ones. The rest of your present is behind the bed," she said.

He took a step forward, but there was nothing on the nightstand or the dresser. He turned back to her in time to see her point to the floor.

"Holy smoke!" His eyes widened and a grin covered his face. "How did you…where did you…oh, Josie, they're beautiful." He dropped down on his knees and picked up one of six kittens crawling all over a big yellow mama cat.

"I went to a shelter and only planned on bringing home two kittens for your Valentine, since you love them. But they'd just gotten in this family so you get them all." She plopped down beside him.

"You are totally amazing, woman." He kissed her with two kittens between them. "I love you so much." The words slipped out so slick that it amazed him. "Well, dang it, Josie. I planned to say that in a whole lot more romantic setting."

"I love you, too, Deke," she said. "And there's no place on earth as romantic as our home."

He laid the kitties back in the box and held her for a long moment before he took her hand and led her into their bedroom. He pointed at the pillow. "Looks like we both remembered the first time we met and the shelter in Montana. You can trade that stuffed hound in for a real one when you are ready."

She picked up the little animal and hugged it close. "Maybe I will here soon. And red suckers and something else."

Carefully removing the red bow from the velvet box, she opened it slowly and gasped.

"Oh, Deke, it's beautiful. Put it on me." She held the chain out to him with shaking hands. "Two hearts. One love forever."

"That's right. Will you marry me, Josie Dawson, and make this a permanent thing?"

"Yes," she said without a moment's hesitation. "I love you and I'm ready."

He fastened the chain and turned her slowly. "You are branded."

"I think, darlin'," she said as she cupped his face in hers, "that I was branded from the first time I laid eyes on you."

Chapter Twenty-nine

Four months later...

The church was packed to overflowing with Dawsons and the regular congregation that morning. The preacher and Deke, along with all three Dawson cousins, stood at the front of the church.

Josie's mama, Amanda, buttoned up the back of the wedding dress and put the veil on her daughter's head. "You are such a beautiful bride, Josie."

Josie turned to look at her reflection in the mirror. "Oh, Mama, I do feel pretty, but then Deke makes me feel like this every day."

"He's a good man, and I'm glad he's going to be a part of our family."

Josie kissed her mother on the cheek. "Mama, I think maybe it was love at first sight from the time I saw him totin' two bags of goat feed out of Lizzy's store. And, Mama, all women like Deke," Josie said. "But he belongs to me."

"There is our music. Your dad is waiting on the other side of this door with your bridesmaids. I'm glad you asked the newest Dawson brides to stand up there with you and Kasey." Amanda turned her toward the door. "But if you have a doubt, we can crawl out that window over there and be in the Bahamas before they catch us."

"No doubts, Mama." Josie handed her the double heart necklace. "Would you put this on me, please?"

"It's lovely. When did you get this?" Amanda asked.

"Deke gave it to me for Valentine's Day. Double hearts, symbolic of our hearts and the ranch. One diamond for our combined love."

"I love it. Deke is such a romantic." Amanda smiled.

"Hey." Martha peeked in the door. "I just had to get one little look before the wedding. Things will get crazy afterward but I did want to tell you to throw that bouquet straight at me."

"I will sure enough give it my best shot," Josie said. "Now come on in here and give me a hug."

"Oh, no, honey, I don't want to wrinkle up that gorgeous dress, but since I never had a daughter, I wanted to give this to you to wrap the stem of your bouquet." She pressed a lace handkerchief into Josie's hand. "I carried it at my wedding and I want you to have it."

"Oh, Martha, you are going to make me cry." Josie took the hanky and held Martha's hand for several seconds before releasing it.

"Don't do that, because I never let anyone cry alone and it'll sure mess up your makeup," Martha said. "There's another little lady who'd like to see you for a second before the wedding."

Martha moved away and Maddie stepped into the room with baby Ford in her arms. "We were so tickled to get the invitation and to get to stay at the new hotel. I wanted you to see how the baby has grown and tell you thank you again for all you did for us."

"Is this the baby you and Deke delivered?" Amanda asked.

"It is." Maddie held him up so they could both see him. "I'm sure we would have died out there and that God sent you to help me."

"Well, he is a gorgeous baby boy," Amanda said. "And I would like to have one just like him in about nine months."

"Mama!" Josie scolded.

"You and Jud have hit oil. He owns a ranch. You bought the place next to the Double Heart and expanded it to twice its size. It's time for a baby now," Amanda shot right back.

"Yes, it is. It's always time for a baby." A short little lady with gray hair popped inside the room. "Hello, you must be Jud and Josie's mama. I'm Dora June O'Dell, Truman's wife. The ranch next to Deke's belonged to us before we got us a big RV and started traveling. I'm so excited to get to be here for the wedding. Deke grew up not far from us, and we just loved his granny and grandpa. Deke asked me to bring this to you." She handed her an envelope. "I think it's your wedding present from him. He told me that yours to him was the deed to our old ranch and a sign to go above his cattle guard. I'm so excited that you bought the place and that you're joining it to the Double Heart to be one big ranch. It makes my goats right happy, I'm sure. But what tickles me most is that the Lucky Penny is finally living up to its name. Lord, I'm talking too much, but I'm so happy that Deke found you. Open your present, honey."

Josie ripped open the envelope to find AKA registration papers for two redbone hound dogs and a note that read, "I love you and can't wait until you are Mrs. Deke Sullivan."

"What is it?" Amanda asked.

"The beginnings of a great future for the Double Heart Ranch. He's bought me a couple of redbone hound puppies." She dabbed tears from her eyes.

"That man is a keeper for sure," Amanda said. "Your dad gave me a prize horse the day we married."

Dora June and Maddie left and Kasey, Lizzy, Allie, and Fiona all pushed their way inside. Dressed in short red dresses and carrying white roses, they all looked beautiful.

"Is he as nervous as I am?" Josie asked Fiona.

"Much worse, but it'll all be done with soon," Fiona said. "There's the music. We just wanted to see you one more time. Now it's time for us to line up."

Kasey blew a kiss her way. "I love you, cousin."

"You are next," Josie said.

"Never! Besides, no man wants to take on three rowdy kids."

"Never say never." Amanda laughed.

Jud held his arm out to his mother when she and Josie stepped out into the crowded church foyer. Amanda put her arm through his and pasted on a lovely smile. "Okay, let's get this started. Your father has been itchin' for a piece of wedding cake."

Brody picked up Katy's arm and looped it into his. She touched her lips and then Josie's forehead. "I feel like Deke is the son I never had so I'm honored that I get to sit in as his mother today. And, darlin', please know that you will now be my daughter."

"I love that," Josie said.

One by one, the Logan sisters made their way down the aisle toward the front of the church. Then Kasey slipped through the door, and they were all gone, leaving Josie alone with her father.

"Well, princess, this is it," Thomas said.

"I love him, Daddy," she said simply. "And more than that, I'm in love with him."

"Then that's all that matters. Your mama was right when she said I've been cravin' a piece of cake, so let's go get the ceremony done. You know how big of a sweet tooth I've got." He grinned.

The shuffle as everyone stood to their feet made her nervous but then she looked over the top of their heads and locked gazes with Deke. Nothing else mattered in the whole world. Kasey sang "From This Moment On" and Deke nodded with every word. The song ended when Deke stepped forward, took her hand in his, and kissed her on the cheek.

"I love you, Josie Dawson," he said.

"Well, I guess this ceremony, like the Logan girls', is going to be unique," the preacher said, chuckling. "Who gives this bride to be married to this man?"

"Her family and I do," Thomas said loudly. "And, son, you better know that I am giving you my little girl. You'd best honor her until your dying day or you will deal with me. I hope that you have daughters of your own and remember this day when you are standing in my place."

"Yes, sir," Deke said.

"Dearly beloved," the preacher said.

Josie heard the words but pictures kept flitting through her mind. There was Deke with an orange lollipop in his mouth; carrying her from bunkhouse to cabin; shoveling out stalls in the barn; in the hotel in Roswell and on their first date in that little hunting cabin.

She said her vows and heard his, but they were just words. What she was giving Deke that day was her heart and what she was taking from him was his heart.

"And now you may really kiss your bride," the preacher said.

Deke gathered her into his arms and hugged her tightly. "I can't believe that you are my wife."

"Are you going to kiss me?" she whispered.

He brushed a soft kiss across her lips and then picked her up and carried her down the aisle to the applause of everyone in the church. When they reached the fellowship hall, he set her down and gave her a proper wedding kiss.

"I love you. That isn't enough, but it's all I've got," he said.

"And I love you, Deke Sullivan. As long as we never lose sight of our love we will be fine. Now let's get this part done so we can go home," she said. "And before they all come swarming in here..." She kissed him again. "I love my wedding present. When do I get them?"

"They're waiting at home, at the Double Heart Ranch where we'll be until we are old and gray."

"Past that, darlin'," she whispered. "We'll be together right on through eternity."

GET AN EARLY LOOK AT THE
FIRST BOOK IN THE
HAPPY, TEXAS SERIES

FEATURING MORE RUGGED
DAWSON COWBOYS

*Toughest Cowboy
in Texas*

Coming in Spring 2017

Chapter One

"Order up," Molly yelled from the kitchen.

Lila picked up a basket filled to the brim with hot French fries just as the door to the Happy Café opened. The hot west sun from behind the cowboy caused nothing but a silhouette, but she'd recognize Brody Dawson anywhere—in the darkest night or the brightest day. He had to remove his cowboy hat to get through the doorway, and his broad shoulders came close to filling the whole space.

Her chest tightened just like it did back when they were kids and she caught a glimpse of him. She gripped the red plastic basket with the fries to keep from dropping it and willed herself to take a step toward the table where a couple of old ranchers waited for their order.

"Well, well!" He closed the door behind him and slowly scanned her from the toes of her boots to her black ponytail. "The wild child returns."

"And the toughest cowboy in all of Texas never left," she smarted off right back at him.

In a few long strides he slid into a booth and laid his hat

on the space beside him. He filled out the butt of his jeans even better than he had when they were in school. Lord, why couldn't he have developed a beer gut and two chins?

She carried the order to a booth on the other end of the café and set it down between Paul McKay and Fred Williams, two ranchers she'd known her whole growing-up years in Happy.

"I'd forgotten that they called you the wild child, Lila." Paul grinned.

"People change," she said. "Anything else?"

Paul picked up the ketchup bottle and squirted streams of it across the fries. "Naw, we're good for now. Might need some more tea before we go, but you go on and wait on poor old Brody. He looks like he's spittin' dust."

"I am and I'd love a glass of half sweet tea and half Molly's fresh lemonade," he said from across the small dining room.

"Anything else?" Lila turned to face him.

His sexy grin made every hormone in her body whine. Twelve years ago, she would've invented trouble to get a smile like that from him, and many nights she'd gone to sleep with the warmth of kisses on her lips. She fought the desire to touch her lips to see if the memory made them as warm as they felt.

"Whatcha got?" He raised an eyebrow laden with silent meaning.

Determined to remain professional, despite her racing heart, Lila took a menu to his booth. "We have chicken fried steak, grilled pork chops, breakfast served all day, burgers of all kinds, and today's lunch special was meat loaf and mashed potatoes. I think there's a little more left if you are interested. You know, I really thought you might learn to read down there at Texas A&M."

He reached out with a callused hand and laid it on her arm. "Still full of spit and sass I see."

She pulled her arm back like he scalded her—which it almost felt like he had—and focused on the menu. "Want me to go on, or have you heard something that appeals to you?"

He raked his fingers through his thick, dark hair. It needed cut but then maybe he wore it a little longer these days. "Just something to drink for now," he said putting emphasis on the last two words.

Her hands shook as she poured the tea and lemonade.

When she'd set it down on his table and backed up a step, he reached out to touch her arm again. "Sit with me. Where have you been? You just disappeared off the face of the earth after we graduated."

She backed up another step and he turned up the glass and drank half its contents before he came up for a breath. His rough hands testified that he had not spent his years just telling ranch hands what to do, but he'd worked beside them. His sweaty T-shirt and his scuffed boots were further proof.

She went back to the counter to bring the pitcher of tea and the one of lemonade to his booth. "You'll need refills the way you're suckin' that stuff down."

He motioned toward the other side. "So?"

She pulled a chair out from a table in the center of the café and sat down a safe distance from him. "Everyone in town knew that Mama and I moved to Pennsylvania. I went to college, then became a teacher. What about you?"

"Granny turned Hope Springs over to me and Jace this past spring. And then Kasey and her three kids came to live on the ranch with us."

"Kasey has three kids? Where's Adam? I heard they married when she finished high school?"

"Died more than a year ago in some kind of classified

mission. So what brings you back to Happy? You gonna teach here?"

"Had to get my horns trimmed. I was getting too wild," she said sarcastically.

"Well, darlin', I can't help you with that." He refilled his glass with straight lemonade.

"Why?"

He leaned forward and whispered, "I liked you as the wild child too much to shave an inch off your horns. God, we had some good times, didn't we?"

"Yeah, but we're not crazy kids anymore," she said.

"Too bad. Being a grown-up isn't nearly all it's cracked up to be."

"No, it's not, but we do have to grow up. So your granny is still alive?"

"Oh, yes, and giving out advice like candy at Halloween. Things in Happy don't change much," he answered. "How long are you going to be here?"

"Just through the summer. Someone needed to be here to help out with Mom's café since Georgia retired."

"Well, they say it's going to be a hot one this year," he said with a wink.

And with that, he polished off his second glass of lemonade and slid out of the booth. She pushed back the chair and stood up.

He tipped his hat toward her and stopped beside Paul and Fred's table. "Gracie know you are having that big load of taters right here at suppertime, Paul?"

Paul shook his head. "Hell, no, and don't you dare tell her, neither."

"See, Lila, Happy does have some secrets." Brody laughed and ducked to get through the door without removing his hat.

Lila whipped a white rag from the hip pocket of her jeans and wiped down the table, spending extra time on it so she could watch Brody cross the parking lot. His distinctive swagger hadn't changed a bit, either, and even from that distance she could see every ripple in his abs through that sweat-stained T-shirt. Her heart jacked in an extra beat and then raced so hard that she was short winded when she tucked the cloth back into her pocket.

Well, crap! So much for time and distance erasing all the old feelings for that cowboy.

The gravel crunched under the tires of two semis out in the parking lot, and a couple of big burly truckers crawled out and headed toward the café.

"Got customers, Molly," she called out.

Molly peeked out through the serving window and tucked a strand of gray hair up into her short ponytail. Short, with a round face, clear blue eyes set in a bed of wrinkles, penciled black eyebrows that made her look as if she were perpetually surprised, Molly hadn't changed much in twelve years. She didn't take guff off anyone and swore that as soon as the café sold, she would retire, like her best friend, Georgia, had done last week.

"That's Buck on the right with the plaid shirt and Wesley with the blue T-shirt. They'll order the special and they'll want coffee. I'll never understand how they can drink something hot when it's past ninety degrees outside," Molly said.

"Hey, guys." Paul held up a hand when the truckers came inside.

"Whoa! What have we got here? Where's Georgia?" Buck grinned as he eyed Lila up and down.

"Georgia retired last week. Went to live close to her daughter down in Austin," Fred said. "Molly is joining her soon as the café sells. This here is Lila Harris. Her mama actually owns this place. Georgia was just leasing it."

"What can I get you boys?" Lila asked.

"I want whatever the lunch special is if there's any left and a cup of strong black coffee," Buck said.

"Make that two." Wesley nodded.

They chose a table beside Fred and Paul's booth and pretty soon they were in deep conversation about weather, politics, and cows.

Lila poured two mugs of coffee and set them on the table. "Food will be out in a minute."

"No hurry. We been runnin' hard so we get to rest a while," Wesley said.

Lila went to the kitchen, where Molly shook a wooden spoon at her. "I saw you talkin' to Brody Dawson. You stay away from him."

"Why?"

"All of them Dawsons is wild and he's the worst in the lot."

"Molly, that was a long time ago, and if you will remember, I wasn't a saint, myself."

Another shake of the spoon and then Molly went back to fixing two meat loaf dinners. "Honey, he'd make you look like a Sunday school teacher. I told your mama I'd watch out for you and that I'd see to it you didn't fall back into those wicked ways. Why your mama named you Lila after that wicked woman in the Bible is a mystery to me. It was like she was askin' for trouble."

Lila laughed. "It was my great-grandmother's middle name. Bessie Delilah."

"Well, she'd have done better to have named you Bessie," Molly said. "Now get this food out to them guys, and don't sell them two pieces of coconut pie we got left to nobody else because them boys is going to want them when they finish with this."

"Yes, ma'am, but, Miss Molly, I'm a big girl. I've changed from that wild child I used to be and I've been takin' care of myself for a long time." Lila put the plates on a tray and headed out of the kitchen.

"Yep, but that wasn't in Happy. Person comes back here, they turn into the same person that left."

Lila would never admit it, but Molly was right. The moment she hit the city limits sign in Happy, she felt every bit as wild as she had been in high school.

*   *   *

Brody sang along with the radio the whole way back to Hope Springs. Seeing Lila again had brought back all the old excitement. Nothing had been the same after she'd left town. Happy, Texas, didn't have a movie theater or a bowling alley or even a Dairy Queen, so they'd had to drive all the way to Tulia or Amarillo to have fun. Or they could stay in town and Lila would come up with some kind of shenanigans to set their blood to racing.

"Like surfing in the back of my old pickup truck. It's a wonder we weren't all killed, but the adrenaline rush was crazy wild." He chuckled as he remembered the two of them planting their feet on skateboards in the bed of the truck and then giving Jace the heads-up sign to take off. No big ocean waves could have been as exhilarating as keeping on skateboards while Jace drove eighty miles an hour down a dirt road.

Blake Shelton's "Boys 'Round Here" started playing, and Brody kept time with his thumbs on the steering wheel. With his right hand he turned up the volume and the air-conditioning off. With his left, he hit the button to roll down the window and pushed the gas pedal to the floor.

Seventy miles an hour, the dust kicked up behind the truck just like the song said. Seventy-five, he checked the rearview and imagined that Lila was back there wearing a pair of cutoff denim shorts, cowboy boots, and a tank top that hugged her body like a glove. Her jet-black ponytail was flying out behind her and that tall, well-toned body kept balance on the imaginary skateboard every bit as well as she did back then.

He was going ninety miles an hour when he braked and slid into a long, greasy stop in front of the barn doors. Dust settled on everything inside the cab of his crew cab truck. He threw back his head and laughed with the adrenaline rushing through his veins.

You are not eighteen, Brody Dawson. The voice in his head was so much like his mother's that it settled him right down.

But it's nice every now and then to go back and visit those crazy days, he argued.

His phone pinged and he pulled it out of the pocket on his T-shirt, rubbed the screen off on his sleeve to remove some of the dust, and checked the message: *Sundance is in a mud bog out on the north forty. Need help. Bring rope.*

Brody put the truck in reverse and headed down the bumpy pathway toward the old pond on the northeast corner of the ranch. When it rained the pond would hold water for a few days and then it would slowly evaporate, leaving a muddy mess. Sundance, their prize breeding bull, loved water but he wasn't too fond of cold spring water on the other side of the ranch where Hope Springs was located.

He was bawling like a baby and thrashing around like a rodeo bull when Brody parked the truck, opened the toolbox on the back, and pulled out a long length of rope. "How long has he been there?" he yelled at Jace.

"Too damn long. He so stressed that we'll have to keep him in the barn for a week to settle him down. We got cows to breed. I'm already muddy from trying to push his big ass out of here. You lasso him and pull and I'll keep pushing," Jace said.

Brody landed the rope around the bull's neck on the first swing. "I'm ready when you are."

"Pull!" Jace yelled.

Brody felt every muscle in his body knot as he tightened the rope. "Son of a bitch weighs a ton."

Jace had his shoulder into Sundance's hind end, pushing for all he was worth. "Maybe more. He's moving. Pull harder!"

Brody wrapped the rope around his hand another time and hauled back, leaning so far that Sundance wasn't even in the picture. All he could see was sky and big fluffy clouds then boom! He was flat on his back with no wind in his lungs and that crazy bull was pulling him along behind him like a little red wagon.

He quickly untangled the rope from his hand and let go, sucked in enough air so he could get some relief, and threw a hand over his eyes to shade them from the blistering hot sun.

Jace flopped down beside him on the ground and groaned. "If he wasn't such a damn good bull, I'd shoot that sumbitch right between the eyes and turn him into steaks and hamburgers."

"Meat would be too tough and rangy to eat if you did. Crazy old bastard. We're going to have to make sure he stays out of this pasture from now on," Brody gasped.

"Heard that you stopped at the café for tea. Lila changed any?"

Brody managed to sit up. "Who told you that? You are a muddy mess."

"Don't change the subject. You sure don't smell or look like a pretty little red rose either, brother." Jace pulled himself up to a sitting position. "Gracie called the café lookin' for Paul, and Molly told her that you were in there flirting with Lila."

"I was not flirting," Brody protested.

"Yeah, right." Jace laughed. "Remember windsurfing and sneakin' into old Henry Thomas's barn on Saturday nights? You always flirted with Lila. Hey, come to think of it, Henry disappeared the same weekend that Lila and her mama moved. Did she say anything about him? We always thought maybe he hitched a ride out of town with them."

Brody shook his head. "We weren't talking about the great Happy, Texas, mystery of Henry Thomas's disappearance."

Jace poked him on the shoulder. "Were you talking about all the crazy, fun things we did? It never was the same after Lila left."

"No, it wasn't," Brody agreed. "But we're all grown-ups now and times change."

"Too damn bad we all have to be adults." Jace stood up. "Let's tie Sundance to the back of your truck and get him to the barn. His sides are heaving and I bet he's lost ten pounds over this."

That reminded Brody of the night they had chased down a bull so that Lila could show the whole bunch of them that she could ride a bull as good as any of the boys. She'd stayed on for the full eight seconds. Brody could see her long legs wrapped around that big bruiser's body as she held on to one of his horns with her right hand while her left one waved in the air. Her laughter rang out through the night, and when the ride was over, she'd whipped off a well-worn straw hat with a glittery headband and bowed to the applause of the whole crowd.

He got into the truck and slowly backed it down to the shade tree where Sundance and Jace waited. He had to stop thinking about her and remembering how alive he'd felt in the café when he saw her standing there in those tight jeans with the waitress apron slung around her well-rounded hips right below the cowgirl belt with a lot of sparkle on it. And that jet-black ponytail swinging from side to side like it did in the halls of good old Happy High School. Add that to her full lips that begged to be kissed and those big brown eyes full of mischief all the time, and the perfect woman was right there within arm's reach. But Brody was not that crazy kid anymore. He was a ranch owner with responsibilities. She was a teacher, for God's sake, so she'd changed too.

"Lord, I've missed those days...and her," he muttered.

About the Author

Carolyn Brown is a *New York Times* and *USA Today* bestselling romance author and RITA finalist. Presently writing both women's fiction and cowboy romance, Brown has also written historical single title, historical series, contemporary single title, and contemporary series. She lives in southern Oklahoma with her husband, a former English teacher, who is not allowed to read her books until they are published. They have three children and enough grandchildren to keep them young. Follow her on Facebook and sign up for her newsletter at: www.carolynbrownbooks.com

Fall in Love with Forever Romance

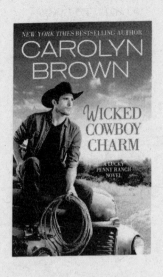

WICKED COWBOY CHARM
By Carolyn Brown

The newest novel in Carolyn Brown's *USA Today* bestselling Lucky Penny Ranch series! Josie Dawson is new in town, but it doesn't take long to know that Deke Sullivan has charmed just about every woman in Dry Creek, Texas. Just as Deke is wondering how to convince Josie he only has eyes for her, they get stranded in a tiny cabin during a blizzard. If Deke can melt her heart before they dig out of the snow, he'll be the luckiest cowboy in Texas...

THE COTTAGE AT FIREFLY LAKE
By Jen Gilroy

In the tradition of Susan Wiggs and RaeAnne Thayne comes the first in a new series by debut author Jen Gilroy. Eighteen years ago, Charlotte Gibbs left Firefly Lake—and Sean Carmichael—behind to become a globetrotting journalist. But now she's back. Will the two have a second chance at first love? Or will the secret Charlie's hiding be their undoing?

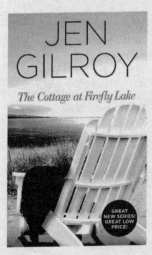

Fall in Love with Forever Romance

TOO WILD TO TAME
By Tessa Bailey

Aaron knows that if he wants to work for the country's most powerful senator, he'll have to keep his eye on the prize. That's easier said than done when he meets the senator's daughter, who's wild, gorgeous, and 100 percent trouble. The second book in *New York Times* bestselling author Tessa Bailey's Romancing the Clarksons series!

THE BACHELOR AUCTION
By Rachel Van Dyken

The first book in a brand-new series from #1 *New York Times* bestselling author Rachel Van Dyken! Brock Wellington isn't anyone's dream guy. So now as he waits to be auctioned off in marriage to the highest bidder, he figures it's karmic retribution that he's tempted by a sexy, sassy woman he can't have...

Fall in Love with Forever Romance

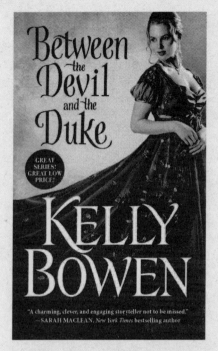

BETWEEN THE DEVIL AND THE DUKE
By Kelly Bowen

The third novel in Kelly Bowen's A Season for Scandal series—perfect for fans of Sarah MacLean, Elizabeth Boyle, and Tessa Dare! When club owner Alexander Lavoie catches a mysterious blonde counting cards at his vingt-et-un table, he's more intrigued than angry. Instead of throwing her out, Alexander offers her a deal: come work for him. For Angelique Archer, refusing him means facing starvation, but with a man so sinfully handsome and fiercely protective, keeping things professional might prove impossible...